T0128695

LIZ, Inc.

LIZ, Inc.

"Diamond" Jim Halter

Book Edited By: Sandy Griffis

iUniverse, Inc.
Bloomington

LIZ, Inc.

iUniverse books may be ordered through booksellers or by contacting:

iUniverse
1663 Liberty Drive
Bloomington, IN 47403
www.iuniverse.com
1-800-Authors (1-800-288-4677)

Because of the dynamic nature of the Internet, any web addresses or links contained in this book may have changed since publication and may no longer be valid. The views expressed in this work are solely those of the author and do not necessarily reflect the views of the publisher, and the publisher hereby disclaims any responsibility for them.

Any people depicted in stock imagery provided by Thinkstock are models, and such images are being used for illustrative purposes only.
Certain stock imagery © Thinkstock.

ISBN: 978-1-4697-6794-9 (sc)
ISBN: 978-1-4697-6795-6 (ebk)

Library of Congress Control Number: 2012901936

Printed in the United States of America

iUniverse rev. date: 01/30/2012

TABLE OF CONTENTS

CHAPTER 1

THE MEETING

I t had been several weeks, since I had the occasion to wear a suit. My meeting this morning was with an old friend, however, I make it a point to dress in business attire when conducting business. Discarding the cello-wrap from the cleaners, I donned the gray Hickey Freeman and tied a red power tie. Even though it had been over twenty years since reading the book "Dress for Success", it still dictated many of my dress habits. My imagination conjured the image of a Medieval Knight putting on his suit of armor and riding off to adventure.

I strode to the garage and raised the door to reveal my midnight blue Cadillac with blue leather interior. When I was a teenager delivering newspapers, I had always wanted a Cadillac. Entering the car, I strapped on the seat belt and keyed the ignition. The Northstar engine in the Sedan DeVille roared into life, and I drove the mile and a half to Don's Enterprises.

Don Smith had been my best friend, for as long as I could remember. We had met years ago, at one of those Chamber of Commerce networking events. They call them "Business After Hours".

Don had built a chain of women's clothing stores and had sold them for around five million dollars, before the recession of the early 1990's. Since he had signed a no-compete clause, Don decided to go into the wholesale ladies' clothing business.

Don's home is in an older section of Valdosta, Georgia. The homes were built in the 1960's. His is a two-story, old southern plantation style. It has Doric columns across the entire front of the building and is painted the traditional white. The front porch is slightly raised and is floored with marble quarried in North Georgia. Don painted the front door red, to give it his personal touch. The grounds are heavily planted in azaleas and camellias. Tall, stately pine trees are scattered throughout the estate. On the edge of an old millpond behind the main house is a boathouse with adjacent screened dock area. Several rocking chairs occupy much of the screened dock. The screening is necessary to enjoy the evenings, because of the mosquitoes that come out at dusk.

The view across the fifty-acre-or-so millpond is spectacular. Don's home is on a five-acre tract and is the only one on the south side of the pond. The north side of the pond is lined with homes on one-acre lots. A major road borders the west side of the property. People living on the north side of Valdosta use the road to get to the Valdosta Mall. The dam that forms the pond is at the northwest corner of Don's estate. Its water cascades over the dam, then immediately goes under the road through a series of large pipes.

One of the things Don and I share is the love of fine, hand rolled premium cigars. Many evenings we have enjoyed the setting sun over the millpond, while smoking an aromatic Churchill or double corona cigar. There's something about the lit end of a cigar in the dark that brings visions of earlier times in America. Times when Native American hunter-gatherers sat around a campfire in the evening and enjoyed fellowship while smoking tobacco. Over the years, and many cigars, Don and I had become friends.

Don's family consists of a wife and two children. The son and daughter are both students at the University of Georgia. Don is 6' tall with a full head of Red Hair and weighs about 200 pounds. Don can make people laugh with his ability to remember jokes and humorous stories. He easily fits into groups and becomes the center of attention. Dressing casually, yet stylishly, is Don's dress code. He only wears a suit when absolutely necessary.

I came into the world at the end of World War II and was baptized Joseph J. Hall, Jr. Since my father went by the name of Joseph, they called me Joe to prevent confusion. I was born prematurely and almost died at birth. From my earliest days, I can remember being called by the nickname "Lucky" Joe.

My mother's family is Irish and my father's is Welsh, so St. Patrick's Day was a major celebration in our household. There were plenty of shamrocks, the color green, and beer. While our family was not wealthy, we were not poor, either. My father was an engineer on the railroad, and mother's role was that of taking care of the family.

I worked my way through Valdosta State College, which, at the time had just gone coed and had about 1,000 students. Valdosta State has since become a university and grown to some 10,000 students. My wife and I graduated from Valdosta State together and got married the same week. We immediately moved to Atlanta to embark on our careers. She went to work in the bookkeeping department of a large insurance company and I took an assistant-manager job with a chain of furniture stores.

The retail furniture business was interesting. It required long hours and most weekends. After several years, I was promoted to store manager and learned a lot about retail. In 1977 we had saved enough money, with both of us working, to move back to Valdosta and open our own furniture store. We wanted our two children to grow up in Valdosta as we had. My wife, Suzanne, did the bookkeeping. I did the buying, advertising, hiring and firing. Business went well and we opened other stores in Georgia, Florida, and Alabama. We called them "Lucky" Joe's Furniture.

We used four leaf clovers on each end of the signs and in all our advertising. Our customers loved the concept. In 1994 a national conglomerate bought our endeavor for some two million in cash and four million in stock. Suzanne immediately retired and started spending her time with volunteer work and clubs. She also started spending a lot of time at the country club, dramatically increasing her consumption of alcohol.

Part of the buyout agreement retained my services as consultant for one year. I spent the year mostly playing golf, going to coin and collectible shows, and doing a small amount of consulting to fine-tune the buyout. After a year of taking it easy, I needed a challenge, but I also had a non-compete agreement, so I couldn't retail furniture.

My friend, Don, also was operating under one of these contracts, so I decided to brainstorm with him about ideas.

Over the years, I had listened to dozens of motivational and educational tapes in my car while traveling between the furniture stores. I had also attended numerous seminars on business, motivation, and public speaking. While running the furniture stores, I talked live, on the air with the radio station disc jockeys or deejays as they are commonly called. They would broadcast, live, from my stores during big sales. They were the personalities and had the listeners and following. However, they didn't know anything about furniture. We learned that the public likes to hear two people joking while giving sale information, rather than one person droning on about sale prices. It worked and I became a minor celebrity in the towns where we had stores. I also appeared in the television ads.

I had been thinking that I didn't want to tie myself down to one thing for years and years on end, as had been the case in the furniture stores. So I got my attorney to incorporate "Lucky" Joe's Consulting, Inc. My accountant had been after me to incorporate, after the sale, for tax advantages.

Now, I had a new consulting business and no customers.

Don and I were enjoying a Macanudo cigar on his screened dock. He happened to mention that a friend of his was having problems in the radio business. Between puffs, I told Don that I was starting a consulting business and that it sounded like an interesting challenge. As we finished our cigars, Don agreed to introduce us over lunch, and set up a meeting for the next week. It hadn't been a week and I had a lead.

Our meeting was set at Muldoon's restaurant where they serve great food and are a local "watering hole". Over Muldoon Burgers, I met Sam "The Man" Martin. Sam had been in radio since he lied about his age in high school. He had become one of the most sought-after deejays in this part of the country, then had come into an inheritance. Based on this combination, he bought a local radio station with his money, along with that of some investors.

To conserve assets, he was trying to do everything himself. His forte was his air personality, musical programming, and building an audience. In just six months, he had taken the station to number two in the market, in audience share. However, it was near the bottom in sales, and was still losing money.

The number one station in the market had the same format and was getting the lion's share of advertising dollars. Most people placing advertising don't like to buy two stations with the same format.

We finished lunch and Don left. Sam "The Man" and I went to the covered patio area of Muldoon's. We worked out a consulting deal where I would get a percentage of increased sales and a percentage of the sale price of the station, if and when it was sold. The investors and Sam were looking for some quick money in the deal.

I spent a year turning the station around. The first part of the plan was to change the format to "oldies music" from the 50's and 60's. We started a large promotion by arranging some advertising swaps with a billboard company, the local television station, and a free shopper publication in order to publicize the changed format. While we remained the number-two station in the market, in audience share, we went from near the bottom in sales, to number two in sales. The hardest part was recruiting and training a sales team.

The station sold for five million dollars. Sam and the group of investors had only paid a half million for it a year and a half earlier.

Now I had worked myself out of a job. The year I had spent turning the station around was one of the happiest of my working career. Unfortunately, that was not the case at home.

The 1996 Olympic Games were taking place in Atlanta while I was doing the consulting job at the radio station. I had been chosen to carry the Olympic Torch, in the crosscountry Coca-Cola Olympic Torch Relay. This was prior to the actual games in Atlanta. I guess all the volunteer work I had done over the years won the honor for me.

The torch is the symbol for all the volunteers involved in the Olympic Movement. The sacred flame is kindled in Greece then it is transported around the world and carried to the stadium, where the Opening Ceremony for the games takes place. Each "Local Hero" torchbearer, like me, carried the torch for one kilometer. We were supposed to jog slowly, allowing, everyone along the route to get a good look at the Olympic Flame. That was easier said than done. When you actually carry the flame and have hundreds of people screaming, you want to run like the wind. The adrenaline surge and elation I felt while carrying the Olympic Flame was awesome. I was proud to be a small part of the Olympic Movement. It is the one organization which tries to bring the whole world together in understanding, through competition.

I spent two weeks in Atlanta while the games were going on. Every day, I made live broadcasts to the station's listeners back in Valdosta. My press pass gave me access to many places the general public could not go; I got media tours through Coca-Cola's Olympic City, A.T.&T.'s Global Olympic Village, Budweiser's Pavilion, Swatch's Pavilion, and many other places. I informed our listeners of parking situations, transportation, and anything else of interest.

It was awesome to be in the middle of a million people in downtown Atlanta during the games. The Centennial Olympic Park was a magnet to crowds, day and night. Olympic pin trading was "the" spectator sport. Each sponsoring company made commemorative pins. Each contingent from all over the world had pins. Even the law enforcement groups had pins. Virtually everyone got "pin fever" and bought and swapped these brightly colored, enameled, metal pins. By understanding merchandising and having access to some highly sought after media pins, I turned a handful of pins into a sack full.

My senior year at Valdosta State College I had attended an Amway presentation. I learned about networking and residual income at the presentation. I didn't join, as I was too busy at the time. However, I liked the concept. After the station sold, I was looking for another consulting job. I bumped into an old friend while having breakfast at the local Shoney's restaurant. He asked me if I was interested in nutrition. I told him I was, so he gave me a cassette tape, which I threw in the car. It stayed there a week or so, until I made a trip to Atlanta.

On the trip I got bored with the radio and remembered the tape on nutrition. It turned out that the tape was on a new product to the United States called Pycnogenol. It had been in Europe for years. A Doctor of Chiropractic had made the tape. He had gotten interested in natural medicines and spoke of the different positive things Pycnogenol had done for his patients. The most striking thing to me was that many patients had used it to eliminate hay fever. I was in the middle of one of my two miserable times of year. The spring and fall brought miserable bouts with hay fever allergies.

I stopped at a health food store in Atlanta and got some Pycnogenol. I took one milligram for each pound of body weight. The next morning, miraculously, my symptoms were gone.

The tape was designed to be an educational recruiting device to attract people to enroll in a new networking company. Having some spare time, and a curiosity about networking, I sought out the friend who had given me the tape.

He went over the program and also showed me that the Pycnogenol was slightly cheaper from the networking company than at the health food stores. I enrolled and started working it as a business. Over a six-month period my network grew to over 500 people. The company scheduled a national convention in June of 1997. I was invited to attend, receive an award, and be recognized for my accomplishments.

Over the six months spent building my network, the public's awareness of the product had increased dramatically. It was now being sold in discount stores at a lower price than the Network Company's was.

I attended the convention in Dallas, Texas with a friend who was in my network. Everyone had a good time with all the hoopla!

I met a dozen or so people who were making some big money with the company, having gotten involved when the company started two years earlier. I saw that there were two thousand people at the convention, but only a handful were making any serious money.

The motivational speakers explained some new products coming out, and at my turn, I got up on stage, received my award, and gave a short talk.

When I returned home, I had only put in two weeks of actual networking time for the month. When I got my check the next month, it had dropped by hundreds of dollars. People were dropping out almost as fast as I was enrolling them. Even though I was making several thousand dollars a month, I was spending at least half of it on expenses. Realizing I was not building residual income, I ceased to network for the company. Now I was out of work again.

Don had been in my network. He had gotten results on the products, as had I. He had not been networking on a full time basis, as I had, because he was too busy running his own wholesale company. We went over the decision together to stop networking. Those visits on his screened dock brought about a lot of business decisions, while enjoying fine cigars. These were H. Upmann Coronas, Habana.

One of my attorney friends had received a box of the Cubans, from one of his clients. He was from the Miami Area and had gotten caught on I-75 with something he shouldn't have. It has been illegal to import Cuban cigars into the U.S. since President Kennedy signed papers banning imports from Cuba. However, it's been said, he held up signing the papers until he procured over a hundred boxes. For some reason, the Cuban Cigars are the best in the world. It has something to do with the soil and climate. I guess it's sort of like the "Vidalia Onions", for which Georgia is noted.

A few days after our discussion on getting out of networking, I got a call from Don. He said that he had been thinking about something and would like for me to meet with him. I didn't know what the meeting was about, but looked forward to seeing Don, as always.

At a few minutes before our agreed meeting time, I steered the Sedan DeVille onto the entry road and into the office/distribution park off North Valdosta Road. Upon seeing his building, I remembered that he had been the first one to build in the park. It turned out to be a good investment, as the property had increased greatly in value over the years. The building has a modern front with more than adequate parking. There are 5,000 square feet of office space and 15,000 square feet of warehouse.

Admiring the huge oak tree beside the parking area, I got out of the car. Don had planned the layout around the several-hundred-year-old oak tree. He likes to take a break occasionally and smoke a cigar under his 'cigar tree' as he affectionately calls it. I wondered about the history that it could tell if it could talk. It had probably been there before the United States came into being.

Checking my watch, I noted it was five minutes to 9:00 AM. August in South Georgia is noted for stifling, sweltering heat. The humidity gets up near 100% and the temperature stays in the high 90's. From midday until sunset, just walking about will bring about abundant perspiration. The invention of air conditioning brought about the rise of the Southern United States. I checked my suit pocket to make sure the pocket humidor, with the two Dunhill cigars, was there. It was, and I entered the building.

The receptionist chirped, "Come on in 'Lucky' Joe. Don's expecting you." I smiled and told Sally how lovely she looked and how good it was to see her again. The reception room is fairly large and rectangular. It has comfortable office chairs along the walls, is expensively carpeted, and the room is well lit. The walls are hung with numerous watercolors.

The artist, Mary Carlon, did the watercolors. She and her family now reside in Valdosta, having lived all over the world. Her husband retired in Valdosta after serving his final tour of duty at Moody Air Force Base. He had been in a special unit that spent time in sensitive political areas. They had fallen in love with the South Georgia area and decided to stay.

8

Mary Carlon had studied art in her youth. The time the couple spent in Europe was a boon to her. While her husband was on assignments, she had time to spend in museums and study the techniques of the "Old Master Artists". Befriending the museum workers also paid untold dividends. They taught her many of the secrets used by the famous artists. One was how to paint eyes so that they seem to follow you across the room. So much in art has to be seen to be completely understood.

During one three-year tour of duty in Florida, Mary raised tropical fish for resale to pet stores and wholesalers. Having always loved tropical fish, the time she spent raising them taught her how fish "think". She now intuitively knows how they move, how they rest, how they blend in with their surroundings, and other qualities peculiar to them.

Mary used the knowledge she learned in Europe and merged it with knowledge she learned raising fish to come up with her own style of underwater watercolors. She uses a technique with watercolors to paint coral so that the coral is vibrant with color and jumps off the canvas. Other artists have tried to copy her, in vain. Her paintings are like a salt-water aquarium. One can sit and look at them for long periods of time and feel a calming effect. In many of her paintings, she blends small sea creatures into the background. As in nature, they are camouflaged and hard to find, which creates reality and continuing interest, even after seeing the picture numerous times.

Don had met her at an arts and crafts show and had fallen in love with her work enough to start investing in some of them. He introduced me to Mary, and I too, started investing. We had both advised her to raise her prices. After doing so, her sales doubled. A year ago she doubled her prices again. Now she can't keep up with the demand for her originals. If it weren't for prints, she wouldn't have much to sell. The quality of her work demands a lot of time.

The door opened and I saw six foot, red-haired Don Smith. His grin was wide as a stretch limo. Don hollered, "'Lucky' Joe! Come on into my office." I followed Don down the hallway. We walked halfway through the office area. His office is right in the middle and has two doors, which allow him to quickly get where he wants to go in the building. A private bath and storage closet are connected to the back of the office. The indirect lighting around the walls at ceiling level gives the room plenty of light. He has a large power desk, with built in computer setup. The wall behind his desk has floor to wall bookshelves, filled with books, audiocassettes, and souvenirs. In front of the desk are two upholstered padded chairs. There is a conference table with eight chairs and a wet bar with four stools. On the other walls are three of Don's favorite Mary Carlon watercolors.

After Don motioned to the chairs, I took a seat in the one to his left and sank into the very comfortable cushion. I declined his offer of coffee or other beverage. He then asked if my family situation had improved. I told him that it hadn't, but that it was bearable. At my inquiry about his family, he replied that all was well and that they had really enjoyed their recent vacation to Hawaii. We made more small talk, then Don got down to the reason for our meeting.

Don said, "'Lucky' Joe, I've been thinking since our visit a few days ago when we both stopped networking. You don't have any consulting jobs lined up, and, as you know, I lost my biggest wholesale account a few months ago. Since that time, I've been looking for a new direction for income and interest. Premium hand rolled cigar sales have increased every year for the last five years. They've increased around fifty percent yearly. I investigated getting into the manufacture and sale of cigars and found out that there's too much government regulation. There's also a severe shortage of premium cigars, as compared to the demand. This will change next year, because many of the farmers in South America are changing over from vegetables and other crops to cigar tobacco."

Don went on, "I've got an artist friend in Panama City Beach, Florida who has done a lot of T-shirt artwork. It's unique in that it is colorful and lends itself to the silkscreen printing process. I learned from Walt Disney, that merchandise is the tail that wags the dog. When Disney made an animated movie, the merchandise royalties made more profit than the movie. Well, that's the case now with the sudden huge increase in premium cigar popularity. I've commissioned my artist friend to come up with art for a line of cigar T-shirts.

"In the last ten years, the most profitable line of shirts has been a line called Big Jerry. They are colorful, humorous, and mildly risqué. They've had a good run and its time for some new product on the market. Now here's what I had in mind to talk to you about."

I interrupted Don to say, "Don, you know I don't like to mix business and friendship, but I'll listen. However, if we're going to talk business, lets adjourn to the 'cigar oak'. It's still early enough in the day to enjoy a good cigar and I just happened to bring along two Dunhill's." Don said, "Times a wasting, let's go."

The shade of the majestic oak and the clear blue morning sky, with a light breeze, created a little bit of heaven. We used a bullet cutter to pierce the cigar ends. We had both used guillotine cutters, but had recently discovered that the punch method led to a slower, less messy smoke. A butane jet lighter had our cigars lit quickly and we were enjoying what only a cigar aficionado can understand. The Dunhill's were as mild as expected. They were perfect for a nice August morning that was a prelude to a sweltering day and evening.

Don said, "I've decided to go with the cigar T-shirt venture. I want you to work with me on a consulting basis. Your job will be to build a national sales force and head up the sales effort. I've got my hands full working with the artist, the tee-shirt wholesaler, the screenprinter, and the financing people. I know you only work on a percentage basis. I'll supply you with office space, phone, supplies, postage, and travel expenses. Your percentage is two percent of sales and ten percent of the sale, if I decide to sell the line. What do you say?"

I said, "I've got to think about it. What say I give you my answer tonight on the dock? That way we can enjoy another fine cigar." Don said, "That's great. I'll look forward to this evening." By now the Dunhill's had nice white ashes, about three inches long, still holding onto the cigar. A long white ash is the mark of a truly fine cigar. We talked about how hard it was to get good cigars now at a reasonable price. Don's ash fell and mine followed shortly. Sally came out and informed Don that someone he had been playing telephone tag with for a week was holding for him. Don said, "Is eight o'clock okay?" At my confirmation, he went inside to catch the phone.

Another 15 minutes under the tree allowed me to enjoy the rest of my Dunhill. My attention was captivated by a couple of gray squirrels playing around in the tree. I guess they were checking out the up-coming acorn crop.

That reminded me, in less than two months we would be in the nicest weather of the year. October through December and March through May are almost idyllic, weather wise. Temperatures at night are generally in the low forties and during the day in the low seventies. Winters are mild with temperatures in the morning generally in the high thirties or forties. Winter daytime temperatures are normally in the high sixties or low seventies. Usually, there are two or three cold fronts a year, with freezing temperatures. We might see an inch or less of snow every ten years or so. The summers in South Georgia are killers though. From June through August nights are in the sixties and seventies with highs in the nineties. The real problem is the humidity, which stays up near a hundred percent. Thank heaven for air-conditioning.

I took a final puff on my cigar, then headed for the smoke stand near the front door to discard the cigar butt. Don had a no smoking policy in his building. Don and I didn't smoke indoors anywhere as a rule. Exceptions were cigar bars, restaurants with cigar area, lounges in cigar stores, and casinos. In fact, my wife dislikes cigars to the point that I don't smoke at home. Her father had smoked cigars inside their home when she was growing up. He also smoked inside the family car with the windows rolled up. She doesn't like cigars, pipes, or cigarettes. I stubbed out the cigar and headed for my Cadillac. Starting the car, I started thinking about Don's offer.

I had always been cautious about doing business with friends. In any business there can be only one boss. I've seen so many businesses break up where there were too many bosses. But I've also seen successful partnerships where each partner had set areas of responsibility, of which they were the one in charge. I knew that Don and I could work together, as long as we each had our particular areas of responsibility.

I had traveled very little the last few years with the radio station and the networking. I like to travel and this challenge would involve quite a bit of travel, especially on the front end. I decided to take on the challenge, however, I'd ask Don for four percent of sales and settle on three. I've known Don for years. His first offer would not be his best. He likes to negotiate too much for that.

I picked up my cell phone and called my friend Ken Scott. Ken owns Good Stuff Antiques on Plum Street in Remerton. Remerton was a southern mill town where workers for the cotton mill lived. There are three streets with white clapboard houses and duplexes. In the past, there had been the mill, with its company store, and a church. The mill had closed years ago and the houses were now a group of quaint retail shops. They have an association they use to advertise together. They also put on two festivals a year. They do one in the spring and one in the fall. There are a lot of antique stores, craft shops, specialty retail stores, and a few professionals, like architects.

Remerton is unique in that it is incorporated and is completely surrounded by the city of Valdosta. It has a mayor/council form of government and refuses to be annexed into the City of Valdosta. Most of what was vacant land is now apartments. Students attending Valdosta State University occupy them. Remerton allows alcohol sales on Sunday with food. Valdosta does not. Several restaurants have located in Remerton for that reason.

Ken answered the phone with a slight chuckle and said," Good Stuff Antiques." I said, "Are you sure it's all good stuff?" Ken said, "I'm sure, because I picked it out myself." I said, "Well I guess it is, if you will personally vouch for it." Ken said, "Enough insults 'Lucky' Joe, what do you want?" I said, "I'm just checking to see if you're in the mood for a Subway for lunch." Ken said, "I sure am!" I said, "Well I'll see you as soon as I get the mail at the Post Office and do a couple of errands.

I finished the errands and stopped by the Subway shop near the Mall. I ordered Ken a turkey sub with peppers. Then I ordered a roast chicken, on whole grain bread, with peppers for myself. It was only 11:30 AM so there was no line. I took the subs and drove toward Remerton. However, I got caught by a train and sat there in line with the other cars for a good ten minutes. I watched freight cars roll by very slowly as the train slowed down to go through town.

The train cleared the track and I finally made the turn onto Plum Street. The three streets in the village run east/west and are on a long hill that slopes down to the old mill buildings at the bottom. I drove up the hill past a dozen shops and Good Stuff Antiques came into view on the right. Across the street is a vacant lot. One of the buildings had burned long ago. I parked on the grass of the vacant lot and walked across the street to Ken's shop.

The fronts of the old mill houses all have step up porches across the entire front. These were built in the days before air-conditioning, when the pace of life was a lot slower. People used to sit on the front porches during the hot summer evenings and catch whatever breeze was available. For the most part, electric fans stirred the air inside the buildings. The ceilings are high, as was common in tropical and subtropical climates back then. During mill days, all the houses were painted white. Now the shop owners had painted them in eye-catching colors.

Ken's store has a short white picket fence. There is a section on both sides of the sidewalk that leads up to the porch steps. This porch has a white handrail across it and the front below the porch is covered in white latticework. The building is painted bright yellow and has a tin roof. It's really noisy when it rains.

In the middle of the roof, Ken mounted a rectangular red Coca-Cola sign. It had originally been on the roof of an old general store. In the middle of the front porch hangs a three-foot round red Coca-Cola sign. It had been on a pole outside of an old country store/filling station. Ken is an expert on Coca-Cola collectibles. They are a large part of his business.

Ken was relaxing in a double swing hanging on the east end of the porch. He motioned for me to come on up and join him in one of the two wooden chairs and two wooden rockers. Ken had taken on the president's job for the merchants association and had all the meetings on the front porch. There were always people stopping by to "shoot the bull". Ken's blonde hair was waving in the breeze, as he swung his 250 pounds back and forth in the swing. He has a low coffee table between the swing and chairs where I put the sandwiches.

Ken got up, went inside, and got us a couple of Cokes out of an old Coca-Cola vending machine. Ken also collects old Coca-Cola items. Ken handed me one of the Cokes and said, "I really appreciate you getting the subs. You saved me from a can of Vienna sausage and crackers." Ken runs the business by himself and keeps the overhead low. He went through a divorce a few years back and was enjoying the single life.

Ken and I both have a lot of similar interests. I buy and sell coin collections. If he runs across a coin deal he refers it to me. If I run across an antique deal, I refer it to him. We also share an enthusiasm for peppers and cigars. Ken grows some of the hottest peppers around. In the backyard of his store he has a pepper garden with six kinds of peppers. For some reason, the soil and climate around Valdosta are perfect for peppers. Ken makes some of the best pepper-sauce in South Georgia. He keeps a pair of pepper plants, in planters, on the top step to his shop.

We both enjoyed our subs and savored the Cokes. When we finished Ken went inside and came out with a couple of Toros. Toro's are Brazilian cigars that are sold locally at the chain drug store. They are good cigars for the money. Ken handed me one and we proceeded to light up. We talked, enjoyed each other's company, and smoked the Toros. He told me of the plans he was making for the Fall Festival and the advertising plan. I told him of the deal Don had proposed and that I was going to accept the deal. I thanked Ken for the cigar and he thanked me for the sub. As I walked to my car Ken yelled, "'Lucky' Joe, don't be such a stranger." I yelled back and promised not to.

I went to my office at home and drew up a simple agreement for my deal with Don. I make it a point to put into writing, in the form of a simple agreement, every deal to which I commit. I corrected the spelling and directed the computer to print it on the HP LaserJet printer. I made a few minor changes to the document; I corrected it and had the computer print out two copies.

The rest of the afternoon was spent calling businessmen I've met over the years and learning what they knew about building sales organizations. It was fun talking with old friends and acquaintances. Unfortunately, I didn't learn much about the task that lay ahead. The one thing that came up repeatedly was that the sales people would be at the trade shows for that industry. I also learned that T-shirts are mainly sold at the gift shows by multi-line road representatives. These reps work shows and call on buyers at their places of business.

I finished up and my wife was nowhere to be found, as usual. The passion in our lives for each other was gone. It had slowly disappeared over the years. I didn't like her drinking and she didn't like my cigar smoking. Although we still shared the same bed, our sex life was as if she were bound only out of duty. I had bought some tapes about rebuilding a loving relationship from a television infomercial, but she was always too busy to watch them with me. I tried to get her to read the book *His Needs, Her Needs* by W.F. Harley, Sr. That effort had also been in vain.

I had quit smoking cigarettes about the time I turned thirty. I found that I was using alcohol too much, about the time I turned thirty-five. So I pretty much quit drinking. In the early nineties, I started reading about the resurgence of cigars. I also found a medical article showing research had discovered there was something in cigars that contributed to longevity. Some of my friends, like Don, had already started smoking cigars. So I started reading and learning about cigars and became a cigar smoker. When they came out with the non-alcoholic beers, I started drinking O'Douls at business functions. I had always liked the taste of beer. Occasionally, I would have a little brandy with a cigar. They just seem to go together.

When I started smoking cigars, my wife had a "Duck Fit". She gave me more hell over that, than anything else in our time together. Out of respect to her, I don't smoke at home. However, I spend more time away from home now. I'm familiar with all the parks in the area. Many days I'll go to a park, read the paper, and enjoy a good smoke. Sometimes I'll go visit a friend, like Ken Scott at Good Stuff Antiques. I stick with the so-called premium cigars. I don't like the taste from smoking paper, or cardboard, that's incorporated in the cheaper cigars.

The sun was just starting to set, as I drove up the winding drive to Don's home. The shadows from the tall pine trees were covering most of the columned porch that makes up the front of the house. The garage is on the right side and is included in the home. I pulled to the back of the concrete parking area near the walk that meanders to the boathouse. Don saw me drive up and joined me as I carried my briefcase and we walked on down to the boathouse. We went out on the end of the dock past the screened area. Don likes to fish occasionally and has a large plastic garbage can at the end. Inside the can is a large bag of pelletized fish food. He reached in and got us each a handful. We threw it on the water and watched the little bream rise to the attack. Soon larger bream streaked in. Finally, some big catfish rolled to the surface. Before long, there was a feeding frenzy.

As it started to get dark the light sensors turned on the outdoor lights. The mosquitoes started their assault and we retreated to the screened-in area. Don had brought out some brandy and brandy snifters. He proceeded to pour us each a jigger or so. He said as he handed me one of the snifters, "I see by the briefcase you've decided to accept my offer." I said, "Only if you make it four percent." Don said, "You know that's way too much. I'll compromise and make it three percent." I responded, "Well I guess we've got a deal." Don raised his brandy snifter and retorted, "To our good fortune!" I clicked my glass against his and took a sip of the brandy. It was very old and mellow. I swished it across my taste buds and delighted at the intricate flavor.

Grabbing my briefcase, I took out the agreement. We each signed two copies and kept one. Then I took out two large cigars. The labels were printed in black and yellow on white. The print was "COHIBA" and "La Habana, Cuba" in smaller letters. These are known as some of the finest cigars in the world. I had gotten them for fifty dollars each from an airman at Moody Air Force Base. He had brought them back with him from overseas. They had been in my humidor for sometime waiting for a special occasion. I handed one to Don and his face broke into one of the biggest smiles I've ever seen. He blurted, "Wow, I know we're going to have good fortune starting out like this."

We both slumped into rocking chairs and proceeded to savor the COHIBA cigars and brandy. The COHIBA is mild but has a medley of flavor that is incredible. COHIBA cigars were originally only made for Fidel Castro to smoke and give away as favors. They became highly sought after. Cuba needed hard currencies so badly that Fidel had production expanded and started exporting the COHIBA brand. Fidel Castro doesn't smoke cigars anymore. However, the COHIBA will always trace its beginning back to his taste, when he smoked. Don blew a big puff of bluish smoke and said, "'Lucky' Joe, when you gonna start?" I said, "Tomorrow soon enough?" Don said, "Great!"

That was all the business talk for the evening. We just relaxed, relishing the good smoke and brandy. We talked about how much fun we had had networking and all that we had learned about nutrition. I had discovered that traditional doctors go to medical schools and learn to treat illness with prescription drugs, surgery, and radiation. They are taught almost nothing about natural herbs and remedies that have been around for thousands of years.

There's no money in natural products for the drug companies because they cannot patent a natural product.

Then you've got the pure naturalists who think natural is the only way. They are zealots for their cause. I had come to realize that somewhere in the middle is the answer—the best of both worlds.

Don and I went on for almost an hour talking about different things until our COHIBA cigars got too short for comfort. We put the butts in his antique cigar stand, which dates back to the turn of the century. It is cast and has sections of marble with a large marble ashtray that nestles into the top. It has two large grooves to rest cigars on. Don found it in an antique store on one of his excursions, possibly on Amelia Island. I said, "I think its time to call it a night." Don said, "Thank you very much for the COHIBA. It was great!" I said, "You're welcome. I appreciate the brandy."

As we walked up the walkway to my Cadillac, the stars sparkled in the cloudless sky. We said our good-byes and I drove home. My wife, Suzanne, was home. I informed her of my decision and what I was going to do. She made a remark about me smelling like a smokestack. So I left the room, showered, and went to bed.

I arrived at Don's Enterprises a little before eight and rang the bell. The front door was always locked before eight AM and after five PM. Don opened the door, gave me a key, and showed me how the alarm system worked. He took me down a corridor and to a room that had been used for drafting. It now had a desk, chair and a World War II-era file cabinet. There was a drafting table and he asked me if I wanted it to stay. I nodded yes. He informed me that he would call the computer service and get a computer terminal which would be connected with the main CPU as soon as possible. He also said he would have a phone in shortly.

We went to the break room and got some coffee and cake donuts. Don is partial to cake donuts over the yeast type. I like the yeast type better. Don said, "I've got a full slate through lunch. Let's get together in my office at 2:00 PM to brainstorm ideas and come up with a plan." I agreed and finished my coffee and donut.

Sally, the receptionist, came in and told me how glad she was that I would be working with them. Don took me around and introduced me to everyone. I then brought some personal things in to my new office and made a list of things I knew were needed. I also made a list of things I wanted to go over with Don in the afternoon session. I took the hammer I had brought and put up some award plaques and a picture Coca-Cola had sent me of when I carried the Olympic Torch.

For lunch I got some carryout at the nearby Wendy's Hamburger's restaurant and went to the nearby park with a *Georgia Times Union* newspaper. I enjoyed a chicken sandwich, fries, and Coca-Cola, then browsed through the paper and worked the crossword puzzle, while enjoying a Bering cigar.

Two o'clock came and I joined Don in his office with my notes and a couple of the white letter-size legal pads I prefer. We took seats at the conference table and got down to work.

We formulated a plan to set up at some gift shows and hire some sales people to represent us in different areas. Don agreed to take care of getting a professional-looking display made for the booth and take care of display-related matters. He also agreed to take care of travel arrangements and reservations. I took on booking the shows and contacting major chains for house accounts.

Comparable T-shirt lines in the market were selling for around fifteen dollars. We set our price to be in the mainstream of the market. Salesmen's commissions varied from six to twelve percent. High volume lines were around six percent. Low volume lines were generally around fifteen. We set ours at ten percent. We both agreed that the key to success was getting a team of experienced, successful sales persons. We adjourned our session and went to work.

I knew from experience in the furniture business, that there are always ten salespeople trying to call on a qualified credit-worthy buyer for every one that he actually has time to deal with. A new salesperson takes years to build up a group of qualified buyers. For every good salesperson, there are ten bad or mediocre salespeople. My challenge was to get referrals to good salespersons because there's no sense wasting time with mediocre salespeople.

Quickly, I discovered all the strong gift shows have waiting lists of one or more years. Another problem is the shows will not let wholesalers in unless they are exhibitors. I had no problem there. I know several people who have retail businesses that will let me use their credentials. The real problem is that the best shows are sold out.

I found a promoter that puts on small regional shows. The first show available was in Galveston, Texas. He also does one in Panama City Beach, Florida. The Galveston show was set for Monday, October 5 through Thursday, October 9, 1997. I faxed in the paperwork and mailed a check.

Don and I made plans to go to Galveston, Texas. Neither of us had ever been to Galveston. We were both looking forward to our adventure.

CHAPTER 2

GALVESTON

It was 6 AM when Don's red custom GMC van came up my driveway. I could not believe two months had passed and it was already Friday, October 3, 1997. Time flies when you're busy. I opened the side door and put my large bag and hanging bag in the van. Don had removed the middle and rear seats. We then motored over to Don's, Enterprises. We did have to make a short stop at his favorite donut shop on the way. He got some assorted cake donuts and a big cup of coffee. I got some yeast donuts and a big cup of decaf.

We backed up to the first loading door at the warehouse and opened the van's rear doors. We had organized the night before. Everything we needed was in a stack behind the overhead door. It only took a few minutes to pack the van. The modular, pop up, show display took up the most room. There were also two folding six-foot tables with custom covers. We went over our checksheet, to make sure we had everything. Then Don said, "Do you have the most important item?" I said, "What's that?" He said, "Your travel humidor. I don't want you bumming cigars from me all week." I laughed and replied, "It's right here and it's locked to keep you out."

We climbed into the captain's chairs and set off on our adventure to Galveston, Texas. I liked traveling with Don. He doesn't like to be a passenger in a vehicle. He likes to do all the driving. I would rather enjoy the ride and let someone else drive. I like to work crossword puzzles and have been known to purchase a newspaper, just to work the crossword puzzle.

By the time we got to Quitman, Georgia, we had finished the donuts and coffee. U.S. Highway 84 has been four-laned between Valdosta and Quitman and the speed limit has been raised to 65 MPH, so we made good time. Quitman was an old cotton town that had quit growing when the Interstates were built, unlike Valdosta, which was touched by Interstate 75. Downtown Quitman was now a group of about two dozen antique stores and gift shops. This had saved the downtown area from destruction. People from all over come to Quitman to browse the antique stores.

We turned off U.S.84 and took the back road to Monticello, Florida. This shortcut is thirty minutes quicker than going through Thomasville, Georgia. You cut out all the traffic lights and it is about fifteen miles shorter. The scenery is great. Cotton fields blooming prior to harvest, hay fields being cut, forests, and fishing lakes border the road. There is also a huge dairy farm, on both sides of the road, a few miles this side of Monticello. They had dug a tunnel under the roadway to get the cows back and forth. I never knew it was there, until one day I happened along while they were moving the cows.

Don and I had learned of this shortcut in our younger days when we would occasionally go with a group to the Greyhound Track located in Monticello, Florida. Dog racing is illegal in Georgia. So for some diversion, lots of people in South Central and Southwest Georgia cross the state line to wager on the dogs. The state dramatically increased the amount of taxes they take out of the betting pool. It ceased to be as much fun and we quit going.

We made a pit stop in Monticello to relieve our bladders and get more coffee, then we drove a few miles south and got on Interstate 10. It would carry us almost all the way to Galveston. I worked a crossword puzzle. With Don's help I finished it about the time we whisked through Tallahassee, Florida.

Don had gotten on the Internet and gotten information on the casinos along the Mississippi Gulf Coast. It was halfway on our two-day trip to Galveston. Friday and Saturday nights are the big nights for the casinos. Motel/hotel rooms in Biloxi were booked solid. However, The Grand Casino in Biloxi referred us to the new Grand Casino in Gulfport. It was only a few miles west of the main group of casinos in Biloxi. So, Don had booked us for tonight.

At the west side of Apalachicola River, in Florida, you enter the Central Time zone. On the West Side of the river is a large rest area. It's on top of a tall ridge or "Florida Mountain". There is a bridge across I-10 that shuttles the westbound traffic back and forth. We stretched our legs and made use of the facilities, then walked over to one of the covered picnic tables at the side of the hill. We each lit up a Bering Cigar. The heroes, in the movie *Independence Day*, lit up a Bering after they had overcome the alien invasion of Earth. After the movie, Don and I tried the Bering's and found them to be good cigars for the money. Not as good as the super premiums, but a decent smoke. We relaxed on the concrete bench next to the concrete table and enjoyed the view. After about 30 minutes of rest and pleasure, we resumed our trek.

We made a quick stop to refuel, grab a snack, and get drinks just east of Pensacola. Passing through Pensacola, we could still see signs of destruction, from the previous year's "Killer Hurricane". Next we passed by the Battleship Alabama Museum. It and Mobile Bay are easily seen from the Interstate. We then drove through the tunnel that takes traffic under the river to Mobile, Alabama. Being midday, traffic through Mobile was light and we made good time.

Our next stop was the Mississippi welcome station. We went in and got a state map and a handful of brochures and coupon magazines. There were two information papers on the casinos. While Don drove, I shared what was in the handouts. I also gave him a choice of routes to the Mississippi Coast. He chose to go in on the East Side and drive by the casinos. Then he took the coastal highway along the shore to Gulfport and the Gulfport Grand Casino. We also found coupons for a ten-dollar discount with a twenty-five-dollar purchase, at a cigar store.

We exited the Interstate and took the road south toward the coast. It was amazing to see all the new motels under construction. The legalization of casino gambling had turned this area into a boomtown. Run down motels that would have been begging before the recent boom to rent rooms at twenty dollars a night in the off season, were getting almost a hundred dollars a night. During the week they were getting around fifty dollars a night. We got to the coastal highway and turned west. As we crossed a bridge, the new high-rise hotels, next to the casinos, came into view.

We noticed that the casinos were in the water and that the hotels were adjacent, with a covered walkway. We drove around and took in the sights. We saw the new Imperial Palace under construction. Don and I had stayed in the Las Vegas Imperial Palace. We went to the ASD show as an excuse to visit Vegas. The Imperial Palace in Vegas has one of the largest collections of rare antique cars in existence. Presidential cars, Hitler's car, Al Capone's car, and many other one-of-a-kind automobiles are on display. The brochure noted that many of the cars in Las Vegas would be moved to the Biloxi Imperial Palace Casino.

Continuing west along the coastal highway, we found the cigar store. Its selection of cigars was surprisingly good and the prices were respectable, especially with the coupons we each had. The girl attending the store was especially knowledgeable and helpful. With her advice we picked out some cigars. We both got some old favorites and some that we had never tried. As we paid for the cigars, we thanked her for her help.

Our purchases in hand, we continued on to the Gulfport Grand Casino. We passed a cruise ship that had been converted into a casino and a huge banana import facility, then we turned into the registration area for the Grand Casino Gulfport. We unloaded our luggage and had the van valet-parked in the security area. Check-in was a breeze. Before we knew it, we were in a surprisingly nice room with two double beds. It was a four-star room at a two-star price. Our room was on the seventh floor and had a view to the west. You could see down the coastline for miles. When the bellman brought our luggage, we inquired about a place we could enjoy a cigar.

Per the bellman's instructions, we got off the elevator on the third floor. Past the pool there was a whirlpool bath and sauna. Opening the doors we found a deck across the south side of the hotel. It was just above the enclosed walkway to the casino. The imposing casino loomed in front of us. It rose up another two stories above us. The deck had heavy wrought iron chairs and lounge chairs. There were some glass-top, wrought iron, side tables. We moved a couple of chairs and a table to our liking.

Before we left the room, Don had pulled out a bottle of brandy that one of his suppliers had given him ten years earlier. It sold for two hundred fifty dollars a bottle back in the 1980's. He opened the seal and poured us each a double shot in the hotel water glasses. Don said, "I knew I forgot something. I left the brandy snifters back in my office."

I set my glass of brandy on the table and half-reclined on the lounge chair. Don sat down in the regular chair he had chosen and sniffed the brandy. He looked up and said, "Ain't we something, smoking expensive cigars and drinking expensive brandy in hotel water glasses." We both laughed and pulled out a cigar. Don took the cellophane off a seven-inch Baccarat Torpedo that he had just bought. I opened the packaging on a Baccarat Churchill. We punched the ends and lit up. The brandy and cigars sure were good. Mine had a nutty flavor with a hint of spices.

Don noticed that a concrete jetty that went out into the Gulf past the actual casino protected the casino. I then noticed that the casino was built on a barge and was actually floating. It was attached to a series of four-story metal pylons. The attachments allowed the casino to go up and down with the level of the water. It was built to go through the extremes of a hurricane. We walked up to the edge of the deck to get a better view.

The water was almost crystal clear and was shallow in the area between the casino and the jetty. The top of the jetty's concrete was flat and as wide as a sidewalk. The jetty rose about five feet above the water. People had walked out and were fishing at the southwest corner. Near shore, there was a horseshoe crab scavenging across the bottom. It was about a foot wide and two and a half feet long. There were some bait-size fish swimming around. Two people walked down the wall and one of them threw a cast net at the school of baitfish. He pulled up the net and had about a dozen fish.

Our cigars played out and we retired to the room to rest and shower. We relaxed for a few hours and dressed for the casino. Don wore a casual, colorful shirt and slacks. I chose a sport jacket without a tie. Then we headed out the door for the excitement and adventure of the casino. You had to pass the hotel gift shop to get to the connecting walkway. The entryway to the casino was under construction. Signage said, "Excuse us as we renovate for your future enjoyment." We passed the construction area and walked into the lights and noises of the casino. There was something magical about the sounds of the slot machines.

They had given us maps of the casino at the registration desk. We negotiated our way to the customer service desk to enroll in the Grand Advantage Players Club. They gave us each a credit card-size card and information on the club. You get points for playing. The longer you play, the more points you accumulate. There are some special items for free if you build up enough points. There was also cash back if you wagered enough. We walked around awhile. As we passed a row of Double Diamond slot machines, Don said, "I hear that machine saying, 'Put a hundred dollars in me'. 'Lucky' Joe, I feel lucky tonight." I replied, "I feel lucky too!"

We pushed our Grand Advantage Players Club cards into the slots and each fed a one-hundred-dollar bill into the bill slot. The machines made noise as they totaled up the credits. These slots were designed to play two credits. If you played one credit and hit the top combination, you were not eligible for the super jackpot. When that happens, as it often does, the house gets a windfall profit.

I lit up a Bering Churchill and ordered an O'Douls from the cocktail girl. Don ordered a Bud Lite. A few minutes later she was back with our drinks. We gave her a two-dollar tip and ordered another round. Over the years, our experience taught us to reorder and tip or it might be an hour before you get another drink. We'd been playing about thirty minutes and Don said, "I'm getting hungry. You know we didn't get any lunch. That snack's been gone a long time. I've been thinking about that buffet. Let's eat." I said, "Sure!" I was down to about thirty dollars and he was down to twenty-two.

The Internet information showed that the Grand Casino Biloxi was famous for an extravagant buffet. The person who had booked us into the Grand Casino Gulfport had assured us that the buffet here was very good. Don also knew someone who frequented the Grand Casino Biloxi. He always bragged about the buffet. This was the first time Don or I had been here since they had legalized gambling.

I had been to a coin show here in the early 80's. The highlight was a trip to Mary Mahoney's Restaurant with a group of friends. The food was excellent. In fact, we had some of their seafood chowder flown into Valdosta for a party. We had driven by Mary Mahoney's in Biloxi, this afternoon. However, there is a three-hour wait to get in on Friday and Saturday night. Neither of us was in the mood to wait three hours.

Don said, "I'm going to pull off these last few dollars and head for the buffet." I said, "I'm right behind you." A few seconds later, Don tapped my arm and said, "Something happened." I looked over and he had a big red seven on the left reel. The other two reels showed wild cards. The light on top of the machine was flashing. However, the machine was not making any noise. Don said, "What's going on?" He then read a lit up sign that said, "attendant summoned". Then he read the small print on the side of the machine. It said, one wild card doubles the payout. Two wild cards quadruple the payout. He looked at the payout chart and saw that three red sevens pay twelve hundred and fifty dollars. Four times that is five thousand dollars. "Holy Cow!" shouted Don.

The attendant showed up and took Don's name and social security number. My credits played out while we waited and I ordered us another round drinks. The attendant showed back up with tax forms and asked him if he wanted Federal taxes taken out. He told them no. They asked if he wanted cash or a check. They told him that Mississippi taxes had to be taken out by law. In about ten more minutes two attendants and two security guards showed up and handed him forty-eight one hundred-dollar bills and change. Don looked over and said, "'Lucky' Joe, dinner's on me tonight. I think I can afford it." I said, "Great!"

We went up the escalator to the floor where the buffet was. We hit the restroom and Don had to use the pay phone to call his wife and share his excitement. I got us a spot in line. There was about a twenty-minute wait. Don finished his call and joined me in line. Ten minutes later we were seated. We explored the buffet. There was a fifty-foot stretch of food arranged around a three-wall alcove. Then there was a four-sided dessert station.

In the middle of the dessert area was a chef making Bananas Foster.

We grabbed a bowl and plate. I got some gumbo and a plate full of Cajun food. There was jambalaya, red beans and rice, Cajun shrimp, and other delicacies. Don also hit the Cajun area heavily. We both heated up our food with some red pepper-sauce. We went through that food and got another plate. Finally, we hit the dessert bar. Don got the Bananas Foster and I settled on cheesecake.

Somehow we got around to talking about Boudin. We both shared a liking for it. Boudin is cooked rice and meat that is formed into sausage links. It comes in many different styles. It is native to Cajun country, along with chicory coffee. The East Texas Coast over through the Mississippi Coast is noted for Cajun cuisine. Don and I both agreed, we had a taste in our mouths for some Boudin. It had been years since either one of us had the dish.

We left a tip and went back to the casino. Don decided to play a little blackjack to pass the time. I don't like blackjack. So I told Don

I'd be at one of the roulette tables. I remembered one of the billboards touting a single zero roulette wheel. There were eight roulette wheels. One of them had a single zero.

In Europe the roulette wheels have thirty-six numbers and zero. When zero comes up, the house takes everything. So once in every thirty-seven spins, the house gets the money. Statistically, they get about three percent of all the money that is bet. In America, the early casinos put zero and double zero on the roulette wheels. That doubled the amount that the house keeps.

I sat down at the single zero roulette wheel, and got a hundred dollars worth of five-dollar chips. When I play roulette, I play the side bets for the first hour. Then I play a number that hasn't come up in the last hour. My favorite number is twenty-seven followed by seven. I settled in and started playing red-and-black or odd-and-even. I lit up a Bering Churchill and ordered an O'Douls from the cocktail waitress. After about thirty minutes, I was dead even.

A player came up to the table. He was obviously feeling no pain. He was at the very end of the table and had to get the attendant to place his bets at the other end. After a few bets, he asked the attendant to put twenty on double zero. The attendant graciously explained that this wheel only had single zero. Indignantly, the player gathered up his chips and muttered, "I'm going to find me a wheel with double zero on it." I had to laugh to myself. He was looking for a wheel to give his money to the house twice as fast.

Don came by and said he was calling it a night. I told him I wasn't tired yet and was going to play a while longer. Thirty minutes later I had lost the hundred, so I quit the wheel. I walked around awhile and saw a bank of Mega-Bucks slot machines. I put my Grand Advantage Players Club card in the slot and "'Lucky' Joe Hall, Welcome to the Grand Casino Gulfport" scrolled across the message board. Next it said, "Your balance is 180 points." I remembered that at two hundred fifty points you could get a prize and free dinner at the buffet. I put in a hundred and started to play. After about twenty minutes, I hit a three-hundred-dollar jackpot. I had already lost two hundred and had put another hundred in this machine. I played a few minutes longer. When the counter got to three hundred even, I cashed out, then joined Don up in the room.

When I walked in Don, said, "How'd you do?" I told him that I had hit a three-hundred-dollar jackpot and had broken even for the night.

He was still excited from winning the Five Thousand and was having trouble getting to sleep. I suggested he take some Melatonin I had brought. He did and before long we were both asleep.

We got up Saturday morning with the sun. We got some coffee and were on the road by 8:00 AM. We talked about how exciting casinos were; the electricity in the air, players betting against the odds, trying to beat the house. Every now and then, one gets lucky and beats the house. Don was evidence of that. We quickly got into Louisiana. We saw hundreds of cars with LSU flags heading the opposite direction. We wondered where they were headed to watch LSU play football. We passed through Baton Rouge easily, since it was Saturday. Then we went over a swamp in bayou country. I-10 was a bridge for miles on end.

West of Baton Rouge, we got into rice country. There were rice fields on both sides of the Interstate for miles and miles. Occasionally, we would see an oil or gas well. We had skipped breakfast and were both hungry. We started looking at the billboards. There were a lot of Cajun restaurants advertised. We picked one and pulled off the Interstate.

The parking lot was full, but we got a space from a car that was leaving. Both of us were hoping they served Boudin. We got seated and looked at the menu. Everything was either fried seafood or crawdad salad. Looking around revealed that all the locals were getting the seafood special or the crawdad salad. We both ordered the seafood plate. The service was slow, but the food was good. However, we both still had a taste for Boudin. We gassed up the van and hit the road.

We still were passing rice fields one after the other. We crossed a long high, bridge at Lake Charles, Louisiana. From the bridge we saw casinos on both sides of the waterway. We saw several huge riverboat-shaped casinos. On shore there were hotels. We continued and crossed into Texas.

The sign for the Texas welcome center was welcome sight, indeed. We pulled in and got some information on Galveston. The lady at the desk informed us of a short cut to Galveston, which would enable us to skip Houston. We got back on the road and I told Don what was in the literature on Galveston. Neither one of us had ever been to Galveston. I excitedly said, "Don, this week Galveston Beach is having an Octoberfest." He got all excited. I thought he was going to kill me when I told him I was lying about the Octoberfest.

We got off I-10 at Winnie and headed southeast toward the coast. At Winnie, we ran into a traffic jam caused by the annual Winnie Rice Festival. We passed through more rice fields. Now there were lots of oil wells, slowly pumping "Black Gold". We saw gas wells also, but they weren't as plentiful as the oil wells. The land was as flat as flat can be in all directions. We could see the bridge over the InterCoastal Waterway from miles away. It was striking against all that flat land. Crossing the bridge, we saw the Gulf of Mexico.

We turned south on the coastal highway and drove the twenty-five miles or so to the ferry. That stretch of road is sparsely populated. Within fifteen minutes, we drove on the ferry and were crossing over the ship channel that goes into Galveston Bay. The ferry ride was free. We went up on the observation deck to get a good view. By the time we landed in Galveston, we had counted six ferries. Four were in service at the time. While crossing the channel, we saw a dozen or so ships waiting for tugs and harbor pilots to guide them through the channel to Galveston Bay.

It had been sprinkling rain, off and on, since we drove through Winnie. Now it was sporadically raining hard. Checking the map we headed for Moody Convention Center and the Galveston Gift Show. As we went down SeaWall Boulevard, we noticed that the sand was a dark gray color. Then we saw there were numerous oil-drilling platforms right off shore. Every two hundred or so yards there were rock jetties going out into the Gulf for fifty yards or so. Evidently, this was done to prevent beach erosion. The tops of the jetties were paved so that people could walk out on them.

Except for a dozen-or-so piers, all development was on the West Side of SeaWall Blvd. Most of the pier is house restaurants, but a couple of the buildings were gift shops. The one at the south end of the group is the Flagship Hotel. It's the only hotel on the waterside of SeaWall Blvd. It is over the water. There are a lot of hotels, motels, and condominiums on the west side of SeaWall Boulevard. We did notice that there are very few gift shops along the beach. We passed The Commodore By The Sea. Our reservations were there. We turned at the Moody Convention Center direction sign and drove to Moody Gardens.

Moody Gardens is a complex, which was endowed by a local entrepreneur. It is adjacent to the Galveston Airport and Offatts Bayou. Offatt's Bayou is an inlet that connects with the InterCoastal

Waterway. The entry to the convention center proved to be confusing. We passed warehouses and the edge of the water park, before we found the exhibitors entrance. The heavy rain didn't help matters. It was now about 4:00 PM. We were in luck and were able to drive into the center to unload. Show set-up is today and tomorrow. Most people had already unloaded. About half the exhibitors would not even come in until Sunday.

Don found the promoter and got our assigned space. We walked to the space. Water was dripping from the ceiling and collecting in a puddle right in the middle of the space. Don got the promoter over to the booth. He gave us the booth to the left and moved the others in the row down one. They had not shown up yet. So they never knew they had been moved, because the numbers stayed the same. Don and I wondered what he would do with the booth that leaked. We unloaded the van and covered everything up at the back of the new space. All we got with the booth rental was the space, draperies, and two chairs. We thanked the promoter and headed to the Commodore Motel.

The Commodore was an older motel that had seen a couple of renovations. We had to wait for the clerk to tell two couples they were sold out before we could check-in. At check-in they gave us some tokens for the ice machine. We saw the area where they served complimentary breakfast. A sign stated that coffee was available throughout the day. Don got in the van and drove around while I walked to the room.

Don parked the van at the stairway nearest our room, which was on the second floor. We unloaded the van and lugged the clothes and other items up the stairs. The room turned out to be small. The best part was the balcony and its two chairs. It reminded me of the Howard Johnson rooms in the 70's. One plus was an extra sink just outside the bathroom. That speeds up things in the morning when you're sharing a room. We got unpacked and Don was ready to explore the island. The rain had subsided and we settled into the van.

We took the map and went down to 61st St. It turned out to be a smorgasbord of fast food restaurants. The McDonald's was featuring a ninety-nine-cent special on Cajun chicken sandwiches. When 61st dead-ended into Broadway, we took a right turn and headed back north. This was an older area and had a lot of vacant buildings. At 32nd Street, I saw a sign that said Leo's Cajun Corner. The property had a chain link fence around it and we thought it was closed down. We continued on down Broadway and proceeded to get lost around the Shriner's Hospital for burn victims. SeaWall Boulevard came into view and we headed back toward the motel. It was now dark and raining again.

We were both starving and stopped at the 24-hour coffeehouse just north of the Commodore. Today's special was the T-bone steak dinner. Don and I ordered the specials and listened to the rain. The steaks were mediocre, but they stopped our hunger pains. About the time we finished eating, the rain let up and we drove back to the motel.

We got back to the room and Don poured us each a double shot of brandy. Don swore that he would get us some brandy snifters at the Wal-Mart Supercenter. We had seen it near the turn to Moody Gardens Convention Center. Both of us laughed about drinking the expensive brandy in the motel glasses. I got a La Gloria Cubana out of my travel humidor. Don got an H. Upmann Souvenir out of his. The Souvenirs come wrapped in cedar. We adjourned to the balcony and got out the butane torch lighters.

It was dark now and we could see lights of over a dozen oil platforms. The rain had let up again and it was nice and cool. Traffic was heavy on SeaWall Boulevard. After all, it was Saturday night. We could see the lights on some big ships north of us toward the ship channel. There were some smaller boats lit up that we figured were shrimp boats. We could see their green lights. They were moving from our left to our right. It was a perfect evening to relax and enjoy our cigars and brandy. It had been a long two days. We finished our cigars and turned in early.

The drapes had been left ajar and the rising sun awoke us. Don showered and shaved first and headed for the Continental Breakfast. I caught up with him and got a bowl of raisin bran and two small cheese Danish, along with some decaffeinated coffee. I was attempting to cut back on caffeine. Don got himself another orange juice and I got a complimentary paper. There were some Rattan chairs and a TV tuned to the Weather Channel. The Weather Channel forecast sporadic heavy rain for the entire time we were to be in Galveston.

We went back to the room to pick up some items, then headed back to the Moody Gardens Convention Center to set-up our booth. We found a good parking spot and carried our things into the building. The show area was buzzing with activity. We headed toward our booth. The mystery about the leaky booth was solved. The promoter had put a sponge dealer in it and the booth next to it. I guess he figured the water wouldn't hurt sponges. There was a bucket under the leak.

The booth on the other side of us was also set up as a double wide. There was a large busted woman about 5'6" with shoulder length Auburn hair. She appeared to be in her forties and had a nice figure and a smile that could light up the night. The sign said "Royal T's". We went over to her and Don said, "It looks like we're neighbors. I'm Don Smith and this is 'Lucky' Joe Hall." She smiled and said, "I'm Candy Royal, it's a pleasure to meet you." She was in the process of hanging T-shirts on her display. Candy asked what we did. I told her that we were also in the T-shirt business. I also told her that Don Smith was the owner of the company and that I was National Sales Manager. We learned that her business was located in Daytona Beach, Florida. She had been in business for over ten years. Her designs are beach—and resort-oriented and are prominently name-dropped.

Name-dropping means putting the name of the tourist location below or in the design. Some examples of name drop are "Daytona Beach", "Galveston Island", and "Gatlinburg, Tennessee". After a little small talk we went to work setting up our booth. By 11:00 AM, we were finished, ready for action, and in high spirits. After securing the booth for the evening, we walked around the show. There were close to 100 exhibitors set up at the show. At least a dozen T-shirt companies and a half dozen embroidery companies had booths. Shell items and souvenirs were plentiful. Costume jewelry and sun tanning products were abundant.

After strolling through the show, which took a good fifteen minutes, we decided to check out the rest of Moody Gardens. We went outside, lit up a cigar, and started walking. In view was a ten-story framework of steel. They were building a convention hotel next to the convention center. Toward the bayou, two four-sided glass pyramids rose up about six stories. To the right of the glass pyramids, was the Water Park. We walked across a lawn for several hundred yards toward the Water Park. Since it was Sunday, there were hundreds of people splashing and riding the water rides. We got to the park and walked to the left along the perimeter fence. It wasn't long before we got to the entrance. People were still streaming into the park.

After watching for a few minutes, we took the sidewalk to the glass pyramids. There was a ticket booth and we found out that there was a museum, an IMAX theater, and multiple garden areas. You could buy individual tickets or a master ticket for all three, at substantial savings. Moody Gardens is a non-profit, tax free, enterprise. It is greatly endowed by the Moody Family and is run by a board. We finished our cigars and walked around the public area and gardens.

Inside the first pyramid, there was a restaurant with a buffet. The buffet menu looked good and the price very reasonable. It was lunchtime so we ate the buffet. The soups were excellent. They had fresh baked bread and a good chef preparing the dishes. The entrees were succulent and the triple chocolate cake was out of this world. Our tip was hefty, as the service was fast and polite. We walked outside the glass pyramid and saw that rain was threatening again. We hurried to the van and drove around Galveston once more.

We passed Leo's Cajun Corner again. Don turned around and we rode back to check it out. The fence gates were closed and locked. From the front it looked as if it were out of business. We drove around the backside. From the back, we could see stacks of wood and other evidence that Leo's was still in business. Evidently, Leo's closes early Saturday and all day Sunday. We had heard that the downtown area was where the action is in Galveston. After some driving, we found the downtown area. There were lots of restaurants and shops. We saw the Galveston Tourist Information Center and got some tourist papers and brochures.

There is a trolley that makes a loop downtown and a second trolley that makes a run to SeaWall Boulevard and back. Both stop in front of the Galveston Tourist Information Center. We bought tickets and rode the downtown loop on the trolley. There are tracks in the middle of the street. Part of the ride took us down to the dock area along the InterCoastal Waterway. We got off there and walked around.

Our ticket was for unlimited use of the trolley for the entire day. There were dozens of shrimp boats. A replica offshore drilling rig was set up and admission is by a three-dollar donation. It has a self-guided walking tour. People were fishing along the seawall. An oriental couple was catching reds. They surely were excited. We saw a sign advertising cigars and walked into the store. The humidor had the door wide open and didn't look like it was working. Some of the cigars had the outside wrapper cracked. The prices were super high and we left without making a purchase.

The trolley was heading back to the waterfront area. We walked over, got back on, and made the rest of the downtown loop. After the rest of the loop, we started walking again. We found an antique and collectibles store that sold sodas and beer. Don got a Bud Lite and I got an O'Douls. They were ice cold and tasted great. The store had some collector coins. They were priced "Full Tourist". However, most of the items in the store were very reasonably priced, especially the beer. We finished the beers and got another round to go. We finished touring downtown and headed back to the motel.

It was starting to get dark. We went through the drive through at the McDonald's on 61st Street. They prepared us a sack full of the 99-cent "Cajun chicken" sandwiches, and fries. We also got a Coke and a Diet Coke. When we got back to the motel, we feasted on the sandwiches. The Weather Channel showed that another heavy rain area was due to hit Galveston in a couple of hours. Don poured us each a shot of brandy in plastic Dixie Cups. We grabbed a couple of Bering Churchill cigars and walked across SeaWall Boulevard to the beach. It was fairly breezy, with the wind coming directly off the Gulf. We lit the cigars with our butane jet lighters and walked out the nearest jetty where there were some people fishing. They had been fishing for an hour or so with no luck. We looked out in the Gulf. The oil platforms and shrimp boats' lights were shining. Looking north we could see the Flagship Hotel about a mile up the beach. Looking south we could see a solitary fishing pier about a mile in the distance. We finished our cigars, headed back to the room and called it a night.

The Monday morning sun woke us up before the alarm went off. It had rained most of the night, which made for good sleeping. We showered, dressed, and hit the Continental Breakfast. I stayed with the raisin bran, cheese Danish, and decaf coffee. We got over to the show about ten after eight and readied for business.

Don had gone by the Sam's Club in Valdosta before we left and bought several bags of the new Hershey's hard candies. Each candy is individually wrapped and there are four flavors. They are chocolate, butterscotch, mint, and caramel. My favorite is the caramel. We put the candy in a big, old fashioned, general-store glass candy jar; the kind that angles toward the customer, with the big round opening, and bright red lid. We left the lid in Valdosta.

Candy Royal opened up her booth and we got started conversing about the candy. She had a bowl of assorted candies on her table. Candy had never seen the Hershey's hard candies except for on TV commercials. She had been coming to this show since it started. She goes to about twenty shows a year, and she told us that this was an extremely slow show, but that there were four buyers that were "heavy hitters". Each one had multiple stores.

Nine o'clock arrived and the show opened up to the buyers. It was nine-thirty before we had a buyer walk by our booth. I had made some computer-generated signs that read, "SALES REPS WANTED". I put one on the show bulletin board and another on our front table. Looking toward the aisle, the front table abutted the left side of the booth. The other table ran down the left side from the front table. Our hottest designs were displayed on the modular show display. On the right side of the booth there was a chrome portable rolling unit that held the rest of our designs. The front table had a stack of color flyers. All eighteen designs were on the flyer. In the middle of the table was the large candy jar.

I looked over and saw that Candy had settled into a paperback novel. Don threw one of the Hershey's candies in a high arc and it landed beside her book with a "bang". It startled Candy and she looked up. We were laughing and she realized what had happened. She said, "I thought you were nice, mild mannered

'Georgia Boys'. Now I know I was wrong. It's going to be one of 'those' kind of shows." She laughed, closed her book and came over. We gave Candy some of the candies and asked her about the show.

She said that although it was a very slow show, she had established one major account that she wrote a big order with. She also picked up a couple of new accounts every year. She also said that her sales rep for Texas was usually here with her. Her rep had called and was in the hospital recovering from surgery.

Don had quit doing shows years ago. He had done major shows like Atlanta, Dallas, New York, and Chicago. They were busy with buyers and a lot of business was written. Don's personality is fairly hyper. I could see that he was going to be bored to tears. Candy tried one of the chocolate candies and remarked, "This is good." I popped one of the butterscotch candies and said, "This is strong. It's real good though." Don tried one of the mint flavored and said, "This is strong too!"

A man in a flashy suit walked up and joined us. Candy introduced us to her boyfriend, Sam Jones. She told us that Sam was National Sales Manager for a hat company that sells embroidered caps. Don and Sam started telling jokes and hit it off immediately. Sam smokes cigarettes and Candy is a non-smoker. Sam's booth was in the middle aisle on the corner of the crosswalk. Sam headed outside for a smoke and Don joined him to smoke a short stogie.

Candy and I continued to talk until a buyer came to my booth and started looking at the Cigar Tees. We wrote a small order. I then realized that she was the buyer for the store we had been in yesterday in downtown Galveston . . . the one that sold cigars. I didn't mention our experience. I informed her that the first order would be sent COD and that she could apply for thirty-day credit terms. I thanked her for the order and she went on her way.

I started working the crossword puzzle in the paper. After a few minutes I got the feeling someone was staring at me. I glanced up and looked around. No one was looking at me. However, I noticed a woman in the exhibit across from us. The company name is Sally Sells Shells. They had taken ten spaces. It comprised the first five spaces from the crosswalk, double wide, and went past us. The first three sections had a metal framework adjacent to the aisles and cross walk aisle. From the framework, large shell mobiles were hanging, along with dried blowfish and other beach souvenirs. The next two sections were tables that had merchandise packed in tight display.

The woman was looking at the large beautiful shell mobiles and had a beautiful inquisitive smile on her face. Sort of like a child that has seen their first teddy bear. She appeared to be about 5'9" and had the currently elegant pageboy styled blonde hair. Her dress was very professional and accentuated her beautiful legs. Her eyes were a beautiful shade of blue. She had on her thin frame a business suit. She wasn't skinny, just thin. I noted her inquisitive smile and went back to working my crossword puzzle.

It wasn't long before Don returned to our booth. I showed him the order. He said, "At least we're not going to be 'skunked'." I agreed. Just then the sponge guy came in. He had set up Saturday evening after we had left, and we hadn't seen him on Sunday. He had an armload of bags from What-A-Burger. I would guess his weight to be around three hundred pounds. His smile was huge and gregarious. Don and

I went over and introduced ourselves. We talked as he waded into the What-A-Burger biscuit sandwiches and coffee.

His name is Angelo Onassis. His business is in Tarpon Springs, Florida. He has a retail tourist shop near the sponge docks. He retails and runs a wholesale operation out of the warehouse in the back. His wife handles the retail and he makes shows and does the wholesale. In his younger days, he was a sponge diver. We asked Angelo if he is related to the famous Aristotle Onassis. He roared, "Would I be at this show, selling sponges and eating What-A-Burger biscuits, if I were related to Aristotle Onassis?" We all laughed and quickly became friends.

I noticed that the lady I had seen earlier admiring the shell mobiles was in the next booth. She was talking with a younger lady. The booth was a double wide and the sign said "LIZ, Inc." There was an array of children's T-shirts.

Angelo had finished with the biscuits, for now, and told us about Tarpon Springs. He was part of the Greek culture that had settled there. The sponge industry had flourished there until the man-made sponges came along. Now, natural sponges were used more for decoration than anything else. Gift Shops on the beaches sold them and that's how Angelo was making his living. He bought sponges from the divers and wholesaled them all over the country. He told us that he wouldn't do this show except for two accounts that bought only at this show every year.

Angelo got up and said, "I've got to have a cigarette." Don told me that he'd guard the booth if I wanted to go. I thanked him and went outside with Angelo. There was a covered triple driveway at the doors on the parking lot side of the building. Several people were smoking. Angelo lit up a Camel cigarette and I got out a Las Cabrillas Robusto. Robustos are fairly big short cigars. They last around twenty to thirty minutes. It just depends on how fast you smoke. I lit up and watched the rain come down in buckets.

Angelo told me that the promoter had given him the second booth for free. He didn't want to have a vacant booth right in the middle of the aisle. That just didn't look good and water can't hurt sponges. I had to listen closely when Angelo spoke. His thick Greek accent was a little hard to understand, but his roaring laugh and jovial smile were easy to understand. He was well liked. He lit a second, then a third cigarette. I put the cigar in the sand filled smoke stand and returned to the booth.

Don was about to go stir-crazy. He had to be doing something. Buyers only walked by every twenty minutes or so. At major shows the buyers outnumber the sellers. At small regional shows like this, the sellers way outnumber the buyers. It was nearing lunch time, so Don took off to ride around and said he would bring me back some lunch.

I finished the crossword puzzle and quickly became bored. Candy was engrossed in her book and Angelo had gone smoking. I thought to myself, Angelo doesn't spend much time in the booth. Someone had already come by and asked about Angelo. Before I could say anything they said, "He's probably outside smoking. I'll catch him there." Some buyers interrupted Candy and asked some questions. They took a catalog and said they would come back. They said they were just looking today and would write business tomorrow and the next day.

I started a conversation with Candy out of boredom. She told me how she had gotten into the T-shirt business. She had been sales manager for a T-shirt business when it went under. One of the partners had been stealing money out of the business to cover gambling debts. Candy's husband bought the equipment and assets from the bank at a fraction of its original cost and she was in business. She later caught him with another woman and wound up with the business after the divorce.

Candy was a good businesswoman. She had hired the artist and the good employees from the former company. The company continued with the same customers and sales force. It just had a different name and a new owner. Overhead was a lot lower and it made more money than it ever had. She kept the sales area and had an assistant, with a detail personality, doing the production and shipping. She had a bookkeeper to do the invoicing and other book work. Candy's personality is "people person". She loves sales and working with people. We got interrupted when some buyers came into my booth and wrote an order for March 1, 1998 shipment.

Many of the gift shops close down for the off season. They open weekends in March and April, then full time, with long hours, May through September. October and November they open for weekends.

Around 2:00 PM, Don showed back up with a bag from Leo's Cajun Corner. There were two smoked Boudin sausages on hot dog buns and a bowl of red beans and rice. There was also a 16-oz. Styrofoam cup of iced tea. Georgia time was now 3:00 PM and I was starving. As I tore into the food, Don told me about Leo's.

Leo is a Cajun and only opened Monday through Saturday. During the week his hours are 10 AM to 6 PM. Saturday's hours are 10 Am to 3 PM. Leo's is a true family operation. Over the years the neighborhood had deteriorated and he added the security fence. The fence cut down on vandalism dramatically. His prices were more than reasonable. For $3.50 you could get the special. The special is two pieces of Boudin sausage, red beans and rice, potato salad, and bread. A Boudin sausage, on a hot dog bun, is only $1.25.

We gloated in our good fortune to find real Cajun food. Don said that Leo's did a lot of shipping around the country. There are a lot of people like Don and me that like Cajun cooking. We just live in places you can't get it. Leo told Don that on many orders, the Red Label UPS shipping was as much or more than the price of the order. I almost cried when I finished. I had savored every bite. It had been uncounted years since I had enjoyed Boudin.

Most people don't understand my passion for Boudin. It's one of those things you either love or hate. I guess you've got to like peppers and pepper-sauce to understand. Pepper-sauce goes great on Boudin. Don and I finally found something in Galveston that impressed us . . . Leo's Cajun Corner.

Candy Royal called over to us, "Don! 'Lucky' Joe! I've got some people I want you to meet." She walked over to our table with them. She said, "This is Anne Moore. She owns LIZ, Inc." Then Anne said, "This is Karen Stark. She manages the showroom in the Dallas Mart that some of my sales reps work out of." Karen was the younger girl I had seen earlier in the LIZ, Inc. booth talking with Anne. Karen appeared to be around 5'4" tall and was overweight . . . not obese or anything, just overweight. She had short blonde hair, a hoarse voice, and a hearty smile. Anne was the lady I had seen in the "Sally Sells Shells" booth. I remembered her 'inquisitive' smile.

Candy said, "Enough formality, let's get into the candy. Anne and Karen haven't tried the new Hershey's hard candies." Anne picked a chocolate. Candy got a mint. Don got a mint. Karen picked a chocolate and I tried a caramel. Everyone agreed that the candy was very flavorful. We kidded around and Don told some jokes. Someone asked if Don and I were going to the show party tonight. We didn't know anything about it.

Candy and Anne informed us that there was a free party for the exhibitors and buyers every year the first night of the show. Candy said,

"The promoter puts it on as part of his show." We made some small talk and got to know each other. Some buyers started coming down the aisle. Anne and Karen headed back to their booth and Candy went to hers. Don went to find the promoter to find out about the party.

Don came back with information about the party. It was to be at the Ocean Grill seafood restaurant from 5:30 to 7:00. The show closes at five thirty. The Ocean Grill is located at 2227 SeaWall Blvd. The promoter told Don that it occupied the first pier north of the Flagship Hotel. There were free heavy hors d'oeuvres and beverages. Don had all of the show that he could stand for one day. He headed for the motel and said, "I'll see you around five."

I made another sale and talked with Angelo. He headed out to smoke a Camel or two. I talked with Candy about the novel she was reading. After what seemed like an eternity, Don appeared. The rules for the show say that the booth is supposed to be manned the entire time the show is open. We cheated a little and left at 5:15 for the party.

We got there about 5:30 and entered the Ocean Grill. The hostess told us the party was at the end of the pier. We walked through the restaurant until we saw a sign. It read, "PRIVATE PARTY, Admittance by Show Badge Only". We put on our badges and went through the door to the party. On the other side of the door was a covered area of the pier. A buffet was set up in the middle of the covered area. There was a bar set up on the side of the covered area. Past the covered area was an open area with round white plastic tables and white Captain's chairs.

We got a table at the end of the pier next to the railing. A waiter came over and asked if we would like anything to drink. Don ordered a Bud Lite and I ordered an O'Douls. He politely explained that the Bud Lite would be free, but mine would be two dollars and fifty cents. I told him to go ahead. Don laughed as I complained that beer was free and non-alcoholic beer wasn't.

We headed to the buffet to get some food. Don went down one side and I went down the other. I got some shrimp and chicken fingers. There were some slow people in front of me, so Don finished the line ahead of me and returned to the table. At the end of the buffet was a big serving dish of what looked like hush puppies. I couldn't imagine them serving hush puppies at a party. They usually go with fried fish and grits. I took the serving spoon and broke one open. They were crab balls. I put several on my little plate that was full of shrimp and chicken. Then I returned to the table.

The waiter showed up with the drinks and I gave him three dollars. I attacked the shrimp and chicken with gusto. Don said, "I can't believe you got hush puppies when there's shrimp." I said, "I thought they were hush puppies too, until I broke one open. They're crab balls." I gave him two of the four I had garnered. We tried them and they were great. In a few minutes the waiter returned and we ordered another round. We asked him about the crab balls. He explained they were the specialty of the restaurant. The Ocean Grill was famous for the crab balls.

We decided to load up on crab balls. We looked up at the buffet and saw a line that was curved around and out the door. One thing Don and I both agree to one hundred percent is that we don't do lines. The waiter brought the drinks and I gave him another three dollars.

The view at the end of the pier was great. The wind was heavy and the spray from the whitecaps was being carried in the air. It was too breezy to enjoy a cigar. We decided to leave. It was a few minutes after six when we got to the van. We both wanted some more Cajun food from Leo's, but he was closed. I said, "Why don't we go to that park we saw from the ferry, on the north end of the island?" Don replied, "Times a wasting."

We had to go around to the westernmost road on the island. To get to it you had to go across like you were going to I-45. We got to the road and passed a sulfur plant and a college. Then we passed a lot of heavy industry. We finally got to the park. The gate was closed and had a sign, which read, "PARK CLOSED, Hours: 6AM to 6PM. From the ferry, We had seen a fishing pier at the tip of the park. Most fishing piers are open 24 hours a day. We were frustrated and headed back to the Commodore. The McDonald's drive through supplied us with a bag of Cajun chicken sandwiches.

At the room we ate the sandwiches and got ready to smoke cigars on the balcony. Don offered me some brandy, which I declined. I had a slight headache and didn't want to aggravate it. He said, "I can't believe we've drunk this much brandy! The bottle must be thick glass." I got a La Gloria Cubana and Don got a H. Upmann Souvenir with the cedar wrapping. We lit up and enjoyed the evening and sights from the balcony. The balcony protected us from most of the wind. We enjoyed our cigars and called it a night.

Tuesday morning we awoke again with the sun. We showered, dressed and hit the Continental Breakfast again. I got one of the complementary papers. I figured I'd get to read every inch at the show, where Don dropped me off, saying he said he would see me around noon, and bring some Leo's Cajun food. When I got to the booth, Anne was at Candy's table.

They asked why Don and I hadn't gone to the party. I explained that we had left a few minutes after six. They hadn't gotten there until six fifteen. They told me that the party didn't break up until after ten. I said, "The information said it was from 5:30 to 7:30." Candy replied, "That's just for the free stuff. It's a cash bar after that."

I asked Anne why her company was called LIZ, Inc. She told me that she knew a company name needed to be short. Anne explained that she also wanted the name to reflect that a woman owned it. Anne said, "My full name is Anne Elizabeth Moore. I took the LIZ out of Elizabeth and added Inc." I said, "It's a great name." She thanked me and headed to her booth as some buyers had turned onto our aisle.

Candy and I started talking about sales reps. I had explained to her that we had done the show in hopes of hiring some sales reps. I also told her that no one had mentioned our sign. Candy told me that if anyone mentioned the sign, chances are we didn't want them. They would be new and just starting out. They would not have the buyer contacts that we were looking for. She verified my thinking that it took years to build up the contacts.

Candy also told me, that in some territories, the sales reps have sub reps. She also told me that commissions for clothing averaged around ten per cent. Anne's buyer had crossed over to another aisle, so Anne rejoined us. I asked her how she had gotten into the T-shirt business.

She thought a second and told me that she had gotten a divorce after twenty years of marriage. Anne had gotten tired of the corporate world. She had been with IBM for twenty years and had risen into top sales management. Her territory covered from St. Petersburg through Orlando on up to Jacksonville. Another manager had the area south of that to Miami. The third Florida Manager had the area from Tallahassee over to Pensacola. Anne got a chance for early retirement and took it.

Anne was fortunate enough to have a father that taught her about wealth and wealth creation. She had saved ten to fifty percent of everything she had made in stocks and mutual funds. She was rather secure financially.

She related that during the six months she waited to retire, she looked for something to do. She and Candy had met when she was training a new salesperson in Daytona. Candy had inquired about an IBM system and over time they had become good friends. Anne told Candy that she was retiring and was looking for some kind of business to get into. Candy told her of a T-shirt business she knew of in Tampa that was for sale. Anne investigated and bought the assets and incorporated as LIZ, Inc.

Anne asked about me. I told her about selling out "Lucky" Joe's Furniture Stores and going into the consulting business. I told Anne and Candy that I didn't realize that it would be this hard to find good sales reps. they sympathized with me.

Don walked up and joined us. He said that he forgot to ask me what I wanted from Leo's Cajun Corner. He asked Candy and Anne if they liked Cajun Food. Anne said that she loved it and Candy said she could take it or leave it. Candy said that she would probably just get a sandwich with Sam. Don got out Leo's menu and went over it with Anne. She asked if Don would get something for Karen. He said, "Sure!" Leo's had four kinds of Boudin. He made regular, smoked, spicy, and crawfish Boudin. I ordered the special with spicy Boudin and a half-pint of gumbo. Anne came back with an order for her and Karen. Don took off for Leo's.

Some buyers came by and I wrote an order. I handed them over to Candy and she wrote an order with them also. Candy read her novel and I perused the paper while I waited on Don. He showed up shortly and we feasted. He asked if I wanted him to hang around long enough for me to smoke a cigar. I told Don that I would much appreciate it. Angelo and I headed out to the covered drive. He pulled out a Camel and I a Las Cabrillas Robusto. When I got back to the table, Don had written an order for March delivery. He said he'd be back by five thirty and took off.

I wrote a couple of orders amid the boredom and Don reappeared a little after five. He told Candy a few jokes. Shortly, it was five thirty. We closed up and headed for Leo's Cajun Corner.

It was the first time I got to see the inside. I spied the smoked riblets and ordered a pound and a half-pint of red beans and rice for supper.

Don ordered some smoked sausage sandwiches and a pint of gumbo. We took our treasures and headed to The Commodore. Don and I were not impressed with Galveston, other than Leo's. We ate most of our food and decided to explore up I-45 toward Houston. We were told there was a big shopping mall. It was across the InterCoastal Waterway and up Interstate Highway I-45.

Don steered the van onto I-45. There was a very long bridge over the waterway. Across the waterway we could see "Texas City". Some people call it the "Toxic Mile". It's a line of chemical plants along the waterway. The lights at night are a sight to see. Once a ship exploded there and sent debris over a several mile radius. We saw a billboard advertising the mall. We got off at the exit and saw a huge greyhound track. It had been years since either one of us had been to the dog races.

We parked and went in. The escalator lifted us up to the second floor. The crowd was sparse and half the food service stands were closed. Over half the betting windows were closed. I got an O'Douls and Don refused a beer when he found out they cost three dollars. He got a Coke instead. We looked in the program. Then we pooled some money and boxed a quinela.

We went outside and lit up a couple of Bering's and watched the handlers lead the dogs to the starting gate. For some reason, there was no excitement in the air. Our dogs came in at the back of the pack. We half-heartedly bet on another race. Our dogs came in first and third. We struck up a conversation with one o f the track workers. He told us the crowds had gotten worse and worse since Louisiana legalized casino gambling. He told us buses carry people from the Galveston Area to Lake Charles every day. He said the people that owned the track were hoping Texas would legalize casino gambling at the dog tracks.

We finished our cigars and headed back to the van. It wasn't long and we were back at The Commodore. We had seen a billboard for the Isle of Capri Casino in Lake Charles, Louisiana. Don remembered there was an ad in this morning's paper. We found the ad. He called and booked us a room in the Isle of Capri Hotel at the newspaper's coupon rate for Thursday night. Since it was for a weeknight, the rate was most reasonable. We were excited about the prospects of being at the casinos that we had seen crossing the Lake Charles Bridge.

Don went to put a couple of cigars in his humidor. He asked me if I had borrowed some cigars. I was into my humidor and noticed that I was missing around five of my La Gloria Cubana Cigars. I told him about my missing cigars. He told me he was missing around five of his H. Upmann's. Then Don went to get a shot of brandy and the bottle was over half empty. Don said, "We've got a maid with a taste for expensive booze and premium cigars." She had not taken any of the less expensive Bering cigars. We fussed and fumed and called it a night.

The alarm clock woke us Wednesday morning. It was raining hard and the sun was nowhere in sight. We hit the Continental Breakfast again. I grabbed a paper and we went to the show. We took all our cigars and the brandy with us. It was raining hard again, as it had off and on the entire time we were in Galveston. When I entered the auditorium, I noticed several of the Moody Gardens Personnel at the end of the auditorium. They had mops and buckets and were trying to "stem the tide". Water was advancing across the floor toward the booths. The roof had been leaking with the rain before. Now it was leaking like a sieve.

Don and I struck up a conversation with the supervisor. He told us they had just spent a hundred thousand with a contractor to fix the roof. The convention center had been built twelve years ago. It had been plagued with a leaky roof since day one. The architect had been more interested in style than function. It was frustrating to the Moody Gardens people.

We headed to our booth and noticed there were two huge garbage cans in Angelo's booth. There was also one of those yellow plastic, fold out, warning signs. Angelo had not appeared yet. It was still too early for Angelo. He would show up about an hour after the show started with bags from What-A-Burger. Then after feasting would adjourn to his office at the covered drive to smoke Camel's. He had written some big orders with the major buyers. His sales dwarfed ours.

There were very few buyers in the building. The torrential downpour was taking its toll. Don and I joined Candy down at the LIZ, Inc. booth. Karen and Anne were both there and so was Candy's boyfriend Sam Jones. We talked about the dog track and how boring it was. They had all gone to a seafood restaurant last night. The plan for tonight was to go to an Italian restaurant Anne had been to the year before. Anne and Candy chimed in for us to join them at the Italian place. We agreed to go and Don started cracking jokes. We were all in tears when Angelo showed up with his What-A-Burger bags.

We had a good time chatting. Don took off with Angelo to the smoking area and Anne joined them with a pack of Dunhill cigarettes. Candy went to her novel. She was almost finished reading it. I perused the paper and worked the crossword puzzle. Don came back about an hour later and offered to guard the booth while I enjoyed a cigar. I headed out with a Las Cabrillas Robusto and found Angelo "holding court" under the covered drive.

He was talking with some buyers and made an appointment to meet with them at 2 PM. Angelo is one of those people who lives life to the fullest and is fun to be around. The rain had just stopped. Thirty minutes later, when I was finishing my Robusto, some buyers started drifting in.

I was beginning to get concerned. We were nearing the end of the show and I had made zero progress on getting sales reps.

Two of the people I had approached told me they had more lines than they could handle. A company owner also reprimanded me for talking to one of his sales reps.

I talked to Candy about my experience. She told me that most good reps handle around twelve lines. Candy said, "Most sales reps have been burned a time or two by companies that "stiffed" them on commissions or went out of business owing them. The good reps are very cautious about taking on a new line. She said they are notorious about not returning phone calls. Her experience was that the reps that stayed on the road did the best. The ones that hang around the mart showrooms do the worst. Some of them make their money on the participation fees they charge the manufacturers.

I asked Candy how she handled the sales she did at the gift shows. She told me they were credited to the sales rep that had the territory. The reason to be at the show was to pick up new business. It was hard to get the reps to "cold call" to generate new business. They spent their time calling on existing accounts. Once you set up a new account, they would add it to their call list. Some buyers stopped to try the Hershey's candy. I wrote a nice order for the Cigar Tees.

Don came back and told me that while he was smoking, two of the other exhibitors were talking about missing liquor and cigars. They were sharing a room at The Commodore on the third floor. They suspected it and had marked their bottle on Monday. Tuesday night it was down about two inches.

Don brought up the idea of taking back some Cajun food to Valdosta. He said we could buy some Styrofoam coolers at the Wal-Mart Supercenter and keep it iced. I enthusiastically agreed. We wrote down an order to pick up tomorrow when we left the show. Don made the daily lunch run to Leo's and placed the order. I wrote another order while he was gone and enjoyed my Leo's Special until he returned. Today I had chosen the Crawfish Boudin.

The afternoon quickly became boring. A quick investigation around 3:30 PM revealed that there were only two buyers in the whole show. It was raining again and the Moody Gardens employees were mopping again. Angelo had a deck of cards he used to play solitaire. Karen, Don, and I had gathered around Angelo's table. I said, "Why don't we play liar's poker."

Angelo heartily laughed and said, "I haven't played that in years. I'm in." Don and Karen had never played. We all got out some pennies. Every one antes a penny and the winner gets the pot and deals the next hand. Angelo complained that he used to play for dollars, not pennies. The hand passes around with each one getting to draw cards to improve the poker hand. After the person draws cards he has to declare the hand. The person getting the hand can either accept the hand or say, "I think you are lying". If the hand is there, the caller wins. If it's different, the challenger wins.

Angelo won the first deal. He dealt to Karen. She drew and declared a pair of Kings. Don accepted it, drew and declared a pair of Kings with an Ace. I accepted it and threw the Kings away. I declared three Kings and Angelo accepted it. I saw his big bushy eyebrows go up as he looked at the hand. He called three Kings with a ten. Karen took the cards and drew two. She told Don three Kings with a Queen. Don took the hand and almost gasped. There were no Kings. He knew someone had thrown away the Kings. He just hoped it wasn't me. He drew one card. He declared three Kings with a Queen and an eight. I said, "Turn em up, I don't believe you." He turned up a hodgepodge with no Kings. Angelo laughed and laughed. We all started laughing and Anne, Candy and Sam came over to watch the fun. Don accused Angelo of throwing away the Kings. Angelo just laughed. He knew I had thrown them away.

We had a good time playing and it was quickly five thirty. Don and I headed to The Commodore and got ready to meet the others at the Italian restaurant at 7 PM.

We drove down the street the restaurant was on. It was entirely residential. Then at a corner we saw the restaurant. It looked more like a house than a restaurant. We were a few minutes early, and having gotten there before the others, we went ahead and spoke for a table for six. We told the waiter we were waiting for more in our group. The history on the menu stated that the founder had started the restaurant in the front of her home and that it had been expanded three times over the years. The restaurant quickly filled up and kept the hostess very busy.

We spotted Candy, Sam, Karen, and Anne as they arrived and motioned them over to our table. I thought I noticed that Anne went out of her way to sit next to me. Sam said, "Please don't blame me for being late", pointing the verbal finger at the girls, who apologized. The waiter took our drink orders and went over the evening specials. Don ordered a bottle of wine for the table.

Candy and Anne named all the menu items they had gotten on their previous visits, saying that it had all been excellent. Anne raved about having gotten the Veal Marsala the previous year, so I ordered the Veal Marsala as did Anne and Don. The food was excellent and Don was the life of the party. I was wishing I had the ability to remember jokes like Don. A good time was had by all and it quickly became 9:30. As we were breaking up, Anne told me they were staying at the Flagship Hotel and were going for a walk when they returned. It was as if she wanted us to join them, but we headed back to The Commodore.

When we got back, the rain had quit. I suggested to Don that we take a walk on the beach, since it was the last night. He said, "Let's go." We each got a Bering and a shot of brandy. We put on windbreakers, as there was a pretty good gale coming off the Gulf. When we crossed SeaWall Boulevard, we saw that the water was all the way up to the protective wall in places. The water was crashing into the jetties, and occasionally, waves rolled right across them.

We stayed on the sidewalk and walked toward the Flagship Hotel.

When our cigars were half-gone we turned and walked back south. We had gotten within a block of the Flagship. We headed to our room and called it a night.

The alarm woke us up Thursday morning. It was raining and dark. We complained to the manager about the missing cigars and brandy. He told us that he appreciated the information and would take it up with the owner. We hit the Continental Breakfast for the last time, then loaded the van in the rain. Don pulled up to the front door of the Wal-Mart Supercenter. I went in and got us a couple of coolers. When I walked outside, he pulled back up to the door and I got in with the coolers.

Don drove out the side entrance to the Supercenter' parking lot and took the road one block parallel to SeaWall Blvd. We passed a convenience store that had premium cigars on the road sign. Don turned the van around and we investigated. To our surprise, there was a walk-in humidifier. The prices were quite reasonable, so we selected several cigars. At the cash register, we discovered that the owner was from Thailand. He had gone to school in the U.S. and stayed. His family had loaned him the money to purchase the convenience store. He enjoyed cigars himself and had built the "walk in" humidor. His cigar sales were a significant part of his business. We talked about cigars and headed to Moody Gardens.

We went into the show and planned our escape. We did everything we could to be ready. It was raining so hard that Don decided to stay at the show. After Angelo finished his What-A-Burger breakfast biscuits, he and Don went out to the covered driveway. I stopped Anne as she walked by and told her that we had gone walking after the dinner. I said, "You and Karen must have walked to the north of the Flagship, because we didn't run into ya'll." She said, "When we got back, the wind was blowing so hard, that we just went to the end of the pier and watched the people fishing. I wish I'd known that you were going to take a walk."

Before Anne could say anything else, Candy joined us and we talked about how good the Italian restaurant was. We went over how much fun we had. I discovered Anne and Candy would both be at the Panama City Beach Gift Show. It was only nine days from now. A buyer came in and I made my last sale for the show.

Candy finished her novel and I joined her in conversation. Then she said, "I'm going to help you out." She pulled out her planner and told me to take a seat at the table. She gave me some paper and suggested I take down some sales reps' names, addresses, and phone numbers. She told me to use her as a reference and to call if I had any questions. Anne walked up and saw what Candy was doing. She told me to give her a call, that she would also help me. We all swapped business cards. I told them both what a pleasure it had been to meet them.

A buyer came into Candy's booth and our meeting broke up. Don came back and offered to hold down the fort. I went out and joined

Angelo in his "office". I lit up a Bering Gold #1. We laughed about the Liar's Poker game and my throwing away the Kings. The rain had slowed some, but it was still steady. I finished the cigar, then got a snack at the concession stand. When I got back to the booth, Don went to the concession stand.

At one thirty, Don pulled the van under the covered parking area. We broke down at the stroke of two and were headed to Leo's by three. We loaded the coolers with Cajun food and got some Boudin sandwiches for the road. Don wanted a change of scenery and was wary of a wait at the ferry. We quickly headed up to Houston on I-45, barely beating the rush hour. We took the loop and headed east on I-10. We were glad to leave Galveston.

CHAPTER 3

VALDOSTA

Galveston was behind us and we were rolling through the rice fields. Each one had a short earthen dike around it. The rice had been harvested and the fields were dry. Every so often we saw silos. There were the oil wells and an occasional gas well among the fields.

We made good time and just past six we turned off I-10 at the exit to the Isle of Capri Casino and Hotel. Menacing looking chemical plants, with their gridwork of pipes, were on both sides of the road. We had to pass through them to get to the casino. We went through the gauntlet of pipes and pulled up at the registration area at the Isle of Capri Hotel. The casino area was a block away down a sidewalk.

At the registration desk, we learned that the hotel was brand new, having only been open for a week. We got our keys and carried in our luggage. Our room was not quite as good as a Holiday Inn. It wasn't in the same class as the Grand Casino Gulfport. We unpacked, grabbed some cigars, and headed to the casino.

There was a huge, brightly-lit building on the shoreline. A dazzling display of neon lights cascaded across the front side of the building. It had gift shops, restaurants, and other amenities. We entered the building through a grand entrance. Escalators took us up to a large landing. On the landing were two signs. There was one for each of two boats. A series of sailing times was posted. When one boat was out cruising, the other was in. Louisiana Law requires the casinos to be on working boats. However, people can gamble on the boats when they are in port.

We talked to one of the employees. She said, "The boats don't sail very often. If a commercial ship is in, or near, the harbor, they don't sail. If it's low tide, they don't sail. If the wind is ten miles an hour or stronger, they don't sail." Basically, they look for any excuse not to sail. She explained that people leave the boats when they sail. When they do sail, it's for less than an hour and a half.

We went on the larger boat. There were no rating signs on any of the slot machines. However, there was an open bar on each floor. You could just walk up and get what you want. I got my customary O'Douls and Don his Bud Lite. Several attendants told us they didn't know anything about the payout on the slots. After exploring the casino, we transferred to the other smaller casino boat.

In the back of the boat we found a bank of eight machines that were rated. None of them were anything we wanted to play, since they were older, tired games. We went to the observation deck. We could see The Players Island Casino and Hotel across the water. We were about to light up a cigar, but decided to go to Players Island. The grass is always greener on the other side of the fence.

Leaving the casino boat, we went back into the shore building. Both of us were hungry. So we headed for the buffet restaurant, which had decent food, but it didn't compare with the Grand Casino Gulfport or Leo's. We satisfied our hunger and headed for Players Island Casino.

At the grand entrance to Isle of Capri was a sign informing about the free shuttle service between the casinos. It ran every fifteen minutes. One was loading as we walked out. We hopped in and were on our way. The entry to Players Island Casino was through the hotel. Just as at the Isle of Capri, the restaurants and amenities were in the dock building.

One of the boats had actually been sailing and was headed back to the pier. We boarded the one still in port. The machines were newer in the Players Island Casino. However, none of the attendants knew anything about rated machines. The bar supplied us with another round of drinks and we settled in on some slots to play. I found a Double Diamond slot machine and Don sat down at a bank of new machines. They were based on *The Wheel of Fortune* TV Show. It looked like they would be a lot of fun. If you hit the right sequence, a Wheel of Fortune at the top of the machine made noises and spun. There were about two dozen of the machines in the group. One of the top wheels was almost always spinning. A congratulatory announcement played with cheers every time one of the wheels spun. There were just about as many people watching as there were playing.

The machines ate our money quickly and we decided to go on top of the boat and smoke cigars. The speaker announced that the boat would sail in five minutes, which prompted a lot of people to leave the boat. We went up to the observation deck and watched the crew cast off before the casino boat headed out into the waterway. We lit up some Bering Churchill's. One of the boats across the water at the Isle of Capri was sailing.

Don and I talked about the casinos and how they didn't compare to the ones over at Biloxi and Gulfport. We decided to turn in early, get up early, and drive to the Grand Casino in Gulfport. We'd play for two or three hours, then get back on the road. The boat landed and we took the shuttle back to The Isle of Capri Hotel.

The alarm woke us. We showered, got some complimentary coffee, and were on the highway. We made good time and were going through Baton Rouge almost before we knew it. We stopped at the Mississippi welcome center and got the current casino news. Then we took the coastal highway. The scenery was great. Piers, shrimp boats, shore birds, and other things native to the area rolled past the van. Some of the old homes along the highway were spectacular.

We drove up to the valet parking at the Grand Casino Gulfport about 11:00 AM. I decided to play a progressive machine that had a top jackpot currently over a million dollars. Don decided to play something else. I lit up a Bering Churchill and put my Grand Advantage Players Club card and a hundred-dollar bill in the slot machine. After about an hour I hit a jackpot that made me a five-hundred-dollar winner after deducting all my losses. I cashed out and quit. Don had already come over while I was waiting for my winnings.

I cashed in the points that I had accumulated on the Grand Advantage Players Club card. I had enough for a free buffet certificate and a commemorative coin. I also got a check for fifteen dollars. I said, "Don, lunch is on me."

After cashing my check at the cashier's cage, we hit the buffet and had a good meal. We were on the road by two. We hit horrible rush-hour traffic in Mobile. The rest of the trip was uneventful and we were back in Valdosta, just before midnight.

I slept in Saturday morning and went to my office at Don's Enterprises. I did the paperwork on the sales we made. Then I organized the sales reps' names that Candy had given me. Don came in and we took some time out at the 'cigar tree'. Don brought out some Bering Gold #1's. They are packaged in golden aluminum tubes. They were very good. The centuries-old oak tree shaded us as the smoke from the cigars curled up into the branches.

We talked about Galveston and the up-and-coming Panama City Beach Gift Show. Don had a lot of friends in Panama City Beach. It was decided that each of would drive a car. That way we would have more mobility. It's only a three and a half-hour drive from Valdosta to Panama City Beach.

Don and I did a lot of our brainstorming under the 'cigar tree'. The contractor had wanted to cut it down when he constructed the building. Don Smith would hear nothing of it, much to my delight. We finished our cigars and went back inside. I finished up my work and took in a movie. My favorite way to relax is a movie at the theater. There's nothing like the big screen. There are no telephones or other interruptions.

Monday morning I got to the office early. Sales reps are hard to catch. Most of the time they are on the road, calling on buyers or at the trade shows. Miraculously, I did talk with two on the list. I told them that Candy Royal had referred me and told them about our company and line of Cigar Tees. I went over the current craze on cigars. They both were aware of the current growing popularity. Both agreed to look at the line.

I sent each sales rep two sample Cigar Tee's and some of the color flyers by Priority Mail. Priority Mail gives you free boxes in which to mail. The boxes look great and give your contents an air of importance. The postage is also very reasonable. Having gotten the samples out in the mail, I started contacting national and regional chains.

Don had a luncheon appointment. So I called Ken Scott at Good Stuff Antiques. He wanted to have lunch with me. I got his sub sandwich order and went to the nearest Blimpie sub shop. I got him the special with lots of peppers and a roasted chicken, with extra peppers, for me. Traffic was light and I was at Remerton in no time.

I parked across from Good Stuff Antiques in the vacant lot. As I was getting out of my Cadillac, I heard Ken hollering. He shouted, "I'm glad you called. I'm starving." He brought out some Diet Cokes and we made short work of the subs.

Then Ken brought out a couple of Toro cigars. We lit up and I told him about my adventure to Galveston. He was jealous of all the good Cajun food we got from Leo's Cajun Corner. I promised to bring him some of the Boudin and a taste of the smoked sausage I had brought back from Leo's.

Ken complained about how slow business was. He told me he was planning a trip to Atlanta to the monthly Lakewood Antique Show. He would sell of some of the pieces he had picked up that didn't sell in the Valdosta area. He would also purchase some items from some of the northern dealers. He explained how some things are popular in the South and unpopular in the North and vise versa. By going to the shows he could trade out with the northern dealers. He also needed to build inventory for the coming Christmas selling season.

We finished our Toro cigars and Ken gave me a bottle of this year's hot sauce. This part of South Georgia is great for growing peppers. Ken grows some of the hottest peppers in the world in the back yard of his store. Mostly, he grows Tabasco-type peppers for the pepper-sauce he makes. However, he also grows habanero and datil peppers. Habanero peppers are, supposedly, the hottest peppers in the world. Habanero's are native to the Caribbean Islands. Datils are locally famous to St. Augustine, Florida and are grown in that area. He had purchased some small plants while on a trip to St. Augustine.

During the late summer months, Ken keeps some pepper plants on the front steps to his store. The colorful red peppers add additional color to the front of the business. They are also good conversation starters. I thanked Ken for the pepper-sauce and headed back to Don's, Enterprises.

I spent the rest of the afternoon working on national accounts. The office and warehouse staff gets off at five. About five fifteen, Don and I went out to the 'cigar tree', to enjoy a cigar and go over details on this weekend's Panama City Beach Gift Show. Don had gotten us reservations at the Sea Kove Condominium. He told me that he had stayed there before, saying, "They are located at the West End of Panama City Beach. The beach is great for walking and isn't crowded like the main beach area. There's also a donut shop across the street and two blocks west. The rooms have a full kitchen setup and are reasonable in the off season."

Don told me more about all the time he had spent in the Panama City Beach area. He had done a lot of business there over the years. He also had spent many vacations in Panama City Beach with his family. Over the years, he had bought and sold a dozen or so condominiums at a good profit. He bought them during a recession and real estate glut, then held them for a few years and sold them when the market took off.

We finished our cigars and I took in another movie. The last few years saw me spending less and less time at home. The joy of the past was no longer there. Fighting with Suzanne had come to be a common occurrence.

Tuesday morning I went into the office about 10:00 AM. I called Candy Royal and thanked her for the referrals. She told me that both of the reps I had contacted had called her to get 'the skinny' on my company and me. She said, "I told both of them that I've never heard of you." She laughed. Then she said, "Don't worry, I told them that you walk on water." I thanked her profusely.

We talked about the upcoming Panama City Beach Gift Show. I told her that I was looking forward to seeing her again. She said that it was a better show for her than Galveston, there being more buyers. However, it was still a slow show, as compared to the major shows.

The show is in a vacated Wal-Mart store. A year-and-a-half ago Wal Mart constructed a Supercenter a mile west of the location and moved out. The promoter made a deal to use the building until they leased it or did something permanent with it. This was to be the second show in the former Wal-Mart store. Before this, the show had a long waiting list. Nowhere else in the area had this much space. We talked a little more about Panama City Beach. She had a meeting she had to attend, so I said goodbye and worked on contacting national accounts.

Don and I went to lunch in downtown Valdosta at Covington's restaurant. They serve a chicken salad plate that's great. They only use chicken breast to make the salad. A generous portion is served in the middle of a plate with garnishes, cut up fruit, Jell-O, and a wonderful homemade cinnamon roll. We both ordered the chicken salad plate. Don ordered the she-crab soup and I ordered the gumbo. Our food came and we were in heaven. We finished our lunch and headed back to the office. Don invited me to come over to his house Wednesday night and I accepted. We got back to the office and I continued working national accounts.

About three o'clock I called Anne Moore. LIZ, Inc. is located in Waco, Texas, which is in the Central Time Zone, so the time there was only two o'clock. The receptionist answered and with a smile I said, "'Lucky' Joe for Anne Moore." The receptionist asked whom I was with and I told her Don's, Enterprises. She said, "I'll check and see if she's available." A few moments later she informed me that Anne was in a meeting, but she would like my number, and would return my call when the meeting was over. I gave her the number and returned to working accounts.

About four o'clock, the receptionist told me that I had a call from Anne Moore with LIZ, Inc. on line two. I answered the phone, "'Lucky' Joe." Anne said, "It's good to hear your voice. I'm sorry I was tied up when you called." I reminded her of her promise to refer me to some sales reps. She told me that she had already gotten some names and asked for my fax number. She had her assistant fax the names while we talked about going to the Panama City Beach Gift Show.

Sally brought the fax and I went over the names with Anne. She told me that she had talked with Candy earlier in the day and she had mentioned talking with me. She told me that she was driving to the Panama City Beach Gift Show and was leaving from Waco on Thursday. I told her it was only a three-and-one-half-hour drive for us. Anne had a call holding for her and said, "I'll look forward to seeing you at the show."

We disconnected and I started trying to contact the names. I was only successful in getting voice mail and recording machines. I dislike voice mail and recording machines, but that's what we live with in our modern society. By the time I finished calling the list, it was around five-thirty. I went home and my wife was somewhere other than home, most likely at the country club. I spent the evening reading a book and watching *Biography* on cable TV. Suzanne came in around nine thirty and went to bed, more than a little high. I read some more and went to bed around eleven.

Wednesday morning I woke up with the alarm clock. I read the paper and did the crossword puzzle, as was my habit. I had some decaf coffee with the paper. When I left for the office, Suzanne was still in bed. I stopped and filled the Cadillac with gas at the new Chevron station. I bought a *USA Today* newspaper and went to my office.

When I got in, there was a message to call one of the reps I had called the day before. I got the sales rep on the phone and explained that Anne Moore at LIZ, INC had referred me. I told about our line of products and commission rates. She wanted to see samples, so at the end of the conversation, I mailed those out to her.

I was active in the Valdosta, Lowndes County Chamber of Commerce. Today there was a reception at the Valdosta Coca-Cola offices to celebrate their 100th anniversary to which I had been invited, so I went to the Valdosta Coca-Cola plant at noon. I knew most of the people working there because of my consulting job at the radio station. Coca-Cola is one of the station's biggest advertisers.

The Valdosta Coca-Cola manager met me at the door and said, "'Lucky' Joe, I really appreciate your coming today." My reply was that I wouldn't miss it for the world. The Valdosta Plant was the second Coca-Cola bottling plant to be established in the world. I went back to the boardroom where we had held meetings for the Valdosta Olympic Committee. I had served on the committee.

I socialized and got a plate of the bountiful assortment of food; some roll-up sandwich slices, Swedish meatballs, jalapeno cheese squares, and other goodies. There were some foil-wrapped pieces of chocolate in the shape of Coca-Cola bottles. I got a handful of them for the people back at the office.

There were lots of old Coca-Cola items on display. One was a prototype for the classic curved Coca-Cola bottle. Some of the items are worth a lot of money to Coca-Cola collectors. It was like a mini-museum. There was a short program on the history of Coca-Cola in Valdosta. Lots of people from Coke's regional office in Jacksonville, Florida were on hand. When I left, the manager presented me with a Valdosta Coca-Cola 100-year commemorative bottle.

After the Coca-Cola reception, I stopped by The Warehouse, a large discount liquor store. It has a double wall humidor that is about six feet wide by eight feet tall. The manager does a good job of procuring cigars for resale. Valdosta, doesn't have a lot of places to buy premium cigars. The Warehouse had just gotten in a box of Al Capone Churchill Cigars. I bought a couple to try this evening with Don. I had seen ads for the Al Capone cigars in magazines; however, I had never smoked one.

When I parked the car that evening at the back of Don's drive, I could see him feeding the fish. He was at the back of the pier. I walked out to the dock and we went into the screened-in area. Don's eyes lit up when he saw the Al Capone Churchill cigars. He had never smoked one either. We lit up and were happy. The cigars were as good as they were advertised to be. We relaxed, enjoyed, and talked excitedly about our coming adventure to Panama City Beach. The Churchills lasted a full hour and we called it an evening.

I went home and Suzanne was already asleep. That suited me fine. I read some of the book I was reading and went to bed myself. I thought about the upcoming show and quickly went to sleep.

Thursday morning, October 16, I dressed in one of my suits. Don and I had a luncheon meeting at Muldoon's restaurant with John Austin and some other local power people. Suzanne inquired why I was wearing a suit instead of a sport coat. I told her I was meeting with John Austin for lunch about politics. That ended her curiosity. Suzanne couldn't care less about politics.

At 12:10 PM, Don and I walked in Muldoon's restaurant. We went into the private dining room and joined John Austin and the two others. One made his money through the insurance business and the other made his in the bag business. None of us were happy with the current city council.

The council has six seats and a mayor. The mayor only votes in case of a tie vote. The term of office is for six years. Every two years there's an election for two of the council seats. This November, two of the seats were up for election. The election was less than three weeks away.

We all had lunch and talked about the incumbents and their opposition. We all agreed to put up two thousand dollars for each of the candidates we wanted to endorse. Our little luncheon raised twenty thousand dollars or ten thousand dollars per candidate. John Austin agreed to collect the money and get it to the candidates.

Having finished our business, John brought out some Arturo Fuente Coronas. We all lit up cigars and had a lively discussion. When our cigars got short, we ended the luncheon.

Friday, I made phone calls and prepared for the show. Friday night, I went to the Valdosta High School football game. High School football is big in South Georgia. In fact, Valdosta High School has the best win record of any high school football team in America. It has a long and proud tradition. Most nights over ten thousand people show up to watch Valdosta High play football. Most small colleges don't get that much local interest.

The team is taught the basics and has one of the best conditioning programs in high school football. Its coaching staff stresses these basics and implementation while instilling confidence and the pride of tradition. The Valdosta 'Wildcats' won the game as usual.

Saturday morning I arose early, put my clothes in the car and went to the office where I loaded the Cadillac with show materials I was taking to Panama City Beach, then drove to Valdosta State University. This weekend was Valdosta State's homecoming. As an alumnus, I was invited to a breakfast reception at the President's home.

I entered the President's home and was warmly greeted by the President and his wife. She takes pains to have great food for her receptions. They work as a team and are excellent ambassadors for Valdosta State University. The dining room on the left side of the house was where most of the food was set up, so I headed there.

The dining room table was crowded with serving dishes. I got some little Danish pastries and some French toast points that were coated in confectioner's sugar. Then I got a cup of coffee and went into the little breakfast room. I joined some old friends and got into a conversation about the football program. A server refilled our coffee and we continued the conversation.

After about fifteen minutes, I got up and toured the rest of the house. In the great room I socialized with some people I hadn't seen in years. They had come down from Atlanta for the weekend. After about an hour, I headed for Panama City Beach, and the gift show.

CHAPTER 4

PANAMA CITY BEACH

I started my Cadillac and tuned the radio to the Tallahassee, Florida 'Oldies Station'. I got through the town traffic and headed west on U.S. Hwy. 84. I took the same route to Tallahassee that we had taken two weeks earlier on our trip to Galveston. I continued on I-10 through Tallahassee and on to U.S. Hwy. 231.

At U.S. 231, I gassed up, and took a short break. When I resumed traveling, I made good time, since U.S. Highway 231 is four divided lanes. When I got to Panama City, I turned west onto 23rd Street. It took some time to get through all the congestion. I passed the Panama City Mall and several miles of commercial development. Finally, I got to Gulf Coast Community College and started across Hathaway Bridge to Panama City Beach. I crossed St. Andrew's Bay. On the other side of the bay, I came to the intersection of U.S. 98 and Thomas Dr. The show was being held in the Beachwalk Center shopping center on the southwest corner of the intersection.

I pulled into the large center and drove over to the western side. There were already a lot of cars and trucks in the parking lot. A flurry of activity was taking place. People were unloading, carrying displays and samples into the building. I saw several people I had met in Galveston.

Don and I had agreed to meet at two o'clock, which is three o'clock Georgia time. I was over an hour early, so I used the time to go inside and register with the promoter. He gave me our registration package containing information and our ID badges.

I located our booth on the front row, at the right corner of the row. The doors to the former lawn and garden area were across the aisle. They were part of the west wall of the building and it opened into a covered area. Wal-Mart used to have plants and garden implements on display under the covering. A chain link fence surrounds the area. Unfortunately, the promoter did not have the key to the gate; however, I could watch the booth and enjoy a cigar anytime I wanted to. I wouldn't have to depend on Don guarding the booth.

I went back out front and selected a Bering Immensa to pass the time. It was a large cigar and would give me about an hour of pleasure. I stayed in the shade of the front overhang and watched the activity. Several cars pulled up to where I was standing. People asked if the show was open to the public. They had seen the huge banner across the front of the building. It read, 'Panama City Beach Gift Show'. There was also a sign, which stated 'The show is not open to the public'. I politely told them, they had to have a sales tax certificate and a business license to get into the show.

I had been out front about fifteen minutes, when Anne Moore walked out with a pack of Dunhill cigarettes. She saw me, and a big smile lit up her face. She said, "'Lucky' Joe, it's good to see you!" I replied, "Anne, it's good to see you also." I lit her cigarette for her and made some small talk about her drive to Panama City Beach. We started talking about local restaurants. I told her the most famous is Captain Anderson's.

Anne said, "I've always wanted to try it. I just never have." I said, "It's a tourist restaurant, but the food is excellent." She said, "Why don't we get Carol, Sam, and Don to go this evening. It will be like our Italian restaurant adventure in Galveston." I said, "I'll set it up with Don." She knew where Candy's booth was and said, "I'll set it up with Candy and Sam." We agreed on eight o'clock. I was to get with her to verify everything when Don and I got through setting up.

Anne had already finished her cigarette. She returned to setting up. It took a lot longer for her to setup than for Don and me. Don drove up shortly before two and we unloaded and set up the booth. I mentioned Anne and Captain Anderson's restaurant. He told me that he had already made plans to go out drinking with his old friend who was doing the artwork for our Cigar Tees and he invited me along. I told him that I'd rather go with the group to Captain Anderson's. We finished and agreed to meet at the Sea Kove.

Don headed out and I went over to where Anne had told me her booth was. It was on the front row at the east corner. As I walked up, Anne was finishing up the details to the LIZ, Inc. Booth.

She told me that Candy and Sam had already made plans, but that she was looking forward to going with Don and me. I told her that Don had already made plans, too. Don had also told me that he had already made too many plans for this trip and didn't have time to go. Anne said, "Why should we let them spoil our plans? 'Lucky' Joe, let's go anyway." I replied, "That's fine with me."

She gave me the name of the condominium where she was staying. We estimated it was about two miles east of the Sea Kove. I told her I would see her at eight. I took U.S. 98 West to S.R. 79 and turned south to Front Beach Road. U.S. 98 runs across the north boundary of Panama City Beach. By taking it, I was at Sea Kove in about fifteen minutes, while taking Front Beach Road would have taken almost an hour. Panama City Beach is about fifteen miles long, but the developed area is only about one mile wide.

Don had already checked in and was unloading his personal effects from the van. I unloaded my gear and was stowed away in no time. The room was on the second floor, and had a kitchen area on the left, as you walked in the door, with a bath on the right. Along the wall to the bath is a dining table with four chairs. The kitchen had a refrigerator, sink, stove, and microwave. I saw plenty of dishes, silverware, and cook ware. The paper towel holder was sporting a new roll of towels.

This area opens into a wide bedroom. On the right are two double beds separated by a nightstand. A large closet is adjacent to the bath and faces the beds. The TV is to the left, on top of a long, low dresser. A comfortable chair is at the end of the dresser with a floor lamp next to it.

The door at the back opens onto a covered deck with privacy partitions between each unit. The stairs go down to a patio area, which is about eight feet higher than the beach. A gazebo protects a picnic table. There are also numerous other benches and a charcoal Bar-B-Q unit. Our room was the westernmost of two buildings. The pool is located in the middle, between the two buildings.

Sea gulls and little 'wave runner' birds greeted us with their calls. The 'wave runners' were running along the edges of the waves that wash the beach. Some of the sea gulls were circling and diving into the Gulf water. They were in the same general area. The gulls were working a school of baitfish.

The sun was starting to set, painting the clouds with areas of vivid pink. Don and I got a couple of Las Cabrillas Robustos. We enjoyed the peacefulness and beauty before us. The beach curves to the right slightly when you look to the east. All the development merges together and makes a spectacular sight. Looking west one sees sandy beaches and water.

We finished our cigars then I showered and dressed for dinner. Don relaxed. He wasn't supposed to meet his artist friend until nine. Don teased me about being married and going on a date. I blushed. I really hadn't considered myself going on a date. He watched the news and I drove east on Front Beach Road to The Dolphin Condominium.

I pulled up to The Dolphin. It was about ten minutes to eight. I sat in the car for a few minutes. The Dolphin is about a mile and a half east of S.R. 79, on Front Beach Road. It is also about a half-mile east of a big 24-hour fishing pier. The pier goes a long way out into the Gulf of Mexico.

I went to the office area and had the receptionist ring Anne Moore's room. She told the receptionist that she would meet me in a few minutes. I gaze around the lobby area told me that the establishment was a lot newer and nicer than the Sea Kove. I went outside onto the landing, which was at the top of a double stairway to the parking lot. After about ten minutes, I saw Anne coming from my right, as I was facing the road. I went down the stairs and met her in the parking lot.

She apologized for being a few minutes late. We walked over to my car and I opened the passenger door for her. When I got into the car, she immediately told me dinner was to be 'Dutch Treat'. I agreed and drove east on Front Beach Road.

It was Saturday night. I knew there would be a wait at Capt. Anderson's. The later we got there, the less the wait, so we enjoyed the scenery on the way and pointed things out to each other. I had spent a lot of time in Panama City Beach and Anne had been making the show for years. We drove on past the Wal-Mart Supercenter and turned onto Thomas Drive, passing by LaVila and Spinnakers Nightclubs. They are side by side and are, supposedly, the largest in the world. Just before reaching St. Andrew's State Park, Thomas Drive leaves the beach and turns north. We continued north on Thomas Drive and passed The Treasure Ship. It is a huge restaurant in the shape of a pirate ship. The server's dress in seafaring outfits and a Pirate Captain roams around entertaining the patrons.

We took the bridge across Grand Lagoon. Captain Anderson's was on our right. The huge parking lot was nearly full. The parking lot serves three restaurants and a marina complex. We found a space and went into the restaurant.

The reception area was elaborately decorated. In the years since I had dined at Captain Anderson's, they had added on a huge gift shop and reception area. The receptionist told us that the wait was forty-five minutes to an hour. I agreed to the wait and she put my name on the waiting list.

In the waiting area, there is a large salt-water aquarium. Lots of colorful fish were swimming about. Anne said, "Let's look at the fish. I'm planning to put a salt water aquarium in my home." I said, "That's great. I love salt water aquariums." Anne pointed out different species of fish and named them for me. She said, "They don't have any clownfish." I said, "I know what clownfish are. I've got an artist friend who paints clownfish and other colorful salt water fish. I'll tell you about her sometime"

Anne said, "Clowns have a special relationship with the Sea anemone. The Sea anemone is harmful to most fish. However, clownfish huddle within their tentacles and are not harmed." I said, "I didn't know that." Anne said, "I've been reading about clowns and Sea anemones. Certain species of clownfish inhabit certain species of Sea anemones. I'm planning on having some clownfish and Sea anemones in my aquarium.

We were blocking the aquarium, so we moved away as some kids came up and wanted to see it. We meandered into the gift shop.

The gift shop was full of the usual souvenirs and some interesting gourmet foods. We spent about ten minutes in the gift shop, then went outside to the marina. Several deep-sea fishing boats make their home here. A lot of charter boats are for hire. Captain Anderson's also has a ship that makes dinner cruises. It goes out several times a week and has different themes for different nights. One ticket office serves all the boats. Next to it is a refreshment stand. Beyond that are a fresh seafood shop and a fish-cleaning operation where people can get their catch cleaned and iced down, for a poundage charge.

I remembered feeding the fish along the pier the last time I had been to Capt. Anderson's. There are some quarter machines that dispense fish food pellets. I got a handful for Anne and myself. We went to a well-lighted area. In no time, we had a feeding frenzy going on. Our fish food ran out and the fish disappeared. I lit a Dunhill cigarette for Anne and talked with her while she smoked. She finished her cigarette and we went back inside to the receptionist.

The receptionist told us that she was just about to call for us. She sent us to the hostesses. A hostess took two menus and asked us to follow her. I slipped her a five-dollar bill and asked her to put us as close to the windows with a view of the harbor as possible. All the window tables were taken. She put us one off the window, but there was a great view of the harbor. The large ship berth in front of our table was empty.

Our waitress came and told us about the evening specials and asked for our drink orders. I ordered ice water and Anne ordered iced tea. The menus were extensive. She returned with the drinks before we had a chance to decide. When I asked our waitress her name, she said it was Rosie and that she was Irish. I told Rosie that I was half-Irish. Rosie smiled and graciously said, "I'll return when you're ready." I knew we had a good waitress.

We decided and Rosie returned for our order. Anne spilled her water with the menu and got so embarrassed, she turned two shades of red. Rosie quickly returned with some towels. We finished getting up the water and Rosie returned again with fresh linen napkins. Anne said something about being a two-year-old and we laughed. Anne ordered Shrimp Scampi and I ordered the Broiled Captain's Platter. Anne ordered oil and vinegar dressing and I ordered Blue Cheese dressing.

Quickly, Rosie brought the salads. They were very good. Anne asked about my background. I told her about retiring from the furniture business. Our meals came about the time we finished the salad. Anne's Shrimp Scampi had a lot of shrimp. She couldn't eat all of them and shared with me. My Broiled Captain's Platter had two fish filets, six shrimp, a dozen small scallops, and two crab cakes. Anne tasted the scallops and declared them to be fine. The food was excellent.

I told Anne about consulting at the radio station and the fun I had. I then told her about knowing Don and agreeing to take on this challenge. About this time, the Capt. Anderson II dinner cruise ship came into view. It docked in the berth right in front of our window. It was fun to see the passengers leave the ship on the gangplank. They were all smiling and laughing.

We finished our meals and Rosie cleared the plates while trying to tempt us with desserts. We settled on decaf coffee for dessert. She brought our coffee and I lit a Dunhill cigarette for Anne. We sipped our coffee and resumed our conversation.

I asked Anne about LIZ, Inc. She told me how Candy had helped her. She told me about the early days of the business and of her move to Waco, Texas in 1995 where her mother lives. She moved LIZ, Inc. to Waco at the same time. It is near Dallas, where a lot of her family lives. Her early days with IBM had been in there. IBM had transferred her to Tampa, Florida, when she was promoted to Area Sales Manager.

Anne remembered something mentioned in one of our past conversations and asked about my involvement with the Olympics. I told her how awesome it was to carry the torch, and about the other things I had done during the 1996 Atlanta Olympic Games. Rosie refilled our coffee cups for the third time. I looked up and realized it was almost midnight. One other couple and we were the only ones left in the restaurant. Rosie brought our check. Anne got out cash for hers and I got out cash for mine. We left Rosie a nice tip.

As it was late, I took the fast route back to The Dolphin Condominium driving north on Thomas Drive, then turning west on U.S. 98. I followed it to Hill Avenue. Then I went south on Hill Avenue to Front Beach Road. On the way back I chided Anne for getting me to do most of the talking. I told her that I prided myself on being able to draw other people out. She had 'one upped' me. She just laughed and told me that she'd had a good time also. I walked her to her condo unit, which was number 100 and opened onto the beach deck. It was the first unit on the East End of the Condominium. It had a door on the left side and a big picture window took up the space to the right of the door.

We talked a few minutes. Anne said, "I really like walking on the beach at night. However, I'm afraid to walk by myself at night." I asked her if she would like to take a beach walk tomorrow night. Anne said that she was going to go to the show party. However, she would like to walk around eight o'clock. I said, "I'll see you tomorrow night at eight." Anne said, "Your being married concerns me. I just want to be business friends." I said, "That's all we are." Then smiled, said goodnight, and drove back to the Sea Kove.

Don was not in yet. I went on the deck with an Arturo Fuente 8-5-8. I lit up and enjoyed the rich, spicy taste. The Gulf was calm and I thought about how much I had enjoyed the evening. Don had returned and joined me with a Las Cabrillas Robusto. We enjoyed the still of the night and savored our cigars. He said that he'd had a good time. He asked about my evening and I replied in the affirmative. The cigars went out and we called it a night.

Don's alarm went off and we showered and dressed. It was Sunday morning and the first day of the show. We rode over to the donut shop and had breakfast. Don ordered his usual cake donuts and I got a huge cinnamon bun. We both got coffee. Don dropped me at the Sea Kove and we both drove our vehicles to the show. The show opened for exhibitors at eight and to buyers at nine.

We opened the booth and got ready for business. Don told me that he had some friends he was going to meet at the show party. I told him that I was going to make an appearance and take off. I had something else to do this evening. Don said, "I'll bet the something else is spelled A-N-N-E." I said, "You guessed right."

Don started making the rounds of the show and talking with old friends. By noon I had written three orders. Two of them were for March delivery, next year. Don came back to the booth and asked if I had any ideas for lunch. I said, "Leo's Cajun Corner." He said, "Me too!" Then Don said, "Seriously, 'Lucky' Joe, do you have a clue?" I replied, "No." Don said, "I saw a special at McDonald's." I said, "That's fine with me." Don took off for McDonald's and was back in about thirty minutes.

We ate the fast food and went over to the side door to enjoy a cigar. I got about three puffs before having to return to the booth for some buyers. It was a nice order. I returned to the smoking area and relit my cigar. A cigar is never quite as good when it goes out and you re-light it. I finished the cigar and returned to the booth. Don had already started walking around again. An hour later, he came back and asked me if I'd like to walk around the show. Nodding in the affirmative, I started exploring.

I found Angelo's sponge booth on the back row. It was across from the concession/rest room area, which, in Wal-Mart days, had been the Lay Away Department. Angelo's booth was a single wide. Of course, there was no Angelo. Smokers in this part of the show were at the back loading dock. The aisles ran left to right with one center aisle running from the front door area to the back of the building. I found Candy Royal's booth on the second row, around the corner from LIZ, Inc.

Candy saw me and smiled. She said, "'Lucky' Joe, where have you been?" I said, "You know how much Don likes to stay around the booth." She just chuckled. I said, "Candy, I wish you and Sam could have gone to Captain Anderson's last night." She said, "We had already committed to something else, but we would have liked to have gone." She asked if I was going to the show party tonight. I told her I was. She had some buyers come into the doublewide booth.

I went on around the corner to Anne's booth. She smiled when she saw me. Anne said, "'Lucky' Joe, I appreciate you walking with me on the beach tonight. I don't feel comfortable walking alone at night. At Galveston, Karen and I were sharing a room and she would walk with me." Some buyers walked up to the booth. Moving away, I told Anne I'd see her at eight.

I returned to the booth. Don told me he was going to visit some people he knew have a retail store. He said he would be back around five. I made three more sales that afternoon and met some new friends at the smoking area. Don showed up again at five. We took off at five-fifteen for the party, which was a couple of blocks east of the show. It was at the foot of the bridge to Panama City. The restaurant is on the north side of U.S. 98 and overlooks St. Andrew's Bay.

We parked both cars and walked along the adjacent marina, to get to the party. The party was on the north side of the restaurant. It was on a huge, partially covered, outdoor deck. The food was inside, in a fairly large meeting room. Local civic clubs, like Rotary and Kawanis, use it during the week.

There was a buffet serving line and a bar to one side of the room. I got an O'Douls and Don got a Bud Lite. Most of the food on the serving line was not on my list of favorites. I got some cheese and a couple of rolls. In the corner of the room was a huge round of corned beef. The promoter had flown it in from New York City. I got some corned beef and headed outside with Don.

The deck was filling up fast. We grabbed one of the last tables. It wasn't long before Don's artist friend joined us. We saw Angelo and waved. He joined us and pulled out a Camel cigarette. We had a good time at the party.

I saw Anne from a distance. She was with some people I didn't know. She had asked me to be discreet. She didn't want to become the gossip of the show for spending time with a married man. She does about twenty shows a year, so it's pretty much the same people at all the shows and they knew her pretty well.

At seven o'clock, I left the show and returned to the Sea Kove. I showered and dressed casually for the walk and picked up my windbreaker. I drove up to The Dolphin Condominium, again sitting in the car until eight o'clock, then had the receptionist call Anne. She told me to join her on the deck in front of her room. I walked around and joined her.

She, as I, was dressed in a jogging outfit, plus a windbreaker. We laughed at our similarity in dress. I was wearing an Olympic cap. She had her hair flipped under as usual. It was slightly moving with the gentle breeze. I was very much attracted to her.

The Gulf was beautiful. Small, six-inch waves were breaking near the edge of the water. The tide was high, and much of the beach was under the water. The birds had stopped their hunt for food and were huddling together for the night. The sun had gone below the horizon and darkness was quickly overtaking the sky. Some stars were already starting to twinkle in the east. The three-quarter full moon was starting to rise, and sparkled on the waters of the Gulf.

We went down the steps to the beach heading east, in the direction of the rising moon. We came upon a group of people fishing. They were using frozen shrimp for bait. They cast out about thirty yards and bottom-fished. Their white plastic bucket already had a dozen or so whiting. Whiting are a silvery-white fish, generally six to twelve inches long, and abundant along Florida beaches. Anne and I watched them catch some fish, then continued our walk.

I was bound and determined that Anne would do the majority of the talking tonight. We walked and talked for about a mile, when we came upon two huge wooden lounge chairs that were at the bottom of the seawall. There was a townhouse condominium above. None of the lights were on in what appeared to be six units. The area was slightly secluded and the chairs were side by side. We stopped, adjusted the chair backs, and sat down.

Anne got out a pack of Dunhill cigarettes. Selecting one and pulling it out, I lit it for her with my torch lighter. We relaxed in the chairs and I watched her exhale the smoke into the light breeze. She thought for a moment and told me about herself. She was born in February of 1946 and had grown up in Waco, Texas. She went to Baylor University. She had gotten a degree in Business Management. Her father had influenced her to go in that direction. When Anne graduated from Baylor, she was highly recruited by 'big business'. She decided to go with IBM, with her first job being in the Dallas area.

She married a young man after dating him for two years. He went to work in the bookkeeping department of a trucking company. They had met at Baylor and graduated together. They married about six months later. They had two girls, two years apart. Both girls were now in their late twenties. They had both gone to the University of Florida. One was in Atlanta, working with The Southern Company. The other teaches school in Dallas, Texas. Her husband works for one of the oil companies.

Over the years Anne and her husband had drifted apart. Her income had risen dramatically and his had stayed rather stagnant. Anne had taken training and did a lot of reading. She traveled a lot and her husband stayed home. Anne had discovered motivational tapes, and listened to them when she drove between appointments. She had been promoted and they had moved to Florida in 1980. They grew even further apart. He liked to stay home and watch TV. She liked to go out. He was great with the kids and that made up for a lot.

He drank more and more beer, becoming an alcoholic. It was more than Anne could put up with. She tried counseling and treatment centers. Nothing worked. She filed for divorce in 1988. She realized she was drinking too much and quit drinking.

Anne retired from IBM about the time the divorce was final. She got the kids through school. It didn't leave much time for dating and social life. Anne had to hire a live-in housekeeper. She has been attending around twenty shows a year since she started LIZ, Inc.

Anne told me that the second year her daughters were both at the University of Florida she had met a man. They were attracted to each other and it turned into an affair. He didn't tell Anne he was married until after they had become intimate. It was one of the greatest times of her life. She told me, once they put the hold switch on, and made love in an elevator. They did some wild and crazy, exciting things together. She came to have hopes of marriage.

Anne said, "I discovered he was a 'swinger'." I said, "Anne, I don't know what a 'swinger' is." She said, "He invited me to come to his house and participate in a threesome, with him and his wife. He told me his wife knew everything. That he and his wife both had affairs and shared the details." Anne told me it almost broke her heart and she ended the affair. She added,

"However, it was one of the most exciting times of my life." Anne told me that it had been about four years since they broke up. She also told me that I bore an uncanny resemblance to him. She said that seeing me startled her and brought back the good memories of the times they shared.

I lit another Dunhill cigarette for her. She told me she was dating a guy by the name of Herb Rhodes when she moved everything to Waco. That was in 1995. After three months, he moved to Waco and they lived together. They did some shows together and he helped in the business. He had some problems that got worse as time went on. The last six months of the relationship, they didn't sleep together. Six months ago, they had separated and he moved to Orlando.

Anne said, "'Lucky' Joe, I've talked enough. Tell me something about you." I said, "I'd rather learn more about you." She tilted her chin up, and with a stern smile, said, "I insist." I gave in, "If you put it that way, okay."

I told her that I had grown up in Valdosta, that I had attended school there and had graduated from Valdosta State College, with a degree in Business Management. I had been President of my fraternity and had a good time in college. It had taken me five years to get my four-year degree. I had met my future wife, Suzanne, the later half of my junior year. I got serious about my studies as I got more serious about her. We graduated, got married, and moved to Atlanta. I told her about the furniture business. We talked about my moving back to Valdosta and eventually selling "Lucky" Joe's Furniture. Then I told her about my consulting career.

I told her I had now been married for twenty-seven years, that I have a son and a daughter. The son had graduated from the University of Georgia and was now working with a computer company in Atlanta.

He was now twenty-four. My daughter was a senior at Valdosta State University and was in the Nursing Program. She was living in an apartment with three other girls.

I told Anne that Suzanne and I have grown apart, just as she and her husband had. I told her that I had listened to motivational tapes, too, while driving in the car between stores, that I read books, and that my wife is addicted to TV. I told her that our sex life had degenerated to almost nothing. It's like she does it out of duty. There's no emotion, there's no enthusiasm and it's like she is a spectator.

I told Anne about Suzanne's increased alcohol consumption. I went into how I had tried to get her to decrease her drinking. I also told Anne that I had bought a set of videotapes, after seeing an infomercial on how to have a more loving relationship. My wife refused to watch them with me. Someone had told me about the book, *His Needs, Her Needs* by Willard F. Harley, Jr. I had bought the book and read it. Suzanne refused to read it. Anne interrupted me and told me that she had read the book also. I told Anne that Suzanne also had a real problem with my cigar smoking.

I confided with Anne that I was frustrated and unhappy with the relationship. I told Anne that I wasn't angry with my wife, but that we had just grown apart over the years. Anne sympathized with me. I said, "Anne, I can't believe how many similar things we've gone through." Anne said, "It's almost spooky."

I happened to glance at my watch, surprised to find it was almost midnight. We arose and started walking back to The Dolphin Condominium. We were walking and enjoying the stars, the noise of the waves, and the beauty of the surroundings. The backs of our hands lightly brushed. Like two magnets our hands interlocked and we continued walking hand in hand. My hand tingled with her touch. I could not remember the last time I experienced that feeling.

As we neared The Dolphin, Anne said, "I've heard the little restaurant at the front of the nearby fishing pier has a really good breakfast. Would you like to join me for breakfast?" I said, "Anne, I'm not a morning person. If I could, I'd sleep in till ten every morning. Let me pass on breakfast. I'd rather do something with you tomorrow night."

She said, "I've committed to taking my sales reps out to dinner tomorrow night, but I'm free Wednesday night." I said, "I'll pick you up at seven Wednesday night." She answered, "I'm looking forward to it."

We reached her unit. Anne said, "'Lucky' Joe, I want to thank you for a wonderful evening." She gave me a hug, a kiss on the cheek, then disappeared through the door. I reflected on the evening and drove to the Sea Kove.

Don was asleep when I entered our room. I got a Las Cabrillas Robusto and went out on the deck. I punched and lit the cigar. As I enjoyed the smoke I reflected on the evening, I thought, "Anne is some kind of woman." As I finished the cigar, I made plans to surprise Anne in the morning and take her to the restaurant at the fishing pier. I laid out the next day's clothes as Don snored in deep sleep, and set the alarm for six thirty before quickly falling asleep.

I awoke, surprisingly fresh, to the sound of the alarm. I showered, shaved, and dressed. I waited until seven and dialed the number to The Dolphin Condominium. I got a recording machine. It played, "The office hours are 9:00 AM until 11:00 PM. However, if you know your party's extension, you may use a touch-tone phone to enter it." I entered 1-0-0. Nothing happened and I was disconnected. I called again and had to listen to the recording. I entered 1-1-0-0 at the prompt and woke up someone other than Anne. I became frustrated and decided to drive down and knock on her door.

I drove to The Dolphin. Anne's van was in the parking area. I walked to her room and knocked. There was no response. I thought that she was probably walking on the beach, since it was daylight. I decided to smoke a cigar and catch her when she got back from her walk. I walked over to the lounge chairs on the deck and watched numerous people walking up and down the beach. I lit up a Bering Churchill. I could not quite see her room from the chairs. Every ten minutes I returned and knocked on her door.

We had to be at the show by nine, so I decided to try until ten after eight. I knocked a final time at ten minutes after eight. There was still no response. I walked out to the parking lot. I drew a four-leaf clover on a three by five index card and put it on the driver's side window of her van. I got gas and a few personal things at the new Revco store.

I pulled into the parking lot at the gift show. I didn't see Anne's car. I got out and started walking to the door. I took another look from the door and saw Anne drive into the lot. I walked over to her van. She got out and said, "'Lucky' Joe, I got your four leaf clover. I was in the room when you knocked and I was terrified. If only you had called out and told me it was you." I said, "Anne, I apologize. I would never do anything to terrify you. Why were you scared?" Anne said, "It's a long story. I'll tell you tomorrow night." I told Anne that I remembered her telling me, she liked surprises. So I had decided to surprise her by taking her to breakfast at the pier. I told her about the problem with the phone. Anne thanked me for wanting to surprise her. She reiterated that she would tell me why she was so afraid on Wednesday night. We walked into the show and headed for our booths.

Don had not arrived yet. I opened up and immediately wrote an order. Don came in around ten and told me he would guard the booth for awhile. I walked to the back and got some coffee and a great homemade sweet roll. Angelo was not in his booth, however, there was an empty fast-food bag on the table. I went out to the loading dock and found Angelo holding court. I laughed at his jokes while I ate the roll and enjoyed the coffee. I lit up a Las Cabrillas Robusto and he lit up another Camel. Thirty minutes later I relieved Don at the booth. He had written an order for immediate shipment and was happy.

He said, "I guess I'd better find something to do tonight. I've got an idea you'll be with a certain lady. How was breakfast this morning?" I replied, "Don, I missed her for breakfast and I have no plans for this evening. Let's have a great meal. Do you have any ideas?"

Don said, "I've seen a Thai restaurant on S.R. 79 every time I've gone to or from the condo, and I've wanted to try it. Do you like Thai food?" I replied, "I don't know. I've never tried any, but I've always wanted to." Don said, "Great! I'll meet you at the condo after this thing is over this evening." I told him not to worry about me for lunch. There was something at the concession stand I wanted to try.

Time slowed to a crawl. The show had gotten very slow. I did the crossword and smoked two cigars, only occasionally interrupted by buyers. I did make one more sale in the afternoon. Five-thirty came and I headed to the Sea Kove. Don was there. He said he had found a new cigar store and had a surprise for after dinner. I begged him to show me what he had found. He refused. We got in his van and drove to the Thai restaurant.

There was only one car in the lot when we drove up. This was a Tuesday night in the off season. We went in. The decor was nice, but not extravagant. We sat at a table that was adjacent to the front window where we could see out. Our waitress brought us menus and took our drink order. I ordered ice water and Don ordered hot tea. She went to the kitchen and we looked at the menu.

There were four pages of dishes on the menu. Don said, "Let's use an old trick I learned. Are you willing?" I said, "I'm willing and eager. Especially to find out what you found in the cigar store." The waitress returned. She was American and was in her sixties. She asked if we were ready to order. Don said, "Please ask the chef to select and prepare the meal for us. We are not typical Americans. We do like our food spicy." Our waitress went back to the kitchen. We could see her talking with a tall man in his fifties. He had an army airborne tattoo on his arm. Behind him was an Oriental woman assisting him. We quickly surmised he was a Viet Nam veteran who had taken a Thai bride. The man and woman started smiling and we quickly had some soup. It was delectable. Next came Thai spring rolls. Then the main course came. It was a mixture of oriental vegetables and seafood. The sauce was spicy and interesting. There was an Oriental dessert. Don and I really enjoyed the meal.

We told the waitress we really enjoyed the meal and we would like to compliment the chef. She went to the kitchen. The owners came out and we talked for a few minutes. They gave us some cards to pass out at the show. We thanked them again and told them we would be back.

We returned to the Sea Kove, stopping in the room for Don to get the cigars from his travel humidor. He handed me a Leon Jimenes. It measured seven and a half inches by fifty-ring gauge. We went out to the deck. We lit up the cigars and marveled at how great they were. Don told me that these were rated in *Cigar Aficionado Magazine*. Their rating was ninety. They were number three, of the one hundred twenty rated that issue. We enjoyed the beach and the cigars. We turned in early, both having been lacking in the sleep department.

Wednesday morning the sunrise woke us. Both of us showered, shaved, and dressed in jogging suits. We walked to the donut shop. I got some glazed donuts and Don got some cake donuts. We both got coffee. We wolfed them down, savored the coffee, and got refills to go. We also got a dozen cake donuts, "To go".

Don told me that he had plans to go out with some friends again tonight. I said, "I can find something to do." He offered, "You're welcome to go with us." I smiled. He said, "I don't need two guesses to know who you'll be with."

It was still early. We fast-walked back to the Sea Kove. It was now seven-thirty. The 'wave runner' birds and the sea gulls were working the beach. We brought out the bag of plain cake donuts. We tore off small pieces and threw them toward the Gulls. It was like we rang a giant dinner bell. At first we had several dozen Gulls fighting over the donut pieces. Within two minutes, we had over a hundred gulls in a feeding frenzy. Quickly, the donuts disappeared. We scrunched up the bag and tossed it into a nearby trash container.

A fresh set of tire tracks was visible next to the trash container. They went as far as the eye could see in both directions. The tracks passed by every container. Every morning, just after sunrise, they would do trash patrol.

We walked toward the east. There were very few people on the beach. The tide was low and there was a lot of beach. Every so often, there was a small stream of water that flowed into the Gulf. The streams came from pipes under the coastal road. They drained the rainfall into the gulf. It had rained during the early morning hours. There weren't any shells or other relics of the sea, to speak of. The weather had been balmy. After a storm, the beach is littered with treasures and trash. We had been walking for twenty minutes and were about a mile from the condo.

We turned around and started the trek back. A couple of shrimp boats passed by. They were unusually close to shore. Their nets were up. Some of their friends must have told them, by radio where the shrimp are located. One of the boats was half again larger than the other one. They were so close that we waved. They returned the greeting.

We returned to the condo. Don stayed on the beach to have a smoke while I dressed in tie and blazer and headed to the show. Don had told me he would bring lunch. I barely got to the show before nine. I opened the booth and adjourned to the smoking area for a Bering Churchill.

Each day of the show had seen a lessening in the number of buyers. This morning, I had two buyers come by the booth. One of them wrote a respectable order. I thought about what I was doing and the end result I had in mind. I realized that manning a booth was in the way of what I was doing. I was stuck at the booth. The reps I wanted to talk to were stuck at their booths. I would be better off without a booth. Then I could walk the floor and talk with reps. The group of people I had now met could supply me with referrals and cross referrals.

Don showed up around twelve-thirty. He had gone by the Publix Deli. It is located inside the big Publix supermarket. He had brought us each a huge sub sandwich. He had a 16 oz. Coke and I had a 16 oz. Diet Coke. The subs were great. They use Boar's Head meats in the West Florida Publix supermarkets. The Valdosta Publix doesn't carry Boar's Head meats.

We finished eating and I explained to Don my earlier thoughts about recruiting reps. He agreed and volunteered to spend some time at the booth. I headed over to Candy Royal's booth. I talked with her about recruiting a rep for this area. Candy was no help. Her rep for this area had just retired and she was looking for someone also. She asked me to refer anyone I found to her.

I went around the corner to the LIZ, Inc. Booth. Anne wasn't there. I surmised she was on a smoke break. I went to the front of the store. She was off to the side, was smoking one of her Dunhill cigarettes. Anne saw me approaching and gave me a warm smile. She said, "'Lucky' Joe, I'm looking forward to this evening." I said, "Anne, I am too." I told her that I was looking for a rep for this Gulf Coast Area. Anne told me that her rep for this area was part of a rep group. She had one rep group that did about half of her sales. I had decided against a rep group.

Anne did remember a girl who had been out front smoking yesterday. The girl had short blonde hair and wore glasses. She had mentioned an interest in picking up an additional line or two. She was a sub-rep, with a suntan oil company. Anne told me where her booth was located. Anne had finished her cigarette and headed back to her booth. I headed to the suntan oil booth.

I was lucky. The blonde girl was manning the booth by herself, for the moment. I told her that Anne had mentioned she might be looking for another line or two. I gave her my card and told her I was National Sales Manager for Don's Enterprises. She said,

"My name's Jean Stark and I'll be free in about thirty minutes. Tell me where your booth is and I'll come by and talk with you." I told her and went back to the Royal T's booth. I told Candy whom I was going to talk to. I also told her that I would refer her. Candy thanked me.

I walked by Angelo's sponge booth. Angelo was nowhere in sight. I didn't have time for a cigar, so I returned to my booth. Don took off. In about fifteen minutes, Jean Stark walked up. She was impressed with our line and I went over our program. Jean agreed to rep for us. I told her about Candy. She thanked me and headed for the Royal T's booth.

I smoked a cigar, across the aisle, in the smoking area. The other exhibitors and I exchanged jokes as we smoked. I was interrupted and made my final sale for the day. Don had come by and had left the show for the day. Finally, five-thirty arrived and I headed to the Sea Kove.

At the Sea Kove, I showered, shaved, and dressed casually. I went outside and joined Don. He was on the deck enjoying the view and relaxing. I offered him a Las Cabrillas Robusto. He accepted and we enjoyed a good smoke. He said, "'Lucky' Joe, I'm sure glad this show is about over. These slow area shows are not my thing." I agreed, saying, "I understand." I also told Don that I felt I should walk the next shows on the show calendar. He agreed with my reasoning.

I told him the next show was in Gatlinburg, Tennessee. Don took a cheap shot. He said, "I'll bet a certain Anne will be there." I said, "Anne doesn't do that show." Don said, "You got me. I apologize." I said, "Nope, you've got to grovel." Don said, "I ought to throw what's left of this cigar at you. But I don't want to waste it." I laughed.

It was fifteen minutes to seven. I drove down Front Beach Road to The Dolphin. I parked the car and walked around to Anne's room. She answered the door and motioned for me to come inside. The room was fairly large. To the left was a large TV. It was on a dresser. On the right wall was a love seat. Then, a night table with a lamp and a king-size bed. There was a doorway to the rest of the condo on the other side of the bed.

I took a seat on the love seat. In a couple of minutes she told me she was ready to go. I said, "Not so fast. I want to hear why you were so afraid yesterday morning." She took a deep breath and joined me on the love seat. With emotion in her voice, she started talking.

Anne said, "Do you remember my telling you about breaking up with my significant other?" I said, "I do. I think you said you broke up about six months ago and he moved to Orlando." She said, "That's right." Anne told me that she had met Herb Rhodes at an art reception in Tampa. She described him as six feet tall with black hair. Anne had been by herself. He was by himself. He had asked her to go out for coffee after the reception. She related that both of them loved art. They enjoyed talking about art and started seeing each other. Herb had retired from the Navy as a Captain. He was divorced and had his retirement income. His ex-wife had remarried, so he had no alimony payments.

Anne had already put the wheels in motion to move to Waco before she met Herb. After a couple of months they had become intimate. He moved out to Waco three months after she did. Anne said, "Herb has a much more reserved personality than I do. He doesn't have a driving personality as I do." When he first moved in, everything went well. It wasn't long before it turned into a nightmare." Anne related. Herb had prostate cancer before he met me. They did radiation therapy in Tampa. He had lived in Orlando. He moved to Tampa to receive radiation treatment. That was four years ago. Shortly after he moved to Waco, he started having prostate problems again. He had to get up four or five times a night to urinate. After several more weeks he had problems urinating. He went for a checkup. The doctor told him the cancer was back.

Herb had surgery. The surgery cured the cancer. However, it left him impotent. They talked about an implant. He refused to consider it and went deeper and deeper into depression. Instead of making the most of the situation, he felt sorry for himself. His personality changed. He used to be caring and fun to be with. Now he was argumentative and in bad spirits all the time.

I put up with it for several months longer than I should have. It cost me some of my best employees. I tried to talk with him. He didn't want to talk. I told him I wanted him to leave. He threatened me with bodily harm. I backed off and went to my friend, who is the Sheriff of the county Waco is in. I did as he said and took out a peace warrant. The Sheriff and two deputies arrived as planned. They served him with the warrant. I gave him ample money to move back to Florida.

He threatened to kill me in front of the deputies and employees. They asked me if I wanted him locked up. I told them I just want him to take his things and leave. Some employees helped him with his things. I had arranged a storage place, until he decided where he was going. He decided to move back to Orlando. I've gotten numerous letters threatening to kill me or hurt me. I have them saved in a box as the Sheriff suggested.

The Sheriff sent me to a firearms school, after which I got a permit and carry a 38-caliber revolver. He gave me some 'hot loads' for it. He told me to ignore Herb and not to talk with him, but Herb calls several times a week and sends E-mail at least once a day. The sheriff told me to never answer the door to my motel unless I know for certain who it is. He told me not to call out and ask who is there. He told me "under no circumstances" was I to peek out and see who was there. That could be suicide.

Herb knows my show schedule. The Sheriff told me that if Herb did try to do something, it would be at one of the shows. I have a copy of the peace warrant with me at all times. If he tries to approach me, I'm supposed to have him arrested. At every show, I meet with the security people and give them pictures of him. It's been a nightmare for the last year.

The other morning, I hoped it was you, but you never called out. You just knocked loudly every ten or fifteen minutes. I was terrified. I started to call the police. You had told me you don't like to get up in the morning, but I still hoped it was you. I didn't want the police to hassle you. Finally, it was fifteen till nine. I hadn't heard a knock for thirty minutes. I looked from the drape and could see no one. I made a run for my van with my hand on the revolver in my purse. When I got to the van, I saw your four-leaf clover and breathed a sigh of relief.

Anne said, "'Lucky' Joe, I'm so sorry. I would loved to have gone to the restaurant at the pier with you. Do you see why I was so terrified?" I said, "I do," giving her a hug and telling her I would never do anything to frighten her intentionally.

We got up and went to the car. I opened the door for her, then went around and got in, fastened my safety belt and started the Cadillac. The 'oldies station' was playing at a low volume. I asked Anne, "Is there somewhere you would like to go." She said, "I would like to go exploring with you and find a restaurant."

She also said, "There is a movie at nine forty five.
I would like to see it with you."

I told Anne that movies were my getaway. She said they were hers, too. We both smiled, realizing we shared something else in common. The movie was one I had wanted to see.

We headed east on Front Beach Road, passing a Hooter's restaurant. I teased her about going there, but Anne said that was fine with her if I wanted to go there. I told her that I was just teasing, that I really had somewhere quieter in mind. She said that she was looking forward to the same thing.

We passed a restaurant that had a deck over the beach. There were a lot of cars and we had heard people at the show mention the food was good. I turned around and went back. At the door you could go on the deck or go inside the restaurant. We explored the deck. There was only one couple eating out there. It had turned a little cooler this evening and most people had opted to eat inside.

We went in and the hostess greeted us. I slipped her a five-dollar bill. Then I told her that we would like to sit on the deck, close to the water. Anne and I both were dressed for the cool evening. The hostess told me the service might not be as good; that the waitress would be serving tables inside and we would be an add-on. I told her that was OK, so she seated us at the end of the deck.

We both sat facing the water. We could hear the waves breaking and the sea gulls calling. Our waitress came out and I gave her a ten-dollar bill. I told her tonight was a special occasion and asked her to take good care of us. She promised she would. She gave us two menus and asked for our drink order. Anne ordered iced tea and I ordered ice water. I told Anne, "One of the tapes I listened to explained what TIPS stood for." Anne quickly said, "'To Insure Proper Service'. I listened to the same tape. He also said to give the tip up front, which you just did." I said, "I'm impressed."

We looked at the menu. The waitress had told us about a Grouper Special. It was broiled Grouper, with cheese, grilled vegetables, and chef's surprise sauce. All served over a bed of rice pilaf. We both ordered the special. The food, when it came, was excellent, and the waitress gave us great service. After the meal, she brought us both some decaffeinated coffee. I lit a Dunhill cigarette for Anne. We talked as the waitress refilled our coffee. It was just after nine when the waitress brought our check. Anne tried to pay half. I refused and agreed to let her buy the movie tickets.

We drove to the theater, which was about four minutes from the restaurant, but we didn't know that in advance. Anne purchased the two tickets. The theater was on the north end of The Shoppes at Edgewater shopping center. We still had almost thirty minutes before the movie started. We walked past several stores to a set of tables. They were in front of an ice cream store. It had closed at nine. We sat down. Anne got out her Dunhill cigarettes and I lit one for her.

There was a Christmas store in front of our table. It was a fairly small store. I remarked, that I didn't know how they could stay in business, with only that much square footage. Anne finished her cigarette and we walked over to the store window. They had Christmas trees set up. All the ornaments were shells and shell ornaments. It was time for the movie and we headed for the theater.

We went in the door to the theater. I tried to get Anne to sit on the back row, but she replied, "I don't know you well enough yet, to sit on the back row." The theater only had a dozen or so people in it. We took two seats in the middle of the middle row. The previews began.

When the movie started, I put my right arm around Anne. She leaned over. I smelled her perfume, recognizing the fragrance. It was *White Diamonds*. My senses delighted at the tingly feeling of her hair touching mine. We held hands and enjoyed the show. The touch of her hands against mine was electric. I was wishing the movie would never end. But it did.

We drove back to The Dolphin at about midnight. I walked Anne around to her room and she invited me in. I started to kiss her and she stepped back. I told her I just wanted to give her a kiss. She said that she really liked to kiss. Kissing was one of her favorite things to do. She said, "You're married and I just want to be friends." I said, "OK."

I took her hand and gave her a short kiss on the cheek. She said, "I really enjoyed the evening and it's time for you to go." She walked toward the door and I followed. She started to open the door and our eyes met. There was an awkward moment, then we were kissing. The softness of her lips and the decisiveness of her tongue were overpowering. We finally broke for air. Anne said, "You've got to go or I won't be able to . . . ." She opened the door. I reluctantly said good night and went to my car.

I had never, ever, been kissed like that. She was the best kisser I had ever met. The evening brought back memories of my college days. I had an uncomfortable rigidity between my legs as I drove back to the Sea Kove. Don was not in yet. I went to the deck and smoked a Bering Immensa, my thoughts on Anne as I gazed across the water.

A boat was moving in my direction very fast. It was close to shore. As it got near our condo, it slowed and made a left turn, heading directly out from shore. After a hundred yards or so the lights went out. I could see the lights on two boats approaching each other, about two miles or so out. They came together and stopped. I was curious and kept an eye on the boats. They were directly out from the condo, and the boat I had seen near shore had turned in their direction. About ten minutes later, I saw blue strobe lights flashing and heading for the two boats. One of the boats went toward my right and the other went to my left. The blue lights went off to my left. The lights on the two boats I had seen almost immediately disappeared.

Don came out to the deck. I pointed toward the blue flashing lights. They were well off to the left now. I told him what I had seen. Don speculated that a drug deal got messed up tonight. We watched for a few more minutes. I put out my cigar and we both called it a night. I drifted off to sleep with thoughts of Anne Moore dancing in my head.

The alarm rudely awakened us at 6:30 AM. We put on our jogging clothes and took to the beach. We walked west until we were even with Don's favorite donut shop. We crossed over Front Beach Road to the donut shop where Don got some chocolate cake donuts and I got some sausage biscuits. We both got coffee. Breakfast was really good.

Don said, "I'm ready to leave Panama City Beach and get back to Valdosta." I had mixed emotions. I'd had enough of guarding the booth and the boredom of the Panama City Beach Gift Show. However, I knew I would miss Anne Moore. Now, when I thought of Anne, a warm feeling came over me.

We returned to the beach and enjoyed the peace and tranquillity. It was a little sad. I knew this was my last walk on the beach for some time. Don looked my way and said, "'Lucky' Joe, this almost makes that boring show worthwhile. You know; just to do this." After an hour, we returned to the condo. Don said, "I don't care if we get there by 9:00 AM or not." I said, "Don, stay and enjoy this as long as you can. Checkout time isn't till noon. There's no sense in both of us being bored. You can do me a favor on the way in." Don said, "What's that?" I replied, "Bring me another one of those Publix deli subs, on the way in. You know, the roast beef with plenty of peppers." Don said, "You're a genius!"

I showered, shaved, dressed and loaded my car, almost forgetting my travel humidor until Don brought it out to the car. I got to the show about ten minutes late. I opened the booth. There were no buyers in sight. Some new friends beckoned me over to the smoking area, in the former Wal-Mart garden center. I lit up a Bering Immensa and joined in the lively conversation. They were all happy about leaving today.

My smoke got interrupted by a group of buyers. I wrote an order. Another group of buyers came by. They were from the Wal-Mart Supercenter in Destin. They liked the shirts and gave me the name and phone number of their District Manager. They left and I finished my cigar. Then I worked the crossword puzzle in the paper.

A little after noon, Don showed up with the submarine sandwiches. They were great. He brought some 16 oz. Cokes to wash them down. Don said he would guard the booth for awhile, so I went back to the loading dock. Angelo was holding court. I joined the group for awhile. I found out Angelo was going to be at the Gatlinburg Tennessee Gift Show. I said my good-byes and headed to Candy Royal's booth.

She was in good spirits and was ready to tear down and leave. Candy told me she would be at the Gatlinburg Tennessee Gift Show. She told me I should definitely go to it. She said, "It's well over ten times bigger than this show. People from all over the world come to the GTGS." I told her I was planning on going. She thanked me for referring the rep to her. I said, "You're welcome."

I went by the rest room. Leaving the rest room I saw the *Tursiops* booth. It was next to Angelo's sponge booth. On the last day of the show, most of the exhibitors sell their samples. I asked the lady if she had any samples. She said, "Sure." I bought a bottle. The top of the bottle was a Dolphin. Anne had shown me that she liked fish. I thought I'd surprise her with this.

I headed back to the booth. Don was glad to see me. No one had come by since I left. He headed out to say his good-byes. The people in the smoking area got my attention. I grabbed a cigar and went over to pass the time.

Two o'clock finally came. Don had already gotten us a good place for the van. I had hidden a four-wheel hand truck in the back of the garden center. It was behind a several hundred shopping baskets. We tore down and loaded the van and Don hit the road. I went over to say goodbye to Anne.

Anne saw me coming and walked over to me. She told me she would like to go outside and smoke. We got outside and she told me her sales reps had been giving her a hard time today about me. Evidently, Don had said something to Candy and Candy had said something to them. I assured Anne that I don't talk to Don about what we do. She told me she knew that. She said, "People love to gossip. It makes me a little uncomfortable."

I gave her a plastic Publix bag. She opened the bag and pulled out a box. Inside the box nestled a bottle of *Tursiops Perfume*. The bottle is cast in a wave design. The top is a frosty white dolphin cast in plastic. The dolphin is anatomically correct. Anne took the top off and sprayed the fragrance on her wrist. She said, "The fragrance is delightful. Thank you."

Anne said, "I had a wonderful time." I said, "I had a wonderful time and you are the best kisser, I have ever met." She said, "I told you kissing is one of my favorite things." Anne said, "I'd like to hear from you." She gave me her business card. Anne continued, "I've written my 800 phone number on the back. I know you have to be discreet." I put it in my billfold and made a mental note to transfer it to my personal planner. Anne said, "I'm not going to say goodbye." She walked over and gave me a hug. I said, "I'm not going to say goodbye either." Then I walked over to my car and began the journey home.

CHAPTER 5

VALDOSTA AGAIN

I had left the Panama City Beach Gift Show and was crossing the bridge over St. Andrew's Bay to Panama City in light traffic. In no time, I was turning the corner at Gulf Coast Community College. I drove on, past all the shops and the Mall. Just past the Mall, I turned north onto U.S. Highway 231.

Now that I was through the stop-and-go traffic, I turned up the 'oldies station'. The 'afternoon drive time' deejay was livening up the airwaves. He got through with his break and I heard him say, "Now for you baby boomers, *This Magic Moment* by The Drifters." The radio blared, "This Magic Moment; While your lips are close to mine; Will last to the end of time." Then I heard, "Sweeter than wine; Softer than the summer time; Forever until the end of time."

My thoughts turned to Anne Moore and the kiss we had shared. I got a warm, fuzzy feeling. I remembered the first time I had the warm, fuzzy feeling. I was in third grade. A little blonde girl had gotten my attention. She had also gotten the attention of my best friend. We both fell in love with her. On Valentines Day, we each showed up at her house with candy. We both vied for her attentions. Thank heaven her parents were in the United States Air Force. They were transferred in June that year. It broke my heart for a week or so. But it probably saved my friendship with my best friend.

As I traveled up the highway, I continued to think of Anne. She had brought something into my life; something that had been missing for a lot of years. The radio blared, *"It's too late; To turn back now; I believe,*

I believe, I believe; I'm falling in love." I now realized I was falling in love with Anne Moore.

I got to Interstate 10 and turned east. I couldn't get Anne out of my mind. The oldies songs, on the radio, kept reminding me of happier times in my life. The fraternity dances in the late sixties were some of the happiest times of my life. I was President of my fraternity and was having fun dating a lot of different girls.

A few years before I started college, Valdosta State had been an all-girl school. When I started, the girls outnumbered the boys two to one. When I finished, five years later, the ratio was almost even. The boys coming back from Viet Nam were going to college on the GI Bill.

In my freshman and sophomore years, we would go over to the girl's dorm great room around six in the evening to meet some girls, then return around seven to take them out. It was a great school, if you were a boy.

Before long, I crossed the Apalachicola River. I lost an hour, as I crossed from Central Standard Time to Eastern Standard Time. I reset my watch to five thirty. Around six thirty, I got to Tallahassee. I turned south off the Interstate on to U.S. Highway 27. It is named Monroe Street in this part of the city.

A mile or so south is an ABC Liquor Store, which carries a large selection of cigars. They've got four, upright humidors. I pulled in and went inside. They had some great cigars. I leisurely made my selection and returned to my Cadillac. I went another mile or so south and turned into a city park. I parked easily and picked a cigar.

The park is on the east side of Monroe Street, encompassing about four city blocks. The center of the park is a large lake. It is round, except for a finger of land that goes a short way into the lake. There's a bandstand on the finger. A sidewalk or track meanders around the lake. There are streetlights and landscaping. Joggers and walkers are a constant. A policeman is always in the park. I could usually count on some coeds jogging or walking on the track. Florida State University is only a short distance away.

Along Monroe Street is a row of little stores adjacent to the park. There was a motor lodge there during the thirties and forties. The motor lodge had been converted to stores. The little buildings are constructed of stone. Each one was a duplex when they served motorists. I can envision the Model T's and other vintage cars of that bygone era. Now, they are antique shops and specialty stores.

Ducks and geese are always in abundance. People love to bring kids and feed the waterfowl. Pigeons are everywhere and join in on the feeding frenzies. The park is a great place to relax and enjoy a cigar. I opened a La Gloria Cubana Churchill, feeling fortunate. The ABC store had just got some in. With the shortage of premium cigars, they are usually out of stock.

I punched the end and got it lit. The smooth spicy taste stimulated my senses. These cigars are great for an evening smoke. I chose one of the benches that are out from under the oak trees. The last time I was here I had witnessed someone get bombarded. One of the pigeons that roost in the trees made a direct hit. Her hair was a mess. She was really embarrassed and angry about her misfortune.

I enjoyed my cigar and watched the people exercising on the track. My thoughts kept returning to Anne. I looked forward to calling her next week. The words of the song on the oldies radio station kept returning to my brain. I kept hearing, "It's too late, to turn back now . . . .".

I finished my cigar and was getting hungry. Two blocks north is a Boston Market restaurant. I drove to it and had a home-style meal, then drove on to Valdosta. I got home around 11:00 PM.

Friday morning, I went to the office. I did the paperwork on the sales from the gift show and returned some phone calls and actually connected with one of the reps. She was referred to me by Candy Royal and I mentioned that Candy referred me to her. She sounded interested and I sent her some samples. It was taking a lot longer than I had anticipated to build a sales force.

Lunchtime arrived and I called Ken Scott. He had brought his lunch today. He asked me to join him for a cigar after lunch. I told him I would.

My attorney friend was in. The receptionist transferred my call. John Austin answered, "'Lucky' Joe, where have you been?" I replied, "I've been at Panama City Beach. I can't seem to find anyone to have lunch with." John said, "I've got an opening. I'll go with you and keep the meter running." I said, "Forget it." He laughed and said, "I'm hungry. What are you jabbering for? You could be on the way over here." I responded, "I'm on the way."

John's office is in downtown Valdosta. It's on the second story of a brick building built in 1898. He rents out the first floor. It is less than a block from the Lowndes County Courthouse. I parallel parked and went up to his office. The outside of the building is old and showing its age. However, John's offices are plush. He practices with two junior partners and some legal assistants. There are four legal secretaries. I had a feeling they did most of the work.

John was waiting for me and we walked down the street to Nicky's Restaurant. They have a one time through buffet. Home cooking is their draw and the food is so good that they stay busy. I got salad, southern fried chicken, collard greens, Brussels sprouts, and a vanilla pudding dessert. I grabbed some ice tea and paid for both of us. The cash register is at the end of the serving line. I had maneuvered in front of John. He fussed about my paying and we sat at his usual table.

The meal was great and we returned to his office. He has a huge imposing office. It is really plush and is designed to intimidate. It's part of the game that successful bankers and attorneys play. John went over to his humidor and got out a couple of Punch Churchill cigars. He said, "I wish I had time to smoke one with you but I've got an appointment in ten minutes. I've got to get my meter ticking." I thanked John for the cigars and headed to Ken Scott's Good Stuff Antique's shop.

Ken was on the front porch. When I got out of the car, he said, "I've been waiting for you. Come on up and let's smoke one." I walked up the steps and handed him one of the Punch Churchill cigars. I said, "These are courtesy of John Austin." Ken said, "I know they'll be good. How's John doing?" I said, "Running his meter and making lots of money."

I told Ken about my trip to the Panama City Beach Gift Show. He asked some questions and we enjoyed the cigars. I didn't tell him about Anne. He took me around back. Then he showed me how his pepper garden was growing.

There were six varieties of peppers, including habanero. I spotted a caterpillar that looked exactly like a rolled up leaf. Ken said, "I wondered what was eating the leaves off my pepper plants and leaving the peppers." He killed the caterpillar. We spotted two more and killed them. He fussed about the camouflaged garden pests. We finished our Punch cigars and I headed back to the office.

I made a few more phone calls and called it a day. The weekend was here. It was Friday night and the Valdosta High School Wildcats were playing. I went to the game. They lost to the Colquitt County Packers in a close game. They had a terrible night and should have won by a score of 35 to 10.

Two movies, rest, and catching up occupied my weekend. I was nice to Suzanne and avoided any verbal fights. Before I knew it, Monday morning arrived. I read the paper, did the crossword puzzle, then went to the office.

The only information I had on the Gatlinburg Gift Show was where and when. I called Candy Royal begging for help and she promised to fax me some information. She told me where she was staying and where her booth is located. Candy said, "The show is spread all over town and there are a number of trolleys providing transportation." I thanked her for her help.

The Fax came in just a few minutes. I called the motel she suggested. It had been booked for months. The fourth motel I called had a cancellation. Its name is the Royal Townhouse Motor Inn. I booked it and thanked my lucky stars. They promised to send a brochure and written confirmation. I had learned; people were having to stay up to thirty miles away.

Don and I went to lunch. We went over my planned trip to Gatlinburg. He said, "I'm glad I don't have to go. I've had enough of shows for awhile." I was, however, glad to go. I'd missed traveling for sometime. We returned to the office. Don looked at the 'cigar tree' and said, "I'd like to smoke a cigar; but it's ninety degrees and the humidity is a hundred percent. Why don't you come over tonight? We'll smoke one on the dock." I said, "See you about eight."

It was 2:00 PM. I thought and realized that it was only one o'clock in Waco. I did some work. At 3:30 PM I called the 800 number for LIZ, Inc. The 800 number Anne had written on the back of her card is for her home phone. The receptionist answered and I said, "'Lucky' Joe Hall with Don's Enterprises for Anne Moore." Shortly, I heard Anne say, "Anne Moore." I said, "Anne, it's good to hear your voice. Are you where you can talk?" She said, "No, let me call you back in about an hour." I gave her the regular number to Don's Enterprises and disconnected.

Around 4:30 PM, I was interrupted by the intercom. I heard, "'Lucky' Joe, Anne Moore with LIZ, Inc. is on line two." I punched line two and said, "Good afternoon, 'Lucky' Joe." Anne said, "I can talk now." I said, "I can talk, but people can hear me through the door if they try. When is a good time to call you?" Anne said, "I close the office at five. The workers get off at 4:00 PM. They come in at 7:00 AM. I'm usually home by 5:30 PM. However, on Tuesday and Thursday nights, I go swimming at the 'Y'. I swim with a group of friends. We swim for an hour or so and then go to dinner together."

I said, "I'll give you a call at 5:30. Everyone leaves here by 5:30 PM Eastern Time and I'll have some privacy." Anne said, "I'm looking forward to talking to you." We hung up and I had that warm fuzzy feeling.

I went home around 4:30 PM. Suzanne was actually there. She told me she was going to the 'Club' with friends. I told her I was going to Don's for the evening. She finished her TV program and departed. I made some supper and killed time until six. At 6:00 PM, I went back to the office.

When 6:30 arrived, I called Anne's 800 number. She answered, "Anne Moore." I said, "It's 'Lucky' Joe." Anne replied, "I've been looking forward to your call all afternoon. How are you doing?" I said, "I'm doing great! It's so good to hear your voice. It's like classical music to me." Anne said, "Flattery will get you everywhere." I inquired how her return trip to Waco went. She said, "It went well but it was really long. I could only find oldies stations for about half the trip. I've listened to the motivational tapes so much, I've almost memorized them."

I said, "I've discovered, through a friend's recommendation, the Cracker Barrel restaurants. They have a tape rental program. You buy the tape and listen to it in your car. They've got a big selection of current novels. When you're done, you turn it back in at any of their restaurants. You get a cash refund, except for a two dollar a week rental fee." Anne said, "We've got Cracker Barrel restaurants here in Texas." I said, "They are all over the East and Southeast." Anne said, "I'm going to do that on my next trip."

We talked about LIZ, Inc. Anne said, "Some of my customers call me Liz. They think that Liz is my name. It doesn't bother me, but it infuriates my mother. She helps me out here at the business and watches it for me when I'm at the shows."

I asked Anne about her business. She described the building as a big square. It was concrete block and had about fifteen thousand square feet. It had been a bar and was located on North Lakeshore Drive, near Interstate Highway I-35. Some bigger, newer nightclubs had opened in

Waco. This one had gone out of business. Anne had gotten the building from the bank that had carried the note. It has a lot of open area, which is what she needs. Anne related that she had the outside walls painted pink. There is a big sign and she had "LIZ, Inc." painted on it in Red. Anne informed me that her home was only a mile away.

Anne asked me about my artist friend who paints tropical fish. I told Anne about Mary Carlon. How she had been in Europe and about her raising tropical fish. I promised to see Mary and send Anne one of her brochures. I asked Anne, "How is your aquarium project coming along." Anne said, "I found a book on clownfish and have been reading it. I've found two pet stores in the yellow pages. I'm going to visit them. Then I'm going to check the Internet about stores in Dallas. I'm really looking forward to getting the information from Mary Carlon."

Anne said, "I'm taking antihistamine, so if I sound a little stuffy, you'll know it's my allergies." I said, "Anne, I used to have hay fever twice a year—once in the spring and again in the fall. Then, a couple of years ago, I learned about Pycnogenol. Since I started taking Pycnogenol, hay fever hasn't been a problem. I've got some cassette tapes. They're left over from my networking days. I'll send you one and a printed brochure. You can get Pycnogenol at GNC or one of the big discount stores." Anne said, "I would appreciate your sending the information."

Anne asked about my trip home. I told her about stopping in Tallahassee at the park. I described the park and the lake. She was jealous. I said, "I wish you could have been there to enjoy it with me."

I told Anne about my plans for the Gatlinburg Tennessee Gift Show. She said, "You're lucky to get a room, 'Lucky'." Then she kind of giggled. I said, "Anne, I love to hear your laugh." I happened to see my watch. It was ten minutes to eight. I couldn't believe how fast the time had gone by. I said, "Anne I've got an appointment with Don in ten minutes. It seems like we've been talking for ten minutes. Anne said, "I can't believe we've been talking this long, either."

I said, "When may I call again?" Anne said, "Monday and Wednesday evenings after five thirty are good for me. However, once a month I take my mother and her friend to Sam's Wholesale. We're set up for this Wednesday night. How about next Monday Night." I said, "It's too long a time. I'll talk with you next Monday." We said our good-byes and I took off to Don's.

I arrived at 8:10 PM. Don was already on the pier. I joined him and handed over a HOYO DE MONTERREY Churchill. Don said, "I haven't smoked one of these in a 'coons age'. Where did you find them?" I told him I had stopped at the ABC Store in Tallahassee. I said, "They actually had La Gloria Cubana and HOYO DE MONTERREY in stock." Don said, "I'd have stopped if I'd known that." We used our cigar punches and lit up. The smoke was unbelievably smooth. The HOYO DE MONTERREY is smoother and not as spicy as a La Gloria Cubana is. For an hour we enjoyed the millpond, the night, and our cigars. We finished and I called it a night.

Tuesday I called Mary Carlon and made arrangements to pick up a brochure. I picked it up and she gave me her E-mail address. She told me she had a nice 'Home Page'. I knew what she meant; however, I had not started using the Internet. I also went to my storage warehouse and got a Pycnogenol tape and a booklet. Wednesday I sent the Pycnogenol tape and Mary Carlon information to Anne by Priority Mail.

The week passed. I used the weekend to prepare for the following weekend. I had booked a table at a coin show in Athens, Georgia. I've got a friend in Athens named Bill Cole. He had invited me to stay with him and his wife Sherry. He runs a manufacturing company. Bill's wife has a doctorate and teaches at The University of Georgia. I had met Bill years ago. We both dealt in old coins. I gave him a call to verify my visit with him.

Bill answered, "Bill Cole." I said, "Bill who?" He said, "'Lucky' Joe, I'd know that voice anywhere. Sherry and I are looking forward to your staying with us. There's one catch though." I said, "What's that?" Bill said, "You've got to go to the Chinese restaurant with us." I said, "You'll have to twist my little finger." Bill laughed and said, "Seriously, we're looking forward to seeing you." I said, "I'm looking forward to seeing ya'll, too."

We talked on about set-up time for the coin show and what time I would arrive. He told me that he had gotten me a good table location, since he was part of the show committee. I said, "It's nice to have friends in powerful positions." He said, "Since when is working on a coin show committee a powerful position?" I said, "Ever since you got me a good table location." We talked on for about fifteen minutes and I disconnected.

Monday evening finally came. At precisely 6:30 PM Georgia time, I called Anne's 800 number. There was no answer. The recording machine came on and gave its message. At 6:45 I called; again, no answer, save the recording machine. I tried again at 7:00 with the same results. I was beginning to worry about Anne. I went out to the 'cigar tree' and smoked a cigar. At 8:00 PM I tried again. Anne answered and apologized for not being there earlier. Her mother had asked her to take her to the funeral home. One of her friends had passed away. She wasn't a close friend. But a friend, nonetheless.

I said, "Anne, it's great to hear your voice." I also told her that I had worried about her not being there. She thanked me for the Priority Mail package. She said, "My inside tape player is broken and I've forgotten to take the tape to the car. I promise to listen to it before our next telephone talk."

Anne said she had visited Mary Carlon's web site and was very impressed. She said, "'Lucky' Joe, I'm going to order some of her prints. I'd like one of her originals. However, she doesn't have any originals for sale with clownfish. In fact, she doesn't hardly have any originals listed for sale." I said, "That's because she doesn't have any to sell. You won't believe this, but I own an original Mary Carlon watercolor, entitled 'Clown Parade'." Anne said, "I'm jealous."

We talked and talked. Before I knew it, it was 10:45 PM. Anne told me she was going to Dallas Wednesday afternoon, to an 'Off Broadway' play. I told her I'd try to call her from Gatlinburg. I went home and Suzanne asked me where I'd been so late. I told her I had been calling reps in Hawaii and the West Coast. She said, "Yeah, and smoking cigars." I admitted to the cigars and went to bed. I fell asleep thinking of Anne.

Tuesday morning I got up early and voted in the city election. I ran into John Austin at the voting place. He asked me to join him tonight at Mathis Auditorium when they tallied the votes. I told him I would. He asked me to get Don to join us.

Tuesday evening at 7:00 PM, Don and I joined John Austin at Valdosta's Mathis City Auditorium. The polls closed at 7:00. By seven thirty half the returns were in. At 7:45 PM the last returns came in and all our candidates had won election to the city council.

We congratulated them and enjoyed the moment, then we went to Muldoon's and celebrated. John and Don had Bud Lite beer and I had an O'Douls. We went out to the patio and John Austin passed out some La Gloria Cubana Churchill cigars. We drank, smoked cigars, and partied. Our party broke up about 10:30 and I went home.

Suzanne was watching TV. I told her that all our candidates had won. She had been heavily drinking and made the comment that our new councilmen weren't any better than the old ones. I ignored her attempt to fight and went to bed.

Friday morning I drove to Athens, Georgia. Stopping at the rest area on I-475 near Macon, I rested and smoked a Bering Churchill, then drove on to Athens. Bill was already at the motel. The Coin Show was to be in its meeting room. Bill showed me where my table was located. I set up, covered up, and followed Bill to his home. Sherry wasn't home yet. Bill and Sherry smoke cigarettes and are about ten years younger than I am. We went out on his back deck. I smoked a Bering Churchill while he had some cigarettes.

Sherry came home. We took off to her favorite Chinese restaurant. We ordered four entrees for the three of us and shared. Their 'pot stickers' are some of the best in creation.

When I told them I had to leave tomorrow at 2:00 PM, they chastised me. I invited them to go to Gatlinburg with me. They declined the invitation. I told them about the consulting job I was doing and that it was taking longer than I anticipated. They sympathized. I fought for the check and won. I had to use the fact that I was staying at their home and avoiding a motel bill.

We went back to their home and relaxed on the back deck. We talked about the trip they were preparing to take to Europe. They had met in Europe on a school trip. One of their fun things is to rent Mopeds and explore ancient ruins. We talked until around 1:00 AM and went to bed. When I lay down, I had thoughts of Anne and got that warm fuzzy feeling. I realized that since I had met Anne, Suzanne and I had not had one of our fights. I pondered that realization as I feel asleep.

We arose at 8:00 AM and were at the show by 9:00 AM. I did some business and made some money buying a few coins and selling a few coins. Then at 2:00 PM, I packed up and thanked Bill and Sherry Cole. One nice thing about the coin business is that your entire inventory fits in a brief case. I put my briefcase in the trunk of the Cadillac and drove away.

CHAPTER 6

GATLINBURG

Having left the Coin Show, I headed to the Perimeter Road and over to U.S. 441 North. I set the Cadillac's cruise control and headed up the highway.

It had rained hard during the night and this morning it still threatened rain. The farther north I got, the darker it got. I crossed over I-85 and got farther up in North Georgia. I took a break at Tallulah Falls, joining a mob of tourists and looking at the falls from the top of the valley. I enjoyed a Bering Churchill and went on my way. In another hour or so, I crossed into North Carolina. It started lightly raining.

I stopped at the North Carolina Welcome Center. I almost cried when I got to the door. A sign said, "U.S. 441 closed through Great Smoky Mountains National Park except to vehicles with snow tires or chains." I had planned to take U.S. 441 through the park to Gatlinburg. Inside, I got a map and information on the detour via I-40. I headed north. It got colder and started raining harder. When I got to U.S. 23 and started the detour, it was through a steady rain, making driving hard. I crossed over the mountains on I-40, in the rain. It would have been nice to enjoy the scenery.

Finally, I crossed into Tennessee. It was a relief to stop at the Tennessee Tourist Welcome Station. I got a map and information on the best way to Gatlinburg. Outside, there were some covered picnic shelters. The temperature was in the high thirties. We were pretty high in the mountains and were level with some of the clouds. I put on my down jacket and smoked a Las Cabrillas Robusto in the cold. I had to keep swapping hands because of the cold.

I got off I-40 and took a twisting, curvy road to Gatlinburg. The posted speed limit was thirty-five miles per hour. Most of the time, I couldn't drive that fast. I finally drove into Gatlinburg from the north. They had thousands of Christmas lights erected along the road; however, they had not been turned on yet. I saw hundreds of people on the sidewalks. My motel was on the south side of town. Finally, it came into view on the right. I pulled in and got out of the car to check-in. I couldn't believe my eyes. The main entrance to the Gatlinburg Convention Center is directly across the street. The center is the main headquarters for the show.

At check-in, they gave me a message. The message was from a Jean Stark. I had recruited Jean at the Panama City Beach Gift Show and was bringing samples for her. She had hoped to see me this evening. I had gotten in two hours later than anticipated. It was a longer trip than I had calculated and the rain had added another hour. I called her motel. It was thirty miles away. I left a message for her to call me when she got in.

It was Saturday night and the streets were swarming with people. I saw a lot of University of Tennessee sweatshirts and jackets. Some of the people were wearing badges for the gift show. Set-up was today. I knew it would be very busy tomorrow. I also knew I would not be able to get much work done on the first day of the show. The reps would be too busy writing orders.

I refreshed myself and headed out to the sidewalk on the south end of the commercial area. I started walking north. After about a mile, I saw a sign for a cigar store. It was on the third floor of a tourist shopping mall. The mall contained around three dozen small shops. The cigar store took up two spaces. The walk-in humidor was fairly small. It was a hassle, as the store was full of people. They had some Arturo Fuente 8-5-8 cigars. I bought a handful and left.

When I got back on the side walk, I lit up one of the Arturo Fuente 8-5-8 cigars. The 8-5-8's have a most unique flavor. It is intriguing and I like them a lot, but they are very hard to find. So many people have started smoking premium hand-rolled cigars that there is a big shortage. The prices have also gone up with the demand.

Don told me that in 1998 the supply would catch up with the demand, then prices would go back to a reasonable level. He said the farmers in the Dominican Republic and Honduras had planted a tremendous amount of cigar tobacco in 1997. It takes six months to go from field to finished cigar. Therefore, the first part of 1998 would see an increase in supply.

There were all kinds of shops along the sidewalk. Ripley's Believe It or Not has a museum here. They also have a Motion Master Moving Theater. Guinness has a Guinness World Records Museum. There are many miniature golf courses, arcades, and other adventure opportunities. All kinds of food shops, cafes and restaurants line the street. Candy apples, fudge, taffy, cotton candy, popcorn, and other festive foods are plentiful.

I finished my cigar and got a hot Italian sausage sandwich. It was great in the cold air. I continued my walk as the Italian sausage sandwich ended the hunger pains.

On the road I saw four-wheel-drive vehicles with snow tires. Some of them had put little snowmen on the tops of their vehicles. They had been in the Great Smoky Mountains National Park. The rain had stopped and people were having a good time. I had walked back to The Royal Townhouse Motor Inn and went up to my room.

My room is on the second floor. It is the second room from the front of the building. There is a stairway right in front of the door. Halfway down the long building is an elevator. It provides service to the basement. I finished unloading my car and went in the room to plan.

Jean Stark called, and we talked about the show, then set up a luncheon appointment. We agreed to meet in my motel lobby at noon. I planned the next day, then hit the hay, immediately asleep, dreaming Anne was here sharing Gatlinburg with me.

Sunday morning the alarm woke me. After dressing, I got some coffee and a sausage-with-cheese omelet at the restaurant across the street. I went back to my room and got my things for the show. After walking across Parkway, I got my credentials. During the next hour I talked with several sales reps, having talked with most of them by phone before the show.

Finally, I found Lucy Wall. She had already agreed to rep Southern California for us. We talked about getting together this evening with Candy and Sam. Lucy had been invited to a party by some reps. The party was tonight in the Holiday Inn. Lucy reps for over a dozen companies, Royal T's being one of them. I told Lucy I was going to see Candy Royal after lunch. Lucy asked me to invite Candy and Sam

Jones to the party. She got back to writing orders and I headed for The Royal Townhouse lobby.

Jean Stark arrived a few minutes before twelve. We walked one block north to Lineberger's Seafood Restaurant. We had a wonderful lunch and I answered her questions. After lunch, we walked back to my motel and I gave her the samples and the forms she needed. Jean was now finished with the show and headed back to the Gulf Coast.

I got the box of samples I had brought for another sales rep. I crossed Parkway at one of the crosswalks. In Gatlinburg, pedestrians have the right of way on crosswalks. It feels funny for cars to stop for me without a red light. There are plenty of police and they strongly enforce the crossing rule. They also stop any jaywalking. I went back into the show and found the rep I had been looking for. He took the samples and I answered his questions.

I then went to the north side of the Gatlinburg Convention Center. I waited a few minutes and took the trolley to The River Terrace Convention Hall. The show guidebook informed me that the Royal T's booth is on the first of two floors. The trolley ride took about ten minutes and dropped us at the door of the center. It had taken us several blocks along The Little Pigeon River. The crystal clear water, the rock bottom, and the small rapids are beautiful.

I entered the River Terrace Convention Hall. I got my bearings and found Candy's booth. She was waiting on a buyer, so I looked around the floor. There were only about fifty booths on each floor. After looking around, she was still busy, so I took the elevator to the second floor and looked around. After about fifteen minutes, I went back down to the Royal T's booth.

Candy was by herself and I went to the booth. She saw me coming and said, "'Lucky' Joe, it's so good to see you." I said, "Candy, it's nice to see you too." She asked where I was staying. I said, "The Royal Townhouse and it's across the street from Convention Center." Candy said, "I thought you'd be staying thirty miles from here—somewhere over past Pigeon Forge. You really are lucky, 'Lucky' Joe."

I told Candy about Lucy Wall inviting her and Sam to the party. Candy told me she wouldn't see Sam until about thirty minutes after the show closed. She asked for my phone number and I gave it to her. Candy promised to call as soon as possible after the show closed today.

I went over some reps with her and thanked her again for her help. She gave me some things to take to Lucy Wall and I exited the hall.

I decided to walk back to the main part of the show. I pulled out one of the Arturo Fuente 8-5-8 cigars, punched the end and got it going. I enjoyed the unique flavor as I slowly walked along the Little Pigeon River. The sound of the water rushing over the rocks is very calming.

I walked about a block and a group of ducks decided to check me out. They must have thought I was a good mark for a handout. However, they didn't get anything from me. So they investigated the flowers planted along the sidewalk. There is a fence between the sidewalk and the river. Every fifty yards or so there is an opening to get down to the river. Bridges cross the river every block or so. I tired of watching the ducks and continued walking.

It wasn't long and I was across the river from Christus Gardens. I noticed that their parking lot was almost empty. The main buildings are built with of stone and are impressive. Just past the gardens I turned left onto Maple Lane. I walked up the hill to Parkway and passed the Gatlinburg Ski Lift. People were taking the lift on sightseeing tours. There was no snow. It would be at least another month before the ski season started. I walked south on Parkway for a block and was back at the show.

I found Lucy and went over what Candy had said. I gave her the things Candy had sent. I got her number and told her I would call as soon as I heard from Candy. Lucy introduced me to another rep. A buyer walked up and I told the rep I would see him tomorrow. I headed back to the motel and sorted out the day. I organized what I had done and planned Tuesday.

The show closed at six and Candy called at 6:30 PM. Sam had already made other plans. They had to pass on the party. I called Lucy and made arrangements to meet her at 8:00 PM in the lobby of the Holiday Inn.

I walked up the hill three blocks to the Holiday Inn. I was a few minutes early and sat down on one of the plush couches. Lucy got there about five after eight. She made a phone call on the pay phone and we walked to the back building. The party was going strong when we got there. We joined some people at a table and I went to get us some drinks. I got her a mixed drink and I got an O'Douls for myself.

She introduced me to some people and spent a lot of time with some major buyers. I watched and listened to the steel band. They started doing the Limbo. It was fun to see the people fall on their rear ends. Lucy and I stayed for an hour and a half before calling it a night. I walked her to her hotel, which was adjacent to the Holiday Inn. A stream runs right below her room. We listened to the water for a few minutes and I headed back to The Royal Townhouse Motel. I smoked a Las Cabrillas Robusto and called it an evening.

The alarm woke me Monday morning. I got a phone call from another rep and set up an appointment for noon at the motel lobby. I went over and worked the show till shortly before noon. At noon I met the rep and went to Linberger's Seafood Restaurant. I answered his questions and had a good lunch with him. After lunch, we went to my motel for some samples. He went back to the show. I walked south on Parkway to a stream that crosses the road.

I lit up one of the Arturo Fuente 8-5-8's and followed the stream. It passed the aerial tram to Ober Gatlinburg. I watched the tram take a load of people up the slope, then I followed the stream down to the Little Pigeon River. Turning north, I walked slowly along the river enjoying the cigar. The beauty and sound of the river were refreshing and the walk invigorated me. When I got to Maple Lane I headed back to the show.

I took the trolley to the Park Vista Hotel Convention Center and looked around. I talked to a couple of people and took the trolley to the Ramada Convention Hall. I didn't find anyone to talk with and called it a day. I went back to the motel and rested a couple of hours.

I got up around six and tried to call Anne. The recording machine answered and disappointment and frustration overcame me as I hung up the phone. Hunger and a taste for a good steak overcame me. I walked south a block to Charley O's and had a great salad and a very good steak.

When I finished the meal, I walked up the street, enjoying a Bering Churchill while watching the crowds of people. I went back to the cigar store and got some more Arturo Fuente 8-5-8 cigars. I tried to buy a box, but they limited me to five. Then I went back to the motel and tried to call Anne again, to no avail. Disappointedly, I fell asleep.

Tuesday morning, the alarm woke me. I dressed and went to breakfast. Then I took the trolley over to the Riverview Terrace Convention Hall to see Candy Royal. Candy was busy with a buyer and I had to wait twenty minutes to see her. I talked with her about one of the sales reps we were both trying to recruit. She invited me to the dinner party she was giving tonight for her reps. She told me to be at the Park Grill at 7:00 PM. She told me to bring some of the flyers showing our line.

I walked along the Little Pigeon River and smoked another of the Arturo Fuente 8-5-8's. When I finished the 8-5-8, I had lunch at Cactus Jack's restaurant on Maple Lane. It was convenient to the show. The decor was interesting and the Tex-Mex food was good.

After lunch, I walked back to the main convention center and visited with Lucy. She gave me the name of a rep. His booth is at the Riverside Motor Lodge. I took the trolley and went to the Riverside Motor Lodge and looked around.

I found the rep's booth, however, he had already left the show. A lot of the reps leave the show before the final day, especially if they are working a company-sponsored booth. The sales manager and other company people are there to shut it down and keep the hours. Most of the buyers disappear after the first two days of a show. I had now been to all five of the show locations.

I took the trolley back to the Gatlinburg Convention Center and visited with reps. The show had slowed down considerably and it was much easier to talk with reps. However, the slowest day at this show is much busier than the busiest day at the Panama City Beach Show.

I had fallen in love with the Little Pigeon River. I left the show about 4:00 PM and took a walk along the stream and then the river. I smoked another one of the Arturo Fuente 8-5-8's. The ducks were in a different section of the river. I stopped and leaned on the guardrail as I watched the antics of the ducks. They were leaving no stone unturned as they looked for food. I continued watching the ducks and listened to the rush of the water over the rocks.

A drake and a susie started nuzzling bills. The sight turned my thoughts to Anne and the kiss we had shared. I got that warm, fuzzy feeling again and didn't notice the cold afternoon, while I was thinking of Anne. I missed her terribly and wanted to call her and hear her voice.

My cigar played out and I went back to my room and set the alarm. Then I took a nap. The alarm awoke me at 6:00 PM. I showered and dressed before the fifteen-minute leisurely walk to the Park Grill. Then, about twenty minutes to six, I put on my all-weather coat.

I left the warmth of the motel room, went out to Parkway, and started walking south. It was sporadically sprinkling rain. The rain was snow that had melted on its fall into Gatlinburg. I saw more vehicles with little snowmen on the roof. They were on their way back from the Great Smoky Mountains National Park. About five till seven I walked up to the Park Grill.

I entered and inquired about the Royal T's Party. The hostess told me it was in the meeting room on the north side. I surveyed the interior of the restaurant, which reminded me of the great ski lodges. There are heavy wooden beams supporting the tall ceiling, which creates a large open area. I passed dozens of tables and made my way to the party room.

After passing through the double doors, I saw Candy. She was at a table with twenty-two chairs. It consisted of ten four-person tables in a single row. A fire was roaring in the huge fireplace behind the left side of the table. There were several other groups in the room.

Candy said, "'Lucky' Joe, let me introduce you to some of my reps." I complimented Candy on the nice outfit she was wearing. She blushed and told me to sit on the other side of the table near the fire. I placed my coat on the back of the chair where she pointed. Then Candy introduced me to the three reps that were already there. Sam was there, too, and I greeted him. He told me that the food here was really good which was why Candy booked her rep party here every show.

The waiter started asking for drink orders. I ordered an O'Douls, as was my custom. More sales reps drifted in and I met them. I had a small stack of the Cigar Tees flyers at my seat. The reps started talking about cigars and my line. Some of the reps at the party had already signed on with me. I met a couple in person for the first time. I had previously talked with them by phone.

The waiter asked everyone to be seated. He and his assistant took our meal orders. As soon as he got the orders, people were milling around again. I ordered another O'Douls and talked with some reps interested in the Cigar Tees line. The food came. It was excellent. Everyone enjoyed the meal.

One of the Reps made a toast for Candy. She talked about how great a person Candy is. Candy had tears in her eyes and said, "It's a party. You're not supposed to make me cry." Everyone clapped and laughed. Sam came up and gave her a big hug.

About 9:00 PM, the reps started leaving. Many of them had multiple engagements for the evening. By ten everyone had left except for Candy, Sam and myself. I thanked her profusely. Candy took care of the bill and refused to let me help. We left the restaurant. There was now a steady light rain. All three of us were wearing all weather coats. I put on my rain hat and we walked up Parkway and crossed over U.S. 441 to my motel. They continued up and over one block to their hotel.

I entered the warmth of the room and hung up my coat. I had planned to leave by ten in the morning. I now had to take samples and information to two new reps for the line. I had made several other contacts at the party, and planned to work with them by phone. Candy had really helped me out. I thought about how to repay her. I couldn't think of anything off the top of my head. I called it a night.

Wednesday morning, the alarm rudely awakened me and I got ready for the day. I had breakfast across the street, then made two trips to my car in the basement parking area. I made up two sample packages and went to the show to deliver them. I had trouble finding one of the reps, but finally found him and was finished for the show.

I checked out of the motel at 11:30 AM, then crawled through traffic in Gatlinburg and took U.S. 441 to Pigeon Forge. It had been over twenty years since I had driven through this area. I could not believe how big Pigeon Forge had grown. It was just an intersection with some country stores and antique shops the last time I had come through. Now it has DollyWood, a big family theme park. There are dozens of motels and restaurants, along with many shops and tourist activities. The highway is heavily commercial all the way to Sevierville. At Sevierville, I transferred to SR 66 and drove to Interstate Hwy. I-40.

I put the Cadillac on cruise control and relaxed. It had been tough driving from Gatlinburg to the Interstate. I had to slow to 55 mph as I passed through Knoxville. Just south of Knoxville, I gassed up and had some fast food.

Time passed and I was approaching Chattanooga. One of my favorite places in the world is Missionary Ridge, where a Civil War battle took place. From the top of the ridge, you can see the expanse of the valley and the city of Chattanooga. Across the valley, Lookout Mountain rises above the city. The river flows around the end of the mountain.

I turned off the Interstate and drove up to the top of Missionary Ridge. The top has a lot of large homes. A lot of those homes have cannons and signs that tell about the battle. I drove north on the ridge, I passing a lot of memorials and cannons while driving to a fairly large park with a parking area. After parking the car, I went over to a scenic overlook.

I got out one of the Arturo Fuente 8-5-8 cigars. It was one I had purchased in Gatlinburg. I lit up and enjoyed the view. I thought about the battle and how many men had lost their lives along the ridge. The unique flavor of the cigar was enjoyable. I took in the beauty and wished Anne were with me to share the moment. I spent about an hour with my thoughts and returned to my car. I went down from Missionary Ridge to I-75 and drove south.

Two hours later I went through downtown Atlanta. I always thrill to the sight of the State Capitol Building. The Dahlonaga gold on the dome is an awesome sight. Passing Turner Field, I remembered a trip to an Atlanta Braves baseball game a few months earlier. Turner Field is an exciting place to watch a baseball game.

Before long, I could see the jumbo jets crossing Interstate I-75 on their landing approach south of downtown Atlanta. I pulled off the highway and went to the Dwarf House. The Dwarf House is a diner that Truett Cathy ran for years. He started the Chick-fil-A restaurant chain from it. I stopped in and ordered a Hot Brown, with a tossed salad and a Coke. The regular Chick-fil-A restaurants don't have the Hot Brown. So, when I come through Atlanta, I stop and get a Hot Brown. It's cut up Chick-fil-A chicken in a porcelain dish that's covered in a cream sauce. Two strips of bacon are on top and toast points are around the sides. The hot brown almost melted in my mouth.

After the meal I continued south on I-75. I had made the trip from Atlanta to Valdosta so many times I knew just about every exit. I would have liked to stop at High Falls State Park and walk along the waterfall, but it was getting late, so I drove on by the exit. The miles passed and I was home around 11:00 PM.

CHAPTER 7

THE WAIT

T hursday morning I went to the office and discussed with Don my accomplishments in Gatlinburg. I made phone calls and organized samples. I sent them to the reps I had recruited. It was three weeks until the Myrtle Beach Gift Show. I thought of Anne and looked forward to talking with her Monday evening.

John Austin called about 11:15 AM. His court case had settled and he wanted me to have lunch. Don was free and we drove down to John's office. We found a parking place a block away in a city lot and went upstairs to John's offices. The receptionist informed him that we were there and he joined us in the reception area.

We went downstairs and walked the block to Nicky's Restaurant. Today being Thursday, chicken divan was featured on the serving line. I got a tossed salad with Thousand Island dressing and topped it with Greek peppers and tomato wedges. Chicken divan, fried chicken, collard greens, and snap beans were my choice for today. I got some water and paid for all three of us.

John and Don complained about my paying, but it was too late. They both got fried chicken and chicken divan with assorted vegetables. Every day there is southern fried chicken at Nicky's. The other meats change. However, the meats are the same each day of the week. For example, every Friday there is fried fish and ham along with the fried chicken. The vegetables change with the seasons.

We sat at John's usual table and the waitress brought us cornbread and biscuits. Then she brought us a pitcher of iced tea and another of ice water. We thanked her and dug into our food. Nicky's allows you one plate, one salad bowl, one dessert, and one trip through the buffet line. We were hungry and our plates were piled high.

When we finished eating, we talked about the local political scene and about all of our candidates winning seats on the city council. John suggested that we adjourn our meeting across the street to the park. Don left a tip as we left.

When we got to the park, John took three Dunhill Churchill cigars our of his pocket humidor. He gave Don one and me another. Dunhill cigars are extremely mild and smooth. They are perfect for morning or early afternoon. An early cool front had come through and the temperature was in the mid-seventies. The humidity was also low. We thanked John Austin profusely for the Dunhill's and lit up.

Don invited both of us to his dock tonight for some cigars and brandy. We both accepted. We listened to Don tell some lies and headed back to the office after enjoying the cigars. John told us he was going to check in with his office and take the rest of the afternoon off.

At the office I had some messages. After returning two phone calls and making a dozen others, I left early and went home. Suzanne was busy preparing to go to her Thursday bridge party. She wasn't happy that I was going to Don's to smoke cigars. She probably would have made a scene if she weren't already running late for her bridge party. I took a nap. When the alarm woke me, and I made a light supper. Finishing the meal, I headed to Don's.

It was just getting dark when I joined Don and John on the pier. Don had finished feeding the fish and the mosquitoes were attacking. We went inside the protective screened-in area. Don poured some brandy and opened a box of La Gloria Cubana Churchill cigars. We each got one and prepared to smoke them. John cut off the end of his with a double blade cutter. Don and I used a bullet punch. The earthy, spicy flavor of the La Gloria Cubana Churchill was wonderful.

We'd been smoking and talking about fifteen minutes when Don grabbed a large five-cell flashlight. He shone the beam toward the dam and two red eyes glowed from the dark water. He said, "Every night about this time that six foot alligator checks out the dam. He got a dog across the pond two nights ago. We've called the wildlife people and they're supposed to catch and move him next week. The eyes went underwater and we returned to our smokes.

Don told us that a couple of months back, some beavers took up residence in the millpond. People's small trees started disappearing at night. The wildlife people had a hard time catching the beavers. When we finished our cigars, we thanked Don for the La Gloria Cubana's. Then John and I headed home.

Friday was uneventful at the office. The Valdosta High School Wildcats were playing in Douglas, Georgia. I listened to the game on the radio. They won the game and I went to bed. Suzanne wasn't home when I turned in. I thought of Anne as I fell asleep.

My weekend was spent reading and going to the movies. Both Saturday and Sunday I saw action films. Monday was a boring day at the office. I pretty much wasted my time, as all I got was voice mail and answering machines.

Monday evening finally arrived and I called Anne at 6:30 PM. She answered and I said, "Anne, I've missed the sound of your voice." She said, "'Lucky' Joe, I've missed you, too. I had hoped to hear from you last week." I told her that I had tried several times and had missed her. She asked about the Gatlinburg Gift Show. I told her about The Little Pigeon River and how the show was spread over five locations. I said, "It would have been better if you had been there."

Anne said, "'Lucky' Joe, I listened to the tape you sent me on Pycnogenol and I really owe you. After taking Pycnogenol my allergies to pollen disappeared overnight. It's nice to feel like a real human being again and it's wonderful not having to worry about the pollen." I told her some more about how the Pycnogenol had changed my life and the lives of some other people I'd met. Anne said, "How can I ever repay you?" I replied, "You can kiss me like you did in Panama City Beach when we get to Myrtle Beach." She said, "That will be a pleasure."

I said, "Anne, I've never been to Myrtle Beach." Anne said, "It's a great show and I've been doing it for years. Have you made reservations yet?" I said, "No, I haven't. Where are you staying?" She said, "I'm staying at the Patricia Grand Hotel, at a great rate. My reservations are for Sunday through Wednesday night. However, they are booked for Saturday night and I don't have a place for Saturday night yet." She gave me the phone number for the Patricia Grand.

Anne said, "I really appreciate the *Tursiops* perfume. I adore the fragrance and the bottle is really special." I said, "I'm glad you do." We talked and before long it was 9:00 PM. I could not believe we had talked for two-and-a-half-hours. It seemed like just a few minutes. Anne said, "Are you going to call Wednesday night?" I answered, "I'm looking forward to it."

We said our good-byes and disconnected.

Tuesday morning I called the 800 number for the Patricia Grand. The reservation clerk answered and I told her the dates I wanted. She told me they were booked for Saturday night. However, Sunday through Tuesday was available. I told her to reserve those nights for me. I asked if she knew of a good place to stay Saturday night. She told me they have a sister resort hotel three miles north on the beach which is called the Patricia North. She told me it is ten dollars higher per night and all the rooms are suites. I booked it.

Wednesday night at 6:30 I called Anne. She answered. I told her I had reservations at the Patricia Grand for Sunday through Tuesday nights. I asked if she had gotten a reservation for Saturday night. She said, "No." I told her that I had booked a suite at the Patricia North. I told her it was a sister hotel to the Patricia Grand and it's nicer. She said, "The Patricia Grand is very nice. It must be something." I said, "You're welcome to stay with me Saturday night." Anne said, "I won't say no, but I'll have to think about it." I said, "Think all you want."

We talked on and two hours passed as though they were twenty minutes. We said our good-byes and I promised to call next Monday night.

Monday night finally arrived. Anne answered the phone at 6:30 Georgia time. Anne said, "I'm going to give myself a salt water aquarium for Christmas." We talked about tropical fish and Mary Carlon's paintings. Anne told me about the print that she had decided to order from Mary.

Anne said, I'm frustrated with some of my employees. They aren't getting along with each other as well as I would like. There are a couple I just don't understand." I told Anne that I had the same problem at the radio station. She said, "'Lucky' Joe, how did you solve the problem?" I said, "Anne, I had each of them do a personality profile and share the results with everyone. They all learned a lot about each other. They also learned how to work with each others personalities." Anne said, "That sounds interesting."

I told Anne that I would look and see if I had some of the profiles left. I asked, How many employees do you have." She said, "I have almost twenty." Two hours passed like twenty minutes. I told her I would call Wednesday and disconnected.

Wednesday night I called at 6:30 Eastern Standard Time. No one answered. I called again at 6:45 and Anne answered. She apologized for not being there at 5:30. She had a minor emergency at work and couldn't get away. I said, "I found the personality profiles and have enough for your employees. I said, "I'll bring them to Myrtle Beach and show you how to use them. I'd like to do one with you and see how our profiles match up." Anne said, "That will be fun. I'll look forward to it."

We started talking about Myrtle Beach. Anne had been making the gift show there for years. She told me that Myrtle Beach was where shag music came from. She said, "I love to dance to beach music." I replied, "I love to dance to beach music too." Anne said, "I'm excited that we'll get to dance together. I'm really looking forward to seeing you at Myrtle Beach." I said, "I'm really looking forward to dancing with you. Almost as much as I'm looking forward to seeing you."

I told Anne that I would be going to Orlando, Florida tomorrow morning. I planned to meet with a big house account and have lunch with a sales rep. We've talked on the phone and he sounds interested. We talked for an hour and a half. I promised to call again next Monday night.

Thursday morning I arose early and by 7:00 AM, I was on I-75 heading for Orlando. I stopped at the rest area just below Gainesville, Florida. There is a scenic overlook to Payne's Prairie. The overlook is artistically built in the shape of a snake. It rises up about fifteen feet. The view of the prairie and I-75 is interesting. I walked up the incline to the top of the overlook and lit up a Las Cabrillas Robusto. After about forty minutes, the Cadillac was carrying me south again.

At 10:15 AM I stopped at the AAA/Disney Information Center in Ocala. I got some maps and brochures. A sign said, "Downtown Disney is now open." I got some information on Downtown Disney. I gassed up and resumed driving. Shortly I turned onto the Florida Turnpike. After an hour on the Florida Turnpike, I exited onto Interstate Highway I-4.

I went down I-4 to Sand Lake Drive and cut over to International Drive. I drove a mile south and parked in front of East Side Mario's Italian restaurant. It was 12:15 and I was forty five minutes early. The building next door to the restaurant housed a liquor store. On the sign I read, "Premium Cigars".

I went over and investigated. They had a walk-in humidor and a fair selection of cigars. Their prices were a little higher than I liked to pay, so I only bought a couple of Robustos.

Returning to the front of the restaurant, I smoked one of them while I waited for Eric Hill. I had booked an appointment with the largest chain of gift shops in the Orlando Area for Friday morning. My mind went over Friday's presentation. Eric drove up at five till one. He had told me he would be driving a red Cadillac.

We greeted each other and went inside. The waiter told us about the specials and took our drink order. We looked at the elaborate menu. The waiter brought Eric iced tea and an O'Douls and ice water for me. Eric selected Mamma's Baked Ziti. I selected the Eggplant Parmigiana.

Eric looked at a flyer and I answered his questions about the Cigar Tees. The waiter brought us a 'bottomless' salad bowl and Italian bread. He filled our individual salad bowls and asked if there was anything we needed. We continued our discussion over the salads.

Our entrees arrived. Eric's entree consisted of ziti noodles tossed in Pomodori sauce with fresh basil and garlic. It was baked under a mound of ricotta, mozzarella, provolone, and Parmesan cheeses. My entree consisted of breaded eggplant slices covered with spinach, ricotta, and Parmesan cheeses. It was baked in Pomodori sauce, mozzarella, and provolone cheeses. It was served with a side order of spaghetti. The entrees were excellent.

I noticed that the clientele of East Side Mario's were local business people. Lunch is usually slow for most restaurants on International Drive. The tourists are in the theme parks during the day. I complimented Eric on his choice of our meeting place. We finished our meal and I paid the check.

Eric agreed to rep for us. I told him about the appointment I had for Friday morning. He agreed to meet me at 10:00 AM, at their headquarters. Eric told me he had an appointment with Wild Waters at 3:00 today and asked me to join him.

I went to the car and got samples, flyers, and other items for Eric. We rode in Eric's car up International Drive to Wild Waters. They bought several of Eric's lines and gave him a nice order for the Cigar Tees. Eric dropped me at my car and verified the time and place for tomorrow morning.

I drove down International Drive to U.S. 192 in Kissimmee, Florida. U.S. 192 is the highway that connects with the main entrance to Disney

World. I checked in at the Knight's Inn. I like Knight's Inn Motels because you can drive right up to the door of your room. I moved into the room and browsed through the brochures.

I decided to go to Downtown Disney for the evening. One of the pamphlets had a listing of all the stores that had just opened. I saw The Sosa Family Cigar Store listed, and knew it would be a nice store. Disney insists on quality. I rested for an hour and headed over to Downtown Disney for the evening.

The map in the brochure showed that Downtown Disney is long and narrow. It covers the south shoreline of a lake. In the middle of Downtown Disney is Pleasure Island. There is a charge to get onto Pleasure Island. Once you pay, you have unlimited access to everything on the island. There are comedy shows, dance halls, concerts, and other adult entertainment.

I parked in front of a giant 24-screen AMC Theater. I walked between it and a huge two-story Virgin Megastore. It sells music, books, videos, and other entertainment. When I turned onto the main street, the number of people walking impressed me. This was supposed to be the slow time of year. I knew from the map that Sosa Family Cigars was to the right, just past the theater.

I quickly got to the Sosa Family Cigars store, walked in and was impressed. The furnishings are plush and the interior is designed using expensive woods. The walk-in humidor is large and has a picture window in the connecting wall. The door is mostly glass. The humidor is a large square that is divided into two sections by a partial center wall.

I talked with one of the Sosa's. He told me they had only been open for a few days. He informed me that the family has been in the cigar business in Miami, for many years.

I could not believe the selection. There were Arturo Fuente, Dunhill, Partaga, Ashton, H. Upmann, Macanudo and many other brands. Every size and shape of the Sosa Cigars were available. I had never seen such a selection of premium cigars in one cigar store, even the bigger stores like J.R.'s. I was awestruck by the selection before me. I felt like a kid in a candy store and wished that Don were here to share it with me.

I selected a box of Arturo Fuente 8-5-8's and an Opus X Robusto. I got a Sosa Churchill to try their brand and also got six other brands of cigars I had never smoked. Most cigar stores limit your purchase of Arturo Fuente cigars. I was delighted to be able to buy an entire box of

8-5-8's. The Sosa Family member said, "We get busy around 9:00 PM and stay busy until after midnight." He invited me to smoke a cigar in their smoking area.

They have two plush black leather chairs that are off to one side. Each has an embroidered inset on the chair back. One has the Sosa family emblem and the other has the Opus X logo. He punched the end of the cigar. Then he helped me light the Opus X Robusto, with a jet lighter. I sank into one of the chairs and delighted at the exquisite taste of the cigar. I smoked and chatted with the Sosas and some of the customers who came in. I finished the Opus X and took most of the cigars to my car. I kept out the Sosa Churchill to smoke as I explored Downtown Disney.

I lit up the Sosa Churchill and decided to walk from west to east. I liked the Sosa's mildness with a hint of spice. I walked past the block of stores and came upon the Planet Hollywood restaurant.

It is built over the water of the lake. It's shaped like a planet. It's painted blue and has huge, red neon Planet Hollywood sign. At the entrance, dozens of people were waiting in line. I walked over the bridge and around it.

To my left across a short expanse of water, I could see Pleasure Island. Lots of people were walking around. I heard various types of music as I walked by. I saw a magician across the distance and could hear a comedian working an audience. At the ticket booth people were buying tickets. There were young attendants valet-parking cars. At the east end of the island is a large replica boat. It houses Fulton's Crab House restaurant.

Having passed by Pleasure Island, I came upon the eastern part of Downtown Disney. The first sight is a huge LEGO store. There are many larger than life statues outside the store. They are made completely of LEGO building blocks. I next passed the World of Disney store. It's billed as the newest and biggest Disney Shop on earth.

The variety and quality of the shops impressed me. The Rainforest Cafe is located in an awe-inspiring building. It looks like a volcano and has smoke coming out the top. There was a two-hour wait to be seated. This time of year the theme parks close around six, so it appears the people are leaving the parks and coming to Downtown Disney and Pleasure Island. I reminded myself that this is the slow time of year. I wondered how they would handle the busy time of year.

There is a park-like area beside the lake. The view over the water is nice. I sat on one of the benches and finished the cigar. Hunger pains had now come over me and waiting in line is not my favorite thing to do.

The deli inside the Gourmet Pantry supplied me with a roasted chicken salad and an O'Douls. I sat on one of the wrought-iron chairs and enjoyed the salad and O'Douls. Then I walked back to the car and drove to the motel. It was 11:00 PM when I got back. Sleep came easy as thoughts of Anne danced through my head.

Friday morning arrived. I showered, dressed, and had breakfast at the restaurant adjacent to the motel. The pancake special was wonderful. Checkout was easy and I headed to the headquarters of the gift shop chain. Their headquarters is in an office\warehouse park. It's a block off International Drive. Eric was already there and waiting for me.

We went in together and made our presentation to the buyer. He was familiar with the growing popularity of cigars and gave us a nice order. We left and I had lunch with Eric. Having answered his questions, I drove back to Valdosta. Traffic was heavy going north because it was Friday. I listened to the Orlando 'oldies station' on the radio all the way to Ocala. My thoughts drifted to Anne and how much I was looking forward to seeing her.

The weekend passed quickly. Saturday afternoon was spent with Ken Scott smoking cigars. I talked with him about Myrtle Beach. He had been there often. He also told me that shag music was invented there. He told me that shag music is, more or less, beach music. He said, "There's a great place to dance there."

He picked up his portable phone and called an antique dealer friend in Charleston, South Carolina. Ken asked him the name of the dance club in Myrtle Beach. He told Ken the name. Ken said, "Its name is the Beach Music Cafe. It's located in the Boardwalk-At-The-Beach complex. I wrote the name on the back of one of Ken's cards.

We talked some more about Myrtle Beach and he told me that entertainers like the Gatlin Brothers were building theaters. Ken thinks it will be like Branson in ten years or so. Ken said, "I wish I could go with you."

Sunday afternoon was spent at the Movie Theater. Sunday evening I had dinner with Suzanne at the country club. I managed to avoid fighting with her.

Monday passed slowly. Finally 6:30 came and I talked with Anne. I told her that tomorrow I was going to Jacksonville, Florida, with my attorney friend, John Austin. A promoter had lined up a group of speakers for a success seminar. Some of the speakers are Zig Ziglar, Brian Tracy, and Barbara Bush. Anne said, "'Lucky' Joe, I'm jealous. Brian Tracy is one of my favorite motivational speakers."

I said, "I guess I shouldn't tell you that I'm going to a special VIP luncheon with Brian Tracy." Anne fussed and said that she goes to Dallas occasionally to hear motivational speakers. We both agreed that it is a good way to recharge one's positive thinking. Again, two hours passed, as if it was twenty minutes. I told Anne I would call her Wednesday evening and disconnected.

Tuesday morning at 7:00 AM, I met John at his office and we drove to Jacksonville in his Mercedes. We stopped at White Springs, Florida, on the way and got some Egg McMuffins, eating them in the car. When I asked John if he had any Grey Poupon, he said, "I ought to pull over and let you walk the rest of the way." I just laughed.

We parked in the parking area and went into the auditorium. We both had a great time listening to the speakers, then went to the VIP luncheon and talked with Brian Tracy.

After the VIP lunch we skipped two of the speakers and took the overhead rail to downtown Jacksonville. We went to the Jacksonville Landing. It's on the riverfront of the St. John's River. The Landing is a shopping and dining complex. Don and I found a deck with a great view of the St. Johns River. John had brought a pair of Macanudo Vintage 1988 cigars. We smoked them and enjoyed life and the magnificent view of the river.

We returned to the convention center and took in some more speakers. They were good for the most part. We got back to Valdosta around 9:00 PM. I thanked John for a great day and drove home. Suzanne was in a foul mood. I went to bed.

It was now Wednesday, December 3. When 6:30 PM showed on the clock, I called Anne. She told me she planned to leave early in the morning. She already had her van packed and was ready to go. She asked how I liked the speakers at the seminar. I told her John and I had a great time and had our enthusiasm batteries recharged.

We talked about the tape program at the Cracker Barrel restaurants. She said that she was going to get some books-on-tape from them and see if it made the trip shorter. I assured her that it would.

I said, "I'll be leaving around 6:30 AM Saturday morning. I've never been to Myrtle Beach from here, so, I don't know exactly how long it will take. I could be there as early as two or as late as four. If, for some reason, I'm not there by six, I'll call the Patricia North Hotel and leave a message. She said that she would probably be setting up Saturday until 5:00 or 6:00 PM. However, if she got through sooner, she would call earlier.

I asked if she were going to stay with me Saturday night. She laughed and said she would let me know Saturday. I asked if she had a reservation for Saturday and she said no. Anne told me she felt like she had a fever. She hoped it was just the hectic pace she had been through the last few days.

Anne said, "Last year I went to a great seafood restaurant. Let's go to it Saturday night." I said, "I can't wait. I haven't had good seafood since you and I dined on the deck in Panama City Beach." Anne said, "That's the last time I had good seafood, too. Maybe the company had something to do with it." I said, "Flattery will get you everywhere."

We wished each other a safe trip and ended our phone conversation. I went home and dreamed of the time I would spend with Anne in Myrtle Beach.

The rest of the week seemed like an eternity. I worked at the office making phone calls. Friday I had lunch with Don, telling him I would be back in the office late next Thursday afternoon. I said, "I have an appointment in Atlanta early next Thursday morning. It's with the buyer for a chain of 100 gift shops." Don said, "That's great!"

I wanted to give Anne something nice for Christmas. Something she would cherish, as much as I cherish her. I remembered that I had a Mary Carlon painting, "Clown Parade", stored away. It's a fairly large painting. The painting depicts a small group of clownfish and sea anemones. I got it out of storage and put it with the samples for the reps. I knew Anne would like it.

Friday night arrived. I had the car loaded and was ready to go. My mind was filled with the anticipation of seeing Anne. I turned in early and got a good night's rest.

CHAPTER 8

MYRTLE BEACH

T he alarm woke me at 5:45 AM. It was Saturday, December 6. Today I would see Anne. I showered, shaved, and dressed. By 6:30, I was on the way to the Myrtle Beach Gift Show.

I had watched the Weather Channel last night. The weather for Myrtle Beach was forecast to be cold and clear through Monday. Rain is forecast to come in sometime Tuesday. I had packed accordingly.

U.S. Highway 84 connects Valdosta with Waycross, Georgia. Then U.S. 82 connects Waycross to Interstate Highway I-95. I would take I-95 to South Carolina and stop at the South Carolina Welcome Center for directions. According to the map, there are two ways to go. Which route was quicker, I didn't know.

By 7:30 AM, I was passing through Waycross and listening to the local 'oldies station'. U.S. 84 is mostly two-laned, and is the hardest part of the trip. I turned onto U.S. 82 and started making better time. It is four-laned, much of it divided. It's speed limit is 65 MPH most of the way to I-95. I had gassed up the day before. It would be somewhere in South Carolina before the car would need more gasoline.

About 8:30, I reached I-95 and headed north on the Interstate. I switched the radio to the Savannah 'oldies station'. Traffic was fairly light. By 10:00 AM I was passing by Savannah, Georgia. The sign for the South Carolina Welcome Center appeared a few miles past the state line.

It was 10:15 when I pulled into the parking area. Inside, the hostess gave me a South Carolina map and showed me a large map on the counter. The route they suggested was highlighted in yellow. It showed leaving the Interstate and going to Charleston, then taking the coastal highway north to Myrtle Beach. The hostess said, "It will take about three hours." I thanked her and picked up some brochures on Myrtle Beach.

I hit the rest room and got my down jacket out of the car. I zipped it up and bought a paper. There was a picnic table across the parking area. I lit up a Las Cabrillas Robusto and worked the crossword puzzle. By 11:00 AM, I was strapped in the car and rolling again.

At Exit 33, I left I-95 and took U.S. 17 to Charleston. The route was mostly rural and I stopped for gas in Parkers Ferry, South Carolina. It was at a general store with gas pumps. I pumped the gas and became irritated when I discovered they had no rest room. I stopped again at the next McDonald's and got some triple cheeseburgers. McDonald's was running a ninety-nine-cent special on triple cheeseburgers. I used the rest room and ate the cheeseburgers on the road. I don't normally like to eat and drive. However, I didn't want to take the time to eat in the restaurant.

A "Welcome to Charleston, South Carolina" sign appeared and I turned onto I-526. I-526 is a bypass around Charleston. The tall bridge over the waterway presented a spectacular view. The Interstate Highway ended back into U.S. 17. The ramp put me on U.S. 17 heading north, which is four-lane and divided, for the most part, between Charleston and Myrtle Beach.

I made good time and by 1:30 PM was passing Huntington Beach State Park. I pulled into the Chamber of Commerce Information Center to get brochures. It was closed. I felt that Saturday was the most important day of the week for them to be open to give out information. Nevertheless, they were closed

I started looking for a florist shop. My plan was to surprise Anne with a dozen red roses. The first two shops I saw were closed. Then I saw a Harris Teeter supermarket. They had a floral department and I made my purchase.

I drove up U.S. 17 past U.S. 544 and turned onto Ocean Blvd. Driving north on Ocean Boulevard, I passed amusement parks, restaurants, and other tourist businesses on the left. On the right I could see the Atlantic Ocean and hotels and motels. I passed 29th Ave. N. and saw The Patricia Grand. Its eighteen stories rose high over the beach, creating an impressive sight. After about forty more blocks, I pulled into the Patricia North Hotel Suites. The Patricia North is just less than five miles north of the Patricia Grand.

Following the signs, I drove up the ramp to the second floor. Exiting the car, I entered into the lobby\registration area. The receptionist gave me my keys and told me a little about the Patricia North. The front part of the building is nine stories of parking garage. There are walkways to the suites on each floor. She told me about the other amenities and I picked up some magazines and brochures.

The turns in the parking garage were tight for the Cadillac as I drove up to the seventh floor. It was still early in the day so I got a space right at the walkway to my room. I found the room on the right, across the center walkway. The door opened into a well-decorated bedroom. On the left I saw two queen-size beds. On the right stood a low dresser with a TV on top. A nightstand with phone nestled between the beds. A double closet with folding doors stood open past the second bed.

At the right rear of the room, a doorway opens into a walkway. The left side of the hallway is a lavatory, with a toilet and tub\shower in separate rooms. On the right side is a full kitchen. Included are a sink, stove, refrigerator, microwave, dishes, and glasses. At the end of the walkway, a door opens into a living\dining room. The right side has a dining table and a side desk with a TV on top. A wall phone is between the dining table and the TV. The left side has a couch and coffee table at the far end. The wall on the left has a fold-down king-size bed. The far wall is a double sliding glass door, which leads to a balcony. The balcony has two plastic armchairs and a plastic serving table.

I partially unpacked and stored the things I would need tonight and tomorrow morning. I had to transfer to the Patricia Grand tomorrow and only brought in what I had to. I checked both phones to make sure they had a dial tone. I didn't want to miss Anne's call.

Opening the sliding glass door let in a rush of cold air. I put on a heavy jacket and got a Bering Churchill out of my travel humidor. I closed the door to the walkway to retain the warm air in the kitchen and bedroom areas, then went onto the balcony and left the door open about two feet. That way I could hear the phone if Anne got through early and called.

My watch showed the time as 3:00 PM. The sounds of the waves crashing and the wind were fairly loud. It concerned me about hearing the phone. I lit the cigar and explored the view of the Atlantic Ocean. There was a large group of sea birds to the front and right of the Patricia Grand. Some of the birds were diving. Then I noticed a dolphin roll on the surface. Soon I realized, there were at least three dozen dolphins rolling in the area. They were feasting on a school of beatific. I watched them for an hour and smoked the cigar.

I also watched two bulldozers working. They were moving sand around that had been pumped up onto the beach. Evidently, there was a beach replenishment project going on. Several hundred yards offshore, two tugboats were moving a dredge. The cigar played out about 4:00 PM.

I showered, shaved, and put on my jogging suit, not knowing how to dress for the evening until I talked to Anne. The brochures were interesting. About ten till five, I closed the walkway door and went back on the patio. I smoked a Las Cabrillas Robusto.

At 5:30, I closed the door to the patio and opened the door to the walkway to let the warm air in. I lay down on the couch to rest. The phone rang in the bedroom at 5:45. However, the wall phone across the room I was in, did not ring. I picked up the wall phone by the dining table. The concierge asked me if everything was all right. I told her it was. She said, "There are complimentary drinks every evening in the lobby, from five to seven. I was now concerned that Anne may have called and I missed her call because the wall phone doesn't ring.

I went back to the couch. At about 6:00 PM the phone rang and it was Anne. I told I was on the seventh floor and that she could drive up and I would meet her in the seventh floor parking area. I went out by my car and waited. Ten minutes passed. I was becoming concerned that she had hit one of the walls or something.

I heard someone call "Lucky" Joe and, turning toward the elevator, saw Anne. We walked to each other and she gave me a big hug. She told me her van was too tall for the garage, so she'd had to leave it parked on the first floor. Then I remembered seeing the height restriction bar hanging on the ramp entry.

I walked her over to the Cadillac and got the roses out of the back seat. I handed them to her. She said, "Oh, 'Lucky' Joe, I don't remember the last time someone gave me roses. Thank you so much. I had drawn a four-leaf clover on the card and Anne found it. She said, "I've heard you have good luck when you find a four leaf clover." I said, "You've heard right."

We walked into the suite and I showed her around. Then we went into the living room and looked at the ocean. She sat on the couch.

Anne said, "I got finished early at the show. I tried to call you at 3:15 and 3:30."

She told me that she had been sick ever since she left Dallas. She had stopped at an Urgent Care Center in Monroe, Louisiana with fever and flu-like symptoms. The doctor had given her a shot and some prescriptions. Anne said, "I didn't know what to do, so I got a motel room and rested. I tried to call you again at 5:30. You didn't answer and I was worried your phone was broken. I drove over here and finally got you from the lobby phone.

I explained to Anne that I had been on the patio, with the door to the back room closed. I had been listening for the wall phone. Then I found out at 5:45, when the concierge called, that the front wall phone doesn't ring.

I said, "Anne, do you feel up to going out tonight? We can stay in if you're not up to it." She replied, "I felt real bad when I finished setting up at the show. However, since I've rested, I feel a lot better. I'd really like to go to that seafood restaurant with you. Do you have a phone book? I should be able to find it in the yellow pages."

I found the phone book and asked her how I should dress. She said, "Wear something casual." I went into the bedroom while she searched the yellow pages and put on slacks and sport jacket. I got out my all weather coat. Then I returned to the living room. Anne said sadly, "'Lucky' Joe, I can't find it." I said, "Let's go through these brochures and see what we can find."

We started looking through the brochures. Halfway through the stack, Anne found one to Ripley's Sea Aquarium. Anne said, "This wasn't here when I came to the show last year." I said, "That looks like fun. Let's go!" Anne said, "Great." She said, "I need to go down to the van and get some clothes to wear." I said, "I'll go down with you."

We went down to the first floor on the elevator. We got off the elevator and we could see a huge indoor pool. It was on the other side of huge plate glass windows. We walked through a door into the pool area. The pool is heated and we saw people splashing around having fun. The pool has an opening that connects it to the outside pool. I had seen the outside pool from my balcony. The other half of the huge room has a lazy river indoor tube ride. Lots of people were tubing. Across from that we saw a large whirlpool bath.

We went back out to the garage area and Anne's van. She got what she needed and we returned to my room. She dressed and did her makeup while I looked at the Myrtle Beach map. I deciphered how to get to Ripley's Sea Aquarium. Anne came out of the lavatory area. I said, "Anne, you look very nice." She said, "Flattery will get you everywhere." She was wearing a warm fuzzy outfit. I really liked it.

We got in my car and drove over to Ripley's Sea Aquarium. The building and neon sign are impressive. My digital car clock showed the time to be 7:30 PM. I got out and opened Anne's door for her. She put on her wrap and we started walking to the entrance. Magically, we were holding hands like two teenagers. While we were walking, Anne insisted that we go "Dutch" on everything. We got to the ticket counter and got AAA discount tickets. Anne bought the information booklet for two dollars.

We went in and were awed by the sheer size of the building. Anne was looking at the book and said, "'Lucky' Joe, how much do you think this facility cost?" I answered, "I don't know." She said, "Just guess." I said, "I guess five or six million dollars." Anne smiled and said, "How about 36 million." I was amazed.

The sign directed us down a hallway. We followed the arrows past a reception\grouping area and down the hall. Around a curve we were flabbergasted by what appeared before us. In a twenty foot by ten foot, floor to ceiling, salt water aquarium, we saw hundreds of tropical fish. Anne said, "It 's like a huge Kaleidoscope and the back half is occupied by an artificial coral reef."

A standing sign read, "Next Show at 8:00 PM". Anne started pointing to individual fish and naming them for me. I spied a clownfish. It was swimming inside an opening in the coral reef. Anne ooohed and aaahed over the clownfish. We asked an attendant about the 8:00 PM show. She said, "I'm the moderator and another girl will dive into the tank and feed the fish." It was ten till eight.

We went to the next exhibit; a Lucite tunnel curving through a house-size salt-water aquarium. We noticed the moving sidewalk on the left side. I thought how many times I had been in an aquarium and people had just stood, looking through the glass. The moving sidewalk eliminates that. You can go back to the start of the moving sidewalk, but you can't just stay in one place. A shark swam over the tunnel with his mouth open showing rows of sharp teeth. Anne said, "It's eight o'clock." We went back to the tropical fish aquarium.

A group of people had gathered around. Some were sitting on the floor. Anne and I sat on the floor and I put my arm around her. She grabbed my right hand with hers. The moderator told us about the exhibit. She told us her associate would be diving into the tank shortly. The lady diver got in and moved to the front of the tank. The tropical fish swarmed around her.

The moderator informed us that she would feed the fish brine shrimp from the squeeze-bottle she had in her hand. She started feeding the fish and suddenly the water was roiling with fish in frenzy. The moderator said, "None of the fish have ever been harmed by the diver. Their reflexes are too fast." The show lasted about fifteen minutes and we went back to the main aquarium. We got on the moving sidewalk, looking at the sharks and other fish. We walked on to the next exhibit.

Part of the experience is the music playing in the background. The music makes you feel like you are under the sea. The next exhibit is a colony of moray eels. They look evil. There are at least three dozen living in the rocks of the aquarium. We didn't stay long with the eels. We went on to the next exhibit. It's a series of television screens over a control panel. We played with the push buttons and watched a few short videos.

Anne and I walked over to a shallow pool and talked with the attendant. She told us about the horseshoe crabs in the pool. I asked if the tail had a stinger. The attendant assured me that it didn't. Anne picked up one of the horseshoe crabs, with help from the attendant. She turned it upside down and was careful not to touch the crab's eyes.

Our next experience was a simulated rain forest. It was wet and we didn't stay long. We walked on into the next room. It consisted of a series of smaller theme aquariums.

I couldn't believe my eyes. The first tank has a small reef with sea anemones and clownfish. Anne squealed with delight and gave me a hug. She had told me about the relationship the clownfish have with the sea anemones. We spent about ten minutes watching the clownfish as they swam in and out of the sea anemones' tentacles.

The next exhibit that impressed us was the Sea horse/Sea dragon exhibit. Their fins are almost invisible, because they move so fast. Watching them is like viewing a fairy tale dream.

The other exhibit we enjoyed in the group was the jellyfish aquarium. Their movements are like a fine ballet. The music playing in the background added to the mystery. I looked at Anne's face and saw that it was pale. I said, "Anne, are you feeling bad." She said, "I'm getting tired. I feel kind of washed out. I don't like taking all this medicine."

It was almost nine o'clock when we went into the gift shop where I bought Anne a small ceramic clownfish. She bought a book on clownfish. We enjoyed looking at all the different things in the gift shop and left a few minutes after nine.

Walking out the door, the cold air shocked us. It was now considerably colder than when we had gone in. As we hurried to the car, I asked Anne if she had any ideas about a restaurant. She said, "Let's just ride around until we find something." I said, "Okay by me." I remembered that the map called this area "Broadway at the Beach". It's a huge complex of restaurants, nightclubs, shops and tourist activities, all built around a lake.

We started driving around the complex. We saw a Victoria's Secret shop in a line of shops. Then we saw a big walkway to a group of nightclubs. At the right side of the walkway, we saw a freestanding Hard Rock Cafe restaurant. It was built in the shape of a four-sided pyramid. The color of the pyramid constantly changed. It was striking in the night. We drove past The Hard Rock Cafe and The Planet Hollywood restaurant came into view. It is across 29th Ave. North.

The bright blue building with the bright red neon "Planet Hollywood" sign was like a candle flame to two hungry moths. We looked at each other and knew we had found where we wanted to go. I parked and opened the door for Anne. She said, "My, My, you really are a southern gentleman." I said, "Of course my dear."

We went in and the hostess informed us of a fifteen-minute wait. I put my name on the list and we walked around looking at the movie memorabilia. We had looked at about half of the memorabilia when they called my name. We returned to the entrance and were seated immediately.

Our waiter took our drink order and we looked at the menus. Anne said, "I'm hungry, but not real hungry." I said, "I'm the same way." The waiter brought me an O'Douls and Anne iced tea. We both ordered specialty hamburger plates. I could tell Anne was tiring. I tried to cheer her up. We were still excited about Ripley's Sea Aquarium and continued to talk about it.

I asked Anne if she had stopped by a Cracker Barrel restaurant. Her face lit up. She said, "'Lucky' Joe, I owe you. I got two books on tape. They really made the drive shorter." I said, "What books did you listen to?" She replied, "I listened to *Up Island* and *Men are from Mars, Women are from Venus*. I really enjoyed *Up Island*. I said, "I'll try to rent *Up Island* on my two day trip home." Anne responded, "I think you'll enjoy it. I won't spoil it by telling you anything."

Our meal came and Anne only ate about half of hers. I finished mine and we paid the check. We walked around and saw some of the other memorabilia. We drove back to the Patricia North and I parked on the first floor, next to Anne's van. The elevator took us to the seventh floor.

It was 11:30 when we entered the room. I closed the door and Anne moved up to me and put her head on my shoulder. I tried to kiss her. She put her hand up and tried to say something. She ran to the toilet and threw up. I ran some cold water on a washcloth and gave it to her. She cleaned up and I put my arm around her.

She was embarrassed and sick. Anne weakly said, "I've got to get to bed and rest. 'Lucky' Joe, I'll make it up to you tomorrow night." I asked Anne if she wanted to take one of my rooms, or if I could drive her to her motel. She said that she could drive and asked me to walk her down to her van. I carried her travel case down for her. We got to her van and I opened her door for her. She gave me a hug, got in and drove off.

Sunday morning, I awoke around 9:00 AM. It felt good to sleep in. Today would be the busiest day of the show. The reps would be hard to talk with. They should be writing orders. The ones that weren't writing orders are the ones I didn't want.

I put on some warm clothes and went on the balcony. I lit a Las Cabrillas Robusto. The sea birds were scattered and I didn't see any dolphins. The dolphins would be where the school of beatific had gone. I enjoyed watching the little "wave runner" birds. Their little feet can really move.

I finished the Robusto and took a hot shower, which was heaven. Then I shaved and put on a dark blue pin striped suit. I wore a power tie.

I wanted to look like a National Sales Manager. I also wanted to look nice for Anne.

I looked some more at the brochures. Broadway At The Beach is the main action Mecca. An article about shag music caught my attention. Anne and I had talked on the phone about shag music. The article informed that Myrtle Beach is the birthplace of shag music. It came about in the fifties and sixties. Anne and I were looking forward to dancing.

In my college days, I enjoyed going to the dances. Dancing fast is really enjoyable to me. I don't like the structured moves of classic rock and roll dancing. The freedom of fast dancing is what I like. I still love to dance. Suzanne doesn't like to dance.

The phone rang. They told me my room at the Patricia Grand was ready. I packed up and loaded the car. Around 11:00 AM, I was in the Patricia Grand Hotel lobby getting my keys. The receptionist told me there are two towers and two banks of elevators. One bank serves the north tower and the other serves the south tower. The only connection between the towers is the first floor. You have to go through the lobby to get between towers.

The parking garage is across Ocean Boulevard. The room they gave me is located in the north tower. I went to the elevators and got a bellman's cart. My car was in one of the registration spaces. I loaded the cart and went to the room. I opened the door and saw the room. It wasn't a suite like the Patricia North.

The bathroom is to the right of the door. A double closet is to the left of the door. The room is large. The left side has a king-size bed and nightstand with a phone. The right side has a mini refrigerator, a chest of drawers with TV on top, and a large couch. At the other end of the room, I could see a sliding glass door opening to the balcony.

Unpacking and storing everything was a chore. I missed the table I had at the Patricia North. I finished up and drove in the direction of the show. I'd skipped breakfast, which was not unusual. Hunger pains were starting to grow. I saw a McDonald's and pulled in.

They still had the triple-cheeseburger promotion going. There's something about a bargain. Triple-cheeseburgers for ninety-nine cents is a bargain. I got some triple-cheeseburgers and a Diet Coke. The fast food killed my hunger pains.

I drove to the Myrtle Beach Convention Center. It is only two blocks from the McDonald's restaurant. The center is located at the northwest corner of Oak St. and 21st Avenue. It's one block west of Business U.S. 17 or North Kings Highway. The parking lot was almost full. I had to park at the very back of the lot. My car was almost two blocks from the entrance to the show.

I registered under a friend's retail store credentials and got a show book. I looked up the location for LIZ, Inc. The directory showed the booth to be on the seventh row. I walked over to row seven and up the aisle. Anne saw me, and her face lit up with a big smile.

I told Anne how nice she looked in her business suit. She told me how nice I looked in my suit. She said, "You're wearing a power tie. I like the cartoon ties." I said, "I do to. I thought I'd look like a National Sales Manager today. I've got a lot of Mickey Mouse ties I wear on sales calls." Anne said, "Those are my favorites."

She said, "Lets go to the front of the building. I want to smoke a cigarette and I don't want my sales reps to know about us." I walked to the front of the building where Anne joined me. I told her that I had checked into the Patricia Grand and was in the north tower. I gave her my card, which had my room number written on it. Anne said, "I'll get them to put me in the north tower." I lit her Dunhill cigarette for her.

I said, "Anne, how are you feeling today?" She said, "I was really sick last night. I think it was a combination of all the medicine I took. I've quit taking everything except the antibiotic prescription. I'm feeling much better today and I'm going to watch what I eat. I'll be okay."

I said, "Is there anything in particular that you want to do tonight?" Anne said, "I'd like to go to the show party. It's going to be at the Beach Music Cafe. They play shag music and I've been dying to dance with you." I said, "My friend Ken Scott told me about Beach Music Cafe. He called a friend of his in Charleston, when I told him I was going to Myrtle Beach. His friend said for beach music and dancing, go to the Beach Music Cafe." I pulled Ken's business card from my wallet and showed Anne that Beach Music Cafe was written on the back. Anne said, "I'm excited about tonight."

Anne said, "The show closes at six. I'll call you when I get checked in and get to my room. Where have you been? I thought I'd see you hours ago." I said, "I slept in until nine this morning. I don't remember the last time I got to do that." Anne said, "You know I'm jealous." I said,

"I want to give you a great big hug. I'll resist the temptation since we're in public." Anne said, "You silly. Come back by in a couple of hours. I'll come out and smoke another cigarette as an excuse to get away from the booth. I've got several sales reps here and they can cover."

We walked back into the show. She turned off at aisle seven and I went to aisle one. I planned to walk the show and get a feel for it. I felt a little uncomfortable about tonight. Anne was really sensitive about her reps thinking something might be going on between us and me being married. I wished the show party were somewhere else, then we could go to the Beach Music Cafe without some of her reps being there. I walked the show from aisle 100 to the larger number aisles. I skipped aisle seven. On aisle 1000, I saw Angelo's sponge booth. However, Angelo was not to be seen. His booth was toward the back of the building.

I imagined he would be holding court on the loading dock. I went to the back of the building and asked one of the security officers where the smoking area was. He showed me a curtain and said the door to the loading dock is behind the curtain. I went behind the curtain and out the door. There was a security guard by the door.

Angelo saw me coming and said, "I know I'm going to be lucky today. 'Lucky' Joe, you bring me good luck." I said, "I bring everyone good luck. How are you doing?" He said, "I'm doing fine. Come have a smoke with me." He got out a Camel and I got out a Las Cabrillas Robusto. We laughed and told jokes. Thirty minutes later, I resumed my tour of the show.

I looked and saw that there are twenty-four front to back aisles in the show. I walked over and up to the Royal T's booth on aisle 2000. Candy gave me a big smile. I said, "It's great to see you. I really appreciate your letting me go to your rep party in Gatlinburg." Candy said, "You're welcome. I thought I'd see you this morning." I said, "I kind of slept in. Are you jealous?" She said, "You bet I am. 'Lucky' Joe, you've got two people driving me crazy. They've been by here a dozen times, looking for you to bring them samples."

I told her I would go to the car and get the samples. Fifteen minutes later I returned to the Royal T's booth with the samples. Candy gave me some ideas where they might be. Each one of the reps had over twelve lines. They worked out of several booths at the show. Candy was alone and I asked if I could get her something from the concession stand. She said, "I'm dying for a Coke." I went and got her a Coke and me a Diet Coke.

I continued my tour. When I finished walking the last aisle I returned to aisle seven. Anne saw me before I got there and got her cigarettes. She walked out to the front ahead of me. I joined her outside the front door. We stood beside a trash receptacle, as Anne smoked a Dunhill cigarette. The top of the receptacle was an insert filled with sand. Dozens of cigarette butts were sticking out of the sand.

A friendly lady joined us and lit up a cigarette. She pointed to her booth. It was right beside the entrance to the show. Her husband was watching the booth. The lobby went all the way across the front and left side of the building. Booths are along the outside wall of the show. There were also booths in meeting rooms at the back end of the lobby.

She told us her husband came to the shows with her, but was not part of her repping business. She said, "He guards the booth long enough for me to get a smoke. This is the best booth location I have ever had. I've already written more business today than any other first day at this show."

I told Anne that my number one objective at this show was to get a sales rep for South Carolina. Anne said, "My reps for South Carolina are a husband and wife team. However, they are part of the rep group I use." The lady with us said, "Did I hear you are looking for a rep for South Carolina." I said, "You heard right." She said, "I cover North Carolina and South Carolina." Some buyers walked up to her booth. She said, "I'll be back as soon as I write an order from those buyers."

I knew that might take a while, so I pulled out a Las Cabrillas Robusto and lit it up. Anne said, "She looks like a good rep." I said, "Walking out here to watch you smoke may pay unexpected dividends." Anne said, "You never know what'll happen when you hang around me. I'd better go back to the booth. 'Lucky' Joe, I'm looking forward to this evening." I said, "Anne, I'm looking forward to this evening too."

Anne went inside, and in about ten minutes the rep came back. She had written a nice order. She said, "My name is Judy Long." I said, "It's nice to meet you. My name is 'Lucky' Joe." I asked Judy what kind of lines she repped. She told me T-shirts and gift items. I showed her our flyer. She said, "Cigars are hot right now. I can sell these. Do you have any samples with you? I can put them out today." I said, "I'll go to the car and get you some as soon as I finish this cigar."

I told her about the commission schedule and answered some questions she had. I finished the cigar at the same time she finished her cigarette. Judy said, "'Lucky' Joe, that's the first cigarette that I've been able to smoke all the way today. I usually get two or three puffs and have to go back to the booth." Some buyers walked up to her booth and she hurried over.

I returned to the car and got Judy sales forms, samples, and flyers. I had to wait ten minutes to see her when I got back. I gave her the samples and other items, then walked to the back of the lobby to see the booths in the meeting rooms. I noticed that there were no buyers in the meeting rooms. A group of exhibitors was in the hallway with the show manager. They were complaining that no buyers were coming by their booths.

Every booth I walked by tried to get me to stop. My buyers badge made me a hunted species. I moved it inside my jacket. Now only the most aggressive sales people tried to stop me. I quickly got out of the meeting room area.

It was nearing 5:00 PM. I went back to the Patricia Grand and got a space on the first floor of the parking garage. Parking garages are no fun when you have a large car. I went back to the room to shower and shave. The bed felt good and I decided to rest for a few minutes. I fell asleep and was awakened by the phone. The clock showed 6:42 PM.

I answered and Anne said, "I've finally gotten to the room. It's going to take me about thirty minutes to get ready. I've still got to move my car to the parking garage." I said, call me when you get ready. I'll ride over to the garage with you and let you have my first floor parking space." Anne said, "Wonderful! I'm in room 1027 north." We disconnected and I finished dressing.

I put on a red sweater and a tie. The tie was decorated with little Mickey Mouse figures. The phone rang at 7:12 PM and it was Anne. She said she would be ready in a few minutes and invited me up to the room. I took the elevator up to the tenth floor and knocked on 1027. Anne came to the door and let me in. I noticed that her room was a suite with a kitchen area.

She was dressed in a sixties skirt and had a sweater top. I said, "Anne, you look marvelous. I need a hug." She gave me a hug and said, "You look nice too. Did you wear the Mickey Mouse tie for me?" I replied, "Maybe." She said, "You silly!" Anne pointed to the roses.

She had gotten a container somewhere for them. She said, "Thank you again for the roses." She did her lipstick. We put on our heavy coats and headed for her van.

I rode with her over to the parking garage. She parked in the space I vacated and joined me in the Cadillac. I headed to Broadway At The Beach. The Beach Music Cafe is located in the Celebrity Square section of Broadway At The Beach. The Hard Rock Cafe where we'd been the evening before, is at the entrance to Celebrity Square. I parked near the Hard Rock Cafe and walked to the show party with Anne. We held hands until we got to the entrance to Beach Music Cafe.

We went in the door. Exhibitors and buyers were everywhere. Anne said, "This place is packed." We went to the back and got in the serving line. The party had started at six. It was now seven thirty and the food was getting picked over. The line was moving and we went by a bar area. I got an O'Douls for me and a Coke for Anne. We got to the food buffet and I didn't see anything I really wanted. I got some Swedish Meatballs and Anne made a turkey sandwich.

We walked past the dance floor and I spotted some people leaving a table. I asked them if they were through with the table. They nodded and I held a chair for Anne to sit down. I sat beside her and slowly ate the meatballs.

Anne was halfway through her sandwich when the deejay played a great beach song. I looked at Anne and she looked at me. We headed to the dance floor. We danced to four songs in a row and returned to the table out of breath. For an hour and a half we danced to the good songs and had a good time. Anne was happy and smiling her beautiful smile.

Anne told me about shag music. She said people put a book on their head when they started learning how to shag. Anne pointed out people on the floor that were doing classic shag dancing. She said, "It' too slow for me." I said, "It's way too slow for me."

Around nine, Anne told me that at the show parties she liked say hello to all the people she knew. She said she wanted to make a walk around.

I went to the restroom and she started saying hello to sales reps. The men's restroom was crowded, as there was a lot of beer-drinking going on. At the door was an attendant. He had all kinds of colognes and breath spray. He also had cigarettes and cigars. He had his own convenience store going on. He was making some good tip money and sales were good by the looks of the tip jar. I washed my hands and left two dollars.

I went back to the table and watched people dancing. The deejay started playing modern music instead of oldies. I noticed a lot of the buyers and reps were leaving. There had been around twenty-five couples dancing to the beach music. Now there were only five or six couples dancing to the contemporary music.

Anne returned to the table looking a little pale. I was worried that she was sick again. The deejay only played two oldies over the next hour. We danced to those. However, I noticed that Anne was not happy and smiling as she had been earlier. It looked as if the deejay wasn't going to play any more oldies. I asked Anne if she wanted to leave. She nodded that she did, so we put on our coats and left. Walking to the car I took her hand. Something didn't feel right. I didn't sense that tingling feeling. I opened the door for Anne and we returned to the Patricia Grand. I had to park on the fourth floor of the parking garage.

The elevator was either put on hold or out of service. We walked down the stairs. I had my hand on my derringer in my pocket. I had heard of muggings in parking garages. The thieves had pushed the hold button on the elevator at the top floor, where there were no cars. They then went down the stairwell and held up some people. We exited the stairs and crossed Ocean Boulevard. The elevator carried us up to Anne's room.

She opened the door and we went in. Anne walked over to the kitchen counter by the sink. She partially collapsed and emotionally blurted out, "I can't handle this anymore. It's over! You're a married man. I just want to be friends. No more dates!"

Anne's voice fell to a whisper. She said, "At the dance, one of my sales reps came over to me. He said, 'Is that your new married boyfriend?' It devastated me. I'm sorry. I don't want to hurt you. Please go." I slowly said, "Anne, the last thing I want to do is hurt you. I'll just be your friend." I left and went up to my room.

I was confused and wounded. I could have killed the rude sales rep who had said to Anne, "Is that your newly married boyfriend." I went out to the balcony with a Bering Churchill. I smoked the cigar.

My eyes looked at the ocean and stars. I noticed flashes of light in the water. I realized that hundreds of sea birds were in the water. The water was warmer than the temperature on shore. On shore it was near freezing. I tried not to think of Anne. Inside, I was in an emotional turmoil. I didn't know what to do. The cigar grew short and I went to bed.

I slept fitfully. At 5:30 AM I woke up crying. Unable to go back to sleep, I got up, showered, shaved, and dressed. I thought about leaving the show. However, I needed to recruit reps. After taking some time to think about what I should do, I decided to go ahead and give Anne the painting. In my memories of Panama City Beach, I thought she got up at 6:00 in the morning. If she got up at six, I thought she would probably leave for breakfast around seven.

At 6:00 I went on the balcony and smoked a Las Cabrillas Robusto to pass the time. When the clock showed 6:45, I dialed Anne's room number. The phone rang several times before she answered. I realized that I woke her. I apologized for waking her and told her I thought she got up at six. She said she had set the alarm for seven.

I told her that I had brought her a Christmas present. I asked her if I could give it to her this morning, as I was thinking of leaving the show early. She sounded uncertain and told me she would call when she got dressed and ready to go to the show. She called at 8:15 and said, "'Lucky' Joe, you can come up to the room now."

I got the painting. It was packaged between two layers of cardboard I had taped together and it was heavy. The cold hit me in the face and sobered me as I went to the elevator. In a couple of minutes I was knocking on the door to room 1027. Anne let me in. She said, "'Lucky' Joe, you shouldn't have gotten me anything."

I took the cardboard off the painting and propped it up against the head of her bed. She looked at it in disbelief. Her eyes got teary. Anne said, "It's the most beautiful painting I have ever seen. 'Lucky' Joe, I'll cherish it for the rest of my life. You shouldn't have given this to me." I told her that it had hung in the reception room of the "Lucky Joe's Furniture stores" office building. I said, "It was my painting, not the company's. When I sold the stores, I put it in storage, along with several others. It's been packed away until now."

The painting showed a group of clownfish and sea anemones. I told Anne, "The name of the painting is 'Clown Parade'. It is one of Mary Carlon's paintings." Anne investigated it closer and said, "I've never seen coral this beautiful in a painting. I now understand what you told me about her work. I don't know how to thank you. 'Lucky' Joe, if you go to the show party tonight, please dance some with me." I said, "Anne, if I go, I'll dance with you." Anne said, "I going to put this in a special place in my home." It was after 8:30 and she had to leave to be at the show at 9:00 AM.

I returned to my room and happened to see the personality profile. Since I probably wouldn't see Anne again, I went ahead and did the profile. It turned out virtually the same as the first time I had taken it ten years ago. I got dressed and went to the show.

I planned to find and meet with sales reps. When I got to the entrance to the show, Judy Long ran over to me. She said, "I've already made two sales on the Cigar Tees. One's for immediate shipment and the other's for shipment March 1 of next year." I said, "That's great news." She left and went to wait on some buyers.

I went to the Royal T's booth to see Candy. I walked up to the booth and was surprised to see Anne and Candy talking at the back of the booth. They saw me and Anne said, "Candy, I've got to get back to the booth." Anne looked at me and said, "'Lucky' Joe, if you get a chance, come by my booth and I'll go and smoke a cigarette with you." Then she left.

Candy said, "Good Morning 'Lucky' Joe." I said, "Thank You, Good Morning to you. How is Anne doing?" Candy said, "What do you mean?" I said, "I heard that she's been sick and just wondered how she was doing." Candy replied, "She's taking some antibiotics. When I saw her Saturday morning she was taking all kinds of medicine. She's a lot better now than she was then." I said, "I'm glad to hear that."

I asked Candy about the samples I had left. She told me, "Both reps picked up the samples you left and they left the booth numbers where they'll be today. One left three numbers and the other left six." I thanked Candy and headed off to meet with them.

I thought about Anne and Candy, when I left the booth. I had learned nothing from Candy. Had Anne talked to Candy about us? I had no answer to my question.

I found the reps, both of whom had decided to sell the Cigar Tees. Things were going well for Don's Enterprises, but were going badly for me, personally. I went down Anne's aisle. She saw me coming and waved. I walked slowly. I saw her grab her Dunhill cigarettes and walk toward the front.

I caught up with her outside the front door and lit a cigarette for her. Anne said, "Thank you for 'Clown Parade'. It's one of the nicest things that's ever happened to me." I said, "I thought you would enjoy it more than anyone else in the world."

Anne said, "I still want to go over the personality profiles with you." I replied, "I'd like to do that. I went ahead and did mine this morning and I'd really like to know how yours turns out." She said, "I'm going to the show party tonight at Yesterday's. Tomorrow night I'm going to take my reps out to dinner. I'm going to be here Wednesday night after the show closes. Is that all right?" I answered, "Anne I'm leaving at 6:00 AM Wednesday morning. I've got an appointment in Atlanta I have to get to." Anne said, "I'm taking the reps to dinner directly from the show. I'll be back at the Patricia Grand by 9:00 PM. What about then?" I said, "That's fine with me. I may be a little after nine though. I'm going to a movie tomorrow night." She said, "I appreciate your helping me with the personality profiles." I said, "You're welcome."

Anne said, "Are you going to the show party tonight?" I replied, "If you were serious this morning about me dancing some with you." Anne answered, "I was serious. I just don't want to go as a date." I said, "I understand." I really didn't understand. She said, "When you get bored, walk by the booth and I'll come out with you and have a cigarette." I told her I would and she went back to her booth.

I went back to work recruiting sales reps. The show had been very worthwhile. I now had reps for the East Coast, West Coast, Hawaii, Caribbean, and some interior areas. I'm still missing Miami and extreme South Florida, Texas, and Atlanta. I talked with more people. Walking back and forth, I happened to go by Angelo's sponge booth, not expecting to see him, but Angelo was in the booth. I walked over and greeted him.

Angelo looked up and smiled. He said, "'Lucky' Joe, you're the excuse I've been looking for to go get a smoke. Come on with me." We walked back to the loading dock. He lit up a Camel and I got out a Las Cabrillas Robusto. He made us all laugh. Angelo is fun to be with. After thirty minutes, I told Angelo I had to get back to work. I went back to the show and found the rep I was looking for. He did not like cigarettes, cigars, and smoking in general. I decided not to pursue him any further.

The lack of sleep last night was catching up with me. I returned to the Patricia Grand, set the alarm, and took a nap. The alarm woke me at five. I showered, shaved, and dressed casually for the party. I drove on over to Yesterday's, only one block east and two blocks south of the convention center. It's at the southwest corner of 20th Avenue and North Kings Highway.

Yesterday's has parking all around the building. I got a space right up near the front door. A few minutes to six, I put my badge on and went in with some sales reps. Yesterday's is bigger than the Beach Music Cafe. They directed us to the right and down a short flight of stairs. At the bottom of the stairs is a set of large double doors. They were propped open. Immediately, I grabbed a table for four next to the dance floor.

The dance floor is raised up two steps from the rest of the room with tables on three sides. The wall that runs out from the right side of the double doors is to the rear of the dance floor. On the wall in the middle of the dance floor is a twenty-foot simulated jukebox. It looks just like a sixties juke box. It's rounded at the top and has all the neon lights. Where the records are in a real jukebox, is a booth and equipment for the Disc Jockey. There's a door on the side and stairs up to the deejay booth.

On the far side of the room is a grand stairway to a huge balcony. The balcony comes out almost as far as the dance floor. The wall opposite the jukebox is a long bar except for a set of double doors on the left. They open to the restrooms and a walk-up pizza kitchen. They had set up a buffet line near the grand stairway. I went on over and got some fried shrimp and poppers, then went to the bar and asked for some O'Douls. They said they didn't have any. I got a Coke and went to my table.

Very quickly, the place filled up and the line at the buffet wrapped around two sides of the room. I enjoyed my food and Coke. Angelo came in by himself. He asked if he could join me. I said, "Please do." He put his coat on one of the chairs and got in line. He was back in fifteen minutes with two plates of food. He said, "I told them one is for my wife." We both laughed and I said, "I wish I'd done that."

I saw Anne come in about 6:45. I waved. She came over and put her coat on one of the chairs. She told us that she had gone to the hotel and changed. She was dressed in a different 60's skirt and sweater-top than she had worn to the Beach Music Cafe. She went to the buffet and got some of what was left. The shrimp were long gone. Angelo was finishing up when Anne got back.

In just a matter of minutes Angelo had us laughing. He went back and got a plate for dessert. People started dancing a little after seven.

Angelo came back and started into his 'dessert' plate. I asked Anne to dance. We danced to three songs and went back to the table. She said, "I'm going to socialize. I'll be back later for another dance." Angelo finished up his plate, saying, "Thanks for the good seat and great company. I'm going to smoke a Camel and head out. I only come for the food. This kind of dancing is not my thing. I like Greek dancing." He finished his smoke and left.

I started dancing with the women. There were two women wanting to dance for every man who would dance. It reminded me of my college days. I had a great time dancing. Once the women saw that I was alone and liked to dance, they started asking me to dance.

Occasionally, I would see Anne on the dance floor. She saw me on the dance floor most of the night. About nine, Anne came over and asked me to dance. We danced two fast dances and the deejay played a Chubby Checker Twist Song. I was in trouble. The shoes I was wearing had hard rubber-type soles. I couldn't get them to twist. I told Anne my problem and we left the dance floor. She sat down at the table and a waitress came by. I ordered an O'Douls for me and a Coke for Anne. She brought them and I gave her a dollar tip. I thought to myself, "No O'Douls when it's free. Plenty of O'Douls when you pay."

I'd taken two sips of my O'Douls when a pretty brunette asked me to dance. I got up and danced to *Devil With The Blue Dress On*. It's one of my favorites. We danced to four songs and I stopped for breath. I got back to the table and Anne had gone. I thought to myself, "Good, I've made her jealous." The brunette was at least ten years younger than Anne was.

I danced with a dozen or so women until 10:45. I went and found Anne talking with a sales rep near the bar. He had just bought her a Coke. I interrupted him and asked Anne to dance. We danced three fast dances. Her smile was back. The one she had before the sales rep said, "Is that your new married boyfriend?" The next dance the deejay played was a slow dance. We danced close and I felt the "tingle". The "tingle" that had been missing when I took Anne back to the Patricia Grand last night.

The dance ended and I said, "Anne, thank you for the dance. I'm calling it a night and heading back to the hotel." Before she could say anything, I went to the table, grabbed my coat and left. I didn't look back. It was hard to do because I was still in love with her.

I went to the room and got out a Bering #1. They come packed in a golden aluminum tube. With my down jacket on, I went out on the balcony and lit up. The birds were in the water again tonight. After I had been smoking about ten minutes, little circles started appearing in the swimming pool. A few minutes later, it was raining hard. The wind was from the southwest, so the balcony stayed dry.

I finished the Bering and went to bed. I slept soundly. Tuesday morning the sun awakened me about 7:00 AM. I went on the balcony. The temperature was twenty degrees warmer than it had been the last three days. I put on a light jacket and smoked a Bering Churchill to celebrate.

Around 8:30, I showered, shaved, dressed and went to the McDonald's for two Sausage McMuffins with egg and coffee. I had bought a paper and worked the crossword. I got a refill on the coffee. About 10:00 AM I went over to the show wearing my best suit and Mickey Mouse tie.

Since it was the third day of the show, I only had to park a block away from the entrance. I went in and walked down aisle seven. Anne was at the back of her booth and saw me as I was walking past. She called out, "'Lucky' Joe." I stopped. She said, "Do you have time for a smoke break?" I smiled and we went to the front of the building. I said, "What about that sales rep? The one that gave you a hard time about me." Anne said, "He's gone. He left this morning." I lit her Dunhill cigarette for her.

Anne said, "What movie are you going to see tonight?" I said, "I don't know. I'm going over to the Broadway Cinema around seven. They've got 16 theaters. She said, "I remember what a good time we had at the movie in Panama City Beach." I replied, "I remember too."

I said, "Do you still want me to go over the personality profile tonight?" Anne said, "Most definitely. I'll call you around nine." I answered, "I may be a little later than nine. It depends on the movie." She said, "That's okay." We chatted a little while longer.

Judy Long joined us and lit up a cigarette. She said, "I've sold two more orders of Cigar Tees." I said, "That's great." Anne finished her cigarette and went back to her booth. I talked with more people. I had now reached the point where I'd done as much as I could do at this show. I went by Candy Royal's booth and told her goodbye. She gave me a hug and I left the show.

I drove over to the Broadway At The Beach complex. It was something I wanted to explore. The Visitors Center came into view. After parking, I went in the Visitors Center. I looked at the displays and got a brochure. There were a lot of restaurants on the map. Johnny Rockets was across the main bridge. It got my vote and I headed over for a hamburger. It was good and I explored the Charleston Boardwalk area.

The Charleston Boardwalk area has around two dozen shops. Some of them are The Gap, Perfumania, and Victoria's Secret. I would love for Anne to be here with me. I'd love to buy her something in Victoria's Secret.

When I got to Ripley's Sea Aquarium, I turned around and walked to the Caribbean Village. It also has around two dozen shops. There are a lot of specialty shops and a Planet Hollywood Super Store. I took the western bridge by Landry's Seafood and walked across the lake.

The bridge came ashore between The Crab House and Tony Roma's. The New England Village greeted me when I walked off the bridge. It has close to seventy stores and shops. The Broadway Penny Arcade caught my attention and relieved me of my quarters. Klig's Kites proved to be an interesting shop. When I reached the main bridge, I took a seat on one of the benches by the lake. I got out a Bering Churchill and lit up. It felt great to enjoy a leisurely smoke and people-watch. It took about an hour to smoke the cigar.

I explored the other half of the New England Village and played a round of golf at Dragon's Lair Miniature Golf. It was about five and I walked over to the Broadway Cinema 16. The next movie playing that I hadn't already seen, was *Mortal Kombat II: Annihilation.* The girl sold me a ticket and I went in and waited for it to start.

The movie was an action thriller. It was pretty 'hokey' and I started to leave halfway through the movie. When it was over, I wished I had. It was 6:45 PM and I walked over to Joe's Crab Shack restaurant. It was early and I almost had it to myself. The hostess seated me and gave me a menu.

My waitress came over and I ordered an O'Douls. She brought me the O'Douls and I ordered the Broiled Seafood Platter. When she brought it out, I ordered another O'Douls. It was sad eating by myself. The whole time I was thinking of Anne and how we had planned to go to a good seafood restaurant. Here I was at Joe's Crab Shack, a great seafood restaurant, but without Anne. The meal was excellent, but my emotions wouldn't let me enjoy it. Emotionally, I was still in turmoil.

The check was reasonable and I was back in my room by eight. I brushed my teeth and washed my face. Relaxing on the bed, I fell asleep. The phone rang at 8:55 PM and woke me. It was Anne. She told me to come on up. First, I freshened up and found my personality profile. At 9:15 I knocked on the door to room 1027.

Anne opened the door and let me in. She was dressed in a soft fuzzy sweater and velvet skirt. The roses were still on the counter. I said, "Anne, you look lovely tonight." She said, "Thank You. Why didn't you come by this afternoon?" I replied, "I finished at the show early and spent the afternoon exploring the Boardwalk At The Beach complex. I wish you could have been there." I told her a little about Boardwalk At The Beach.

We sat on the couch and I showed her how to do the profile. She used the marking pen to highlight her most like and least like answers. Neither of us was surprised when her profile came out similar to mine. There was only a slight difference. We talked about how to implement the personality profiles with her employees. We agreed that the main thing is openness. Everyone needs to know everyone else's profile. They also need to know how to deal with different personalities. The booklets explain how.

We got to a stopping point. I said, "I guess it's time for me to go." Anne said, "I guess it is. 'Lucky' Joe, thank you for helping me with the profiles." We got up. I said, "I'll shake your hand and go."

I took her hand and lightly kissed the back of it. I looked up into her eyes. There was an awkward moment. I closed my eyes and felt the softness of her lips against mine. We kissed passionately. Her tongue dueled with mine. I said, "Anne, I love you." She whispered in my ear, "'Lucky' Joe, I love you too."

As if we were marionettes, controlled by a puppet master, we undressed each other, while our mouths were uncontrollably locked together. Free of our clothing, our bodies molded together. Anne's scent aroused me to full sexuality.

Anne felt my firmness as I felt her bosoms against my chest. They were pleasantly round, with fully erect nipples. We fell to the bed and rolled in frenzied anticipation. As our passions flamed, we kissed and fondled each other. Anne's legs opened and I felt her warm, soft, moistness. She moaned softly and moved her pelvis. Magically, we were connected in ecstasy. The two of us became one. We shared nature's gift to man and woman and pleasured each other until we exploded. We collapsed into each other's arms.

The attraction we felt for each other was finally expressed, as it has been expressed through the ages, since the beginning of creation. We spent the night in each other's arms.

The Morning sun awoke us. It was almost 7:00 AM and I had to leave this morning. Neither of us wanted to leave the other. But Anne had to be at the show by 9:00 AM. We showered together and she dressed for the show.

We talked about the next time she would be at a show. It would be January in Orlando. We agreed to meet in Orlando and share a room.

Reluctantly, I walked Anne to her van. At the van I said, "Anne, I won't say goodbye." Anne smiled and said, "'Lucky' Joe, I won't say goodbye either. I love you." I said, "I love you too." We kissed. I helped her in the van. Our eyes filled with tears and Anne drove to the show.

I drove my car to the registration parking and went to the elevators. I took a bellman's cart up to the room. I piled my belongings onto the cart and transported them to the car. By nine AM, I had checked out and was on the road.

CHAPTER 9

THE LONG WAIT

I n a short time, I was headed northwest on U.S. Highway 501. It
is four lanes and is divided. Within ten minutes, it started raining.
Now, I had to concentrate on my driving. At Conway, South
Carolina, I transferred to U.S. Highway 378. It's a two-lane highway.
However, traffic was light and I made good time. The rain had only
lasted for about forty-five minutes.

I put an oldies tape into the cassette player. The music carried me
back to the sixties. I remembered dancing to the tunes while I was in
high school and college. Pink socks and Gant shirts were the rage. My
mother fussed and fumed about my Madras shirts. She had to wash
them separately to keep the dyes from bleeding on the other clothes.

The Valdosta High School I attended was destroyed by fire in the
seventies. A new school had already been built when the fire leveled
it. The old school was standing vacant at the time of the fire. I've been
told the old two story brick building with solid wood interior made
quite a blaze.

The oldies tape played through. I put in a different tape and continued
thinking of those years. They were some of the best years of my life.

When I got to Turbeville, U.S. 378 turned onto a four-lane, divided
highway. The driving was easier and I thought of Anne. I thought of
what we had shared. Around noon, I stopped at a McDonald's in Sumter,
SC. The triple cheeseburger special was still running. I got a bag full of
burgers, along with a large Coke.

In the early eighties, one of my fraternity brothers had been stationed
at Shaw Air Force Base. It's located on the west side of Sumter. The

best part of the visit was an afternoon spent at Swan Lake Park. We picnicked, then fed the ducks and swans. There's a walkway/nature trail around the lake. The walk was memorable.

The McDonald's manager gave me directions and I drove to Swan Lake Park. The temperature was in the low seventies. I found a picnic table with a good view and ate some of the ninety-nine-cent triple cheeseburgers. I robbed the bun from one of the remaining burgers and fed it to two of the Swans. They honked in appreciation. Several ducks waddled up for a handout. Unfortunately for them, I had nothing to feed them.

Then I lit up a Las Cabrillas Robusto and hiked around the lake. It was as peaceful and scenic as I remembered. I wished my beloved Anne were here to share this with me. She was on my mind as I walked. It took about twenty minutes to make the circuit around Swan Lake. On a shady bench, I finished my cigar and returned to the car. In just a few minutes, I was headed west and making good time on U.S. 378.

An hour later, I found a Cracker Barrel restaurant in Columbia, South Carolina. This Cracker Barrel restaurant had two displays of audiotapes. They had a copy of *Up Island*. I rented it and returned to my travels. I got on Interstate Highway I-20 and put the car on cruise control. Excitedly, I replaced the oldies tape with the first *Up Island* cassette. As I listened to the audiotape, the miles flew by. By two thirty, I crossed the Georgia State line and stopped at the welcome center. Since I was now in my home state, I used my cellular phone to call Bill Cole in Athens, GA.

The receptionist answered and transferred me to Bill. I told him I was in Augusta and was headed to Atlanta. He told me to come by and see him. He also asked me to spend the night with them. He asked when I would get into Athens. I told him around 4:30. He said, "I'll meet you at my house. Sherry is due home around six. How does Chinese food sound?" I said, "It sounds great to me." We disconnected and I continued West on I-20.

At Thomson, Georgia I left I-20 and headed northwest on U.S. 78. It's a two-lane highway. When I reached Washington, Georgia, I encountered a lot of road construction. They were going from two lanes to four lanes through town. It's only forty-five minutes to Athens from Washington. I felt good. The tape played on. After thirty minutes, the city limits sign to Elberton, Georgia greeted me. Unknowingly, I had taken the wrong road out of Washington. The construction people must have hidden the signs.

The map showed SR 72 connected Elberton and Athens. The map also informed me that I had added at least forty-five minutes to my trip. Now, I would be late getting to Bill's house and have to face his ridicule.

When I pulled into Bill and Sherry Cole's driveway, it was almost five thirty. Bill came out and said, "'Lucky' Joe, I thought you said you'd be here around four thirty." I said, "That was before I took the scenic tour of Elberton. The road construction must have destroyed the signs." Bill said, "I thought you knew how to navigate. I can't wait for Sherry to get home." We went on the back deck and smoked. I enjoyed a Bering Churchill cigar.

Sherry got home a little after six. She came around to the deck and joined us. She got a good laugh about my unintentional detour through Elberton. I said, "Well, I've always wanted to see Elberton." We laughed and talked another hour, went to the Chinese restaurant. The Chinese restaurant had become a tradition when I visited Bill and Sherry.

We got a pu-pu tray for appetizers. They got Chinese beer and I got an O'Douls. We ordered four entrees to share, as is our custom. The pu-pu platter arrived. In the center of the platter was a cast iron firepot. It was flaming. Fried shrimp, won tons, little Bar B Que ribs, ka-bobs, and egg rolls adorned the platter. We were hungry and tore into the food. We heated the ribs and ka-bobs on the flame. The appetizers were gone in a matter of minutes.

Soon, our entrees arrived and we ordered another round of drinks. The up platter had taken the edge off our hunger. We ate less than half of the entrees. We got a big 'doggie bag' and returned to the Cole's home. The evening air was cool. We kept on our light jackets and went around to the deck.

I got out an Arturo Fuente Churchill. I'd been saving it for a special occasion. We talked about all the food we had ordered and how good the up platter had been. Bill asked how I was doing recruiting sales reps. I filled him in on my progress. Bill made a pot of decaf coffee. We had a couple of cups each and turned in. I fell asleep thinking of Anne.

We all got up at 6:00 AM. Sherry had set the automatic timer on the coffee maker. We all had some coffee and headed out in three directions. My appointment was near the Gwinnett Mall in Atlanta. I took U.S. 78 to SR 316. I then took I-85 to my appointment. I was early and stopped at a Waffle House to get an omelet. Waffle Houses make the best sausage and cheese omelets.

Then I drove to my appointment and set up my samples in the conference room. The buyer was aware of how big cigars have become. He looked at the samples and placed a nice trial order. He put them in ten stores, as a test. He said, "I get a computer printout on sales everyday. If they do half as well as I think they'll do, I'll put them in all our stores." I thanked the buyer and hit the road.

I got on I-85 and went through the middle of Atlanta. Rush hour was over and I made good time. The sight of the gold dome on the state capitol building thrilled me as I drove by. In just thirty minutes, I was cruising south on I-75. Around 11:30, I pulled off the Interstate and went one mile east to High Falls State Park. I paid the two-dollar admission fee and parked next to the river.

The park is on both sides of an east/west road. Several hundred yards north of the road is a large concrete dam. It rises about twenty feet and is probably a hundred yards across. The west side of the dam has a sluice gate. When opened, it dumps water into an ancient sluiceway. The sluiceway goes to an old gristmill. Only the ruins remain today.

High Falls is a series of waterfalls, which start at the foot of the dam. For about a mile, there is a walkway on both sides of the waterfalls. Most of the falls are on the south side of the east/west road. I lit a Bering Churchill and crossed the road. Then I hiked for about a half mile down the falls. I wished that Anne were with me to enjoy the falls. It would be over a month before we could be together again. I missed her terribly.

The sound of the falling water was relaxing. After about another hundred yards, I saw some people trout fishing. One of them even landed a fish while I watched. It was about a foot long. Patience has never been one of my virtues. Trout fishing takes too much patience. It's not something that I enjoy.

In summer time, I've seen dozens of people enjoying the water. On the smaller falls, people like to climb up and slide down the slippery rocks. Most people wear tennis shoes, to avoid hurting their feet on the rocks. The rocks will skin you up if you're not careful.

After about thirty minutes, I walked back up the falls. My cigar got short about the time I got back to the car. The falls are so nice that it's hard to leave. However, I forced myself and headed back to I-75. Once on the Interstate, I started listening to *Up Island* again. It was too hectic in Atlanta traffic to enjoy it.

By two-fifteen, I was in Perry. It took forty-five minutes to gas up and grab some fast food. About Hahira, I finished *Up Island*. I couldn't wait to talk with Anne about it. At 4:45 I drove into the parking lot of Don's Enterprises. I took some things in and Don welcomed me home.

We adjourned to the 'cigar tree' and I filled him in on Myrtle Beach. We were both satisfied with my progress on recruiting reps. He was also happy about the sale I had made in Atlanta. I didn't say anything about Anne. We finished our cigars and I went home. Suzanne was nowhere around.

I'd been home about two hours when Suzanne came home from the club. She'd been drinking, as usual and tried to start a fight. I realized that I didn't care anymore. When I had cared, I would fight with her about her drinking. My thoughts were now on Anne and the possible life we could share together.

Suzanne could sense something was different. I wasn't fighting with her anymore. However, her drinking kept her from thinking clearly. I thought of being free of Suzanne and my possible future life with Anne. I told Suzanne I was going to bed and retired. I still had that warm fuzzy feeling and fell asleep with Anne on my mind.

Friday, I caught up with paperwork and phone calls. Don and I had lunch with Sam 'The Man' Martin. It was good to see him again. We laughed and laughed and laughed. He charmed us with some of his radio stories. We dined in the bar section of Muldoon's restaurant. It's Sam's favorite place. He's been known to spend long evenings there.

When we finished our lunch, we adjourned to the outdoor patio. I got out some Las Cabrillas Robusto's. We smoked them as Sam told us some more radio stories. We laughed and laughed, as we enjoyed our cigars.

After the two-hour businessman's lunch, we returned to the office. I returned a phone call and took the rest of the afternoon off. I did some personal errands and headed home. Suzanne had left a note. She wanted me to take her to supper at the club. I was supposed to meet her at the bar between seven and eight. This was not what I had in mind for the evening. I'd had a nice relaxing movie in mind.

At 7:30 PM, I met Suzanne at the bar. She had been drinking with friends most of the afternoon. We had supper and I drove her home, she being in no shape to drive. She insisted that she could drive and tried to pick a fight with me all the way home. I knew one thing. I'd had enough of Suzanne and her drinking. I got into the house and she passed out on the couch. I left her there and went to bed. Thoughts of Anne danced through my mind as I passed into my dream world.

Saturday morning I slept in. I took Suzanne to the club and had lunch with her in the snack bar. After lunch, I headed to Good Stuff Antiques. Ken and I spent the afternoon smoking cigars. He asked me about Beach Music Cafe. I told him about it and Yesterday's. He had to get up and wait on customers. I got to just sit and enjoy.

Several people joined us on Ken's 'cigar porch'. Ken's porch reminds me of an old-fashioned barbershop. People come by just to socialize. Most of the other shop owners spend some time on Ken's porch. Some of them have the new 900 MHz portable phones. They watch for customers and answer the phone. The merchants in Remerton are pretty close to each other. We talked about the world's problems and told stories.

Around five I headed home. Suzanne was there. I asked her if she'd like to go to a movie with me. She told me she'd rather stay home and watch TV. I knew what that meant drink and watch TV. I went to a movie and relaxed. The weekend passed.

Monday morning I anticipated talking with Anne. The day seemed to take forever. Finally, six thirty arrived and I called my darling Anne.

She answered the phone. I said, "My darling Anne, I love you so much." Anne replied, "I love you more than I can put into words. I've missed you so much. You've been on my mind all the way home to Texas." I responded, "You've been on my mind all the way back to Georgia and then some. I love you."

Anne said, "Did you find *Up Island*?" I said, "Did I ever?! It's a great book. I almost cried about the swan." She said, "I didn't almost cry. I bawled." We talked about the book for almost thirty minutes.

We agreed that we'd like to see the real "Up Island" and that part of the country. I told her how strange it was to be listening to a book about Atlanta while driving to and from Atlanta. Anne said, "I felt the same way. I was listening to the book while driving through Atlanta to Myrtle Beach."

Then I told Anne about stopping at Swan Lake Park in Sumter, South Carolina. I told her how eerie it was to listen to the book about the swans right after having stopped at Swan Lake Park. I hadn't even rented the book when I stopped. I said, "Anne, you must have used ESP on me about the swans. Anne said, "I don't know about ESP. I do know I'm jealous of you stopping at Swan Lake Park without me." I replied, "You were there in my mind. I really wanted to share it with you." She listened to my description of the park and vowed to stop there next year.

I asked Anne about her trip. She told me she had listened to two books on tape. She had found and stopped at the same Cracker Barrel restaurant in Columbia, South Carolina. Anne said, "It's the shortest two day trip I've ever made. The books on tape are wonderful and I've got you to thank." I said, "You're very welcome."

Anne told me she had stayed in Birmingham on the way back. She got a room and immediately went to bed. The next morning, she was up early and on the road by 7:00 AM. She said, "Nothing interesting happened on the trip, like your trip to Swan Lake Park."

I said, "Anne, that wasn't the only place I wanted to share with you. After I made the sale to the chain of gift shops, I stopped at High Falls State Park." I told her about the park. Anne said, "I wish I had ridden home with you. I would have loved to have been with you at both parks." I said, "Almost as much as I would have liked to share them with you."

We talked for three hours. It seemed like less than thirty minutes. We spoke of our reunion in Orlando. We both agreed that it was too long to wait, but wait we must. I told Anne that I would get us a room. She insisted on paying for half of it. We finally, reluctantly disconnected.

I got home at ten. Suzanne was already home and tried to start an argument. I avoided arguing. I didn't care enough to argue anymore. I went to bed thinking of my phone conversation with Anne.

Tuesday morning was spent making phone calls. Don asked me to go to lunch with him. We went to Nicky's restaurant in downtown Valdosta. We stuffed ourselves on the good southern home cooking. Then we walked across the street to a city park.

We found a bench and got out some Las Cabrillas Robustos. They were good after the heavy lunch we had just eaten. The local Warehouse liquor store tries to keep them in stock for Don and me. They are an excellent smoke, for the money.

Don and I talked about the deterioration of the downtown area. Both of us were frustrated at the direction the Downtown Development Authority was taking. We could not make them understand that people do not like to parallel park. The main streets are one way and have three traffic lanes. By reducing from three to two traffic lanes, the parallel parking could be converted to angle parking. Another option would be to have three lanes of traffic and slant park on one side of the street. We finished our cigars and headed back to the office.

Wednesday I called Anne at 6:30 PM Georgia time. She answered the phone. I told her how much I love her. Anne told me how much she loves me. She was just bubbling over. I said, "Anne, what are you giggling about?" She replied, "I've hung 'Clown Parade'. I want to share with you." She proceeded to tell me about her home.

Anne said, "My house is on ten acres of land with a three-acre duck pond in back. Pecan trees surround the house. Being deciduous, they shade it in the summer and let the sun through in the winter. The house is one story, white stucco, with a tile roof. It's rectangular. The front door is oversized solid wood, which opens into a foyer. To the left of the foyer is the living room. Past the living room, on the left side, are a kitchen and dining room. The master bedroom is the back left corner of the house. The back right corner of the house is a two-car garage. The rest of the right side is composed of two bedrooms connected by a common bath.

"The center of the house is a huge sunken great room. The rear center portion of the house is a screened porch area. The great room has a small dinette near the kitchen and a large brick fireplace. The fireplace is on the common wall with the foyer. The master bedroom has a huge walk-in closet and a whirlpool bath. The view from the screened porch is magnificent. The master bedroom also has a picture window on the rear wall. The duck pond is very picturesque from both the master bedroom and the screen porch."

Anne continued, "I spend most of my time in the great room. I hung 'Clown Parade' on the right wall of the great room. That way I can look at the painting for as long and often as I want while relaxing. 'Lucky' Joe, It's just like an aquarium. I'd almost forgotten how much fun an aquarium can be."

Anne giggled and said, "I've got a little secret." I said, "What is it?" She replied, "I'm not going to tell. You'll find out soon enough." Not one hint did she give me. We talked on for three hours and reluctantly disconnected.

I got home at 10:00 and Suzanne was already in bed. I was still warm and happy from my conversation with Anne. I went to bed with Anne on my mind.

Thursday, December 18 I found out Anne's secret. I received a package via UPS from LIZ, Inc. I opened it. It contained a three inch by six inch red Christmas candle. There was a typed note. It read, "Merry Christmas. I appreciate the help. Sincerely, Anne Moore." The candle was decorated with a multitude of small, colored wax, Christmas decorations.

I called the 800 # for LIZ, Inc. An elderly lady answered. I said, "May I please speak with Liz?" She said, "I'll see if she's in." I could tell from her tone of voice that she was irritated. I waited several minutes on hold. Anne answered the phone by saying "Hello." I said, "Is this LIZ?" Anne said, "You silly."

I said, "I found out your secret. It's mostly red and it's beautiful." Anne said, "I had to get you something for Christmas. However, I didn't want to cause you any problems at home. The red has the same meaning as the roses you gave me in Myrtle Beach. You can tell everyone it's a corporate gift, as it's inexpensive." I said, "You're very clever and I love it."

I asked, "Who answered the phone?" Anne said, "It was my mother." I replied, "I made her mad when I asked for Liz." Anne said, "She hates for people to do that. My mother used to correct people when they asked for Liz. I explained that I don't care, because this is a business. Then I told her not to correct people when they ask for Liz. So, now she doesn't correct, but she still doesn't like it." I said, "I won't do it again. I just couldn't resist this one time. Thank you for the candle. I'll call again Monday evening." Anne said, "I'm looking forward to it."

I went to South Georgia Pecan Company. It's at the edge of downtown Valdosta on east U.S. 84. I visited with the manager and got a case (of one pound bags) of pecans. I chose the roasted variety. Every Christmas, I get a case of the pecans for casual gifts. They stay in the trunk of my car. That way, they are conveniently near at hand during the gift-giving season.

Suzanne and I had been invited to John Austin's Christmas party. This year he rented the Crescent. The Crescent is a beautiful, southern plantation style home. Senator West built it in the late nineteenth century. It has magnificent Greek Ionic columns across a curved front porch. They rise up around thirty feet. The porch curves from the front of the house around both sides. There are some huge oak trees in the yard. The Crescent is a very picturesque place.

Years back, a consortium of garden clubs bought and saved the home. They rent it for weddings and other social occasions. I was looking forward to seeing John at the party. However, I would like to be taking Anne instead of Suzanne.

I dropped by The Warehouse liquor store to get some cigars for the occasion. The manager told me they had gotten in a box of Las Cabrillas Robustos. I purchased the box and a handful of other cigars, then got on my cellphone and called Ken. He hadn't made plans for lunch. After a quick stop at the nearest Subway restaurant, I had lunch with Ken. The foot long subs quickly disappeared.

We enjoyed smoking some of my Las Cabrillas Robustos. While smoking, we talked about what we were doing for the holidays. He planned to stay in Valdosta. I returned to the office and made some phone calls.

Friday evening arrived. It was five after seven and I had found a parking place next door to the Crescent. The insurance business allows people to park in their lot after hours. I let Suzanne out of the car. The front yard of the Crescent has about eight large oak trees. There is a little grove on the left side of the double concrete sidewalk. On the right side are two extremely large oak trees. We walked under one of the huge oak trees to the front steps. I was dressed in a tux. Suzanne was dressed in a revealing evening gown.

At the top of the steps, John greeted us. He said, "Suzanne, you are lovely tonight. 'Lucky' Joe, come back when I'm through greeting guests and we'll smoke one." I said, "Looking forward to it." Suzanne frowned. We went in the house. Inside the front double door is a grand entryway. Wide formal stairs curve up to the second floor. The third floor of the mansion is a ballroom.

We went to the left of the stairs to the dining room. A buffet was set up on the large dining table. Sumptuous food lined both sides of the dining table. I got a plate and served myself some of the food.

Suzanne headed left to go to the sunroom. A bar was set up there and two bartenders were mixing drinks.

Suzanne got a mixed drink. By the time I got my food, she was on her second drink. I got an O'Douls and asked Suzanne if she would like to look at the Christmas decorations. She got a third drink. We went through the side rooms and looked at the vintage decorations. The garden clubs each take a room. They decorate them with old ornaments and antiques from bygone years.

We saw some friends and got into a conversation about the season. Suzanne left us and returned to the bar. After about fifteen minutes, I joined her near the sunroom and got another O'Douls. She was with some of her girl friends. I greeted them and adjourned to the front porch. John saw me and motioned for me to come over. I walked over to the top of the steps. It was now about seven forty five. John said, "I've had all this greeting I can stand. Let's adjourn to that oak tree and have a cigar." I said, "I'm with you."

We walked over and John handed me a large Leon Jimenes. It measured seven and a half inches by fifty-ring gauge. He said, "These were highly rated in *Cigar Aficionado Magazine*." I said, "I know." We punched the ends and lit up. For the next hour we sat under the oak tree and enjoyed the cigars. People came up and joined us with cigarettes and other cigars. The conversation was stimulating. I said, "John, these Leon Jimenes live up to their rating." He answered, "They surely do."

Just before nine, I went in to find Suzanne. She was drunk. She made some disparaging remarks about my cigar smoking as she wobbled. I told her it was time for us to leave. She informed me that she was just starting to have a good time. Suzanne refused to leave. Her friends were far from sober. I left and returned to the large oak tree.

There was still a group under the tree. I gave John an Opus X Robusto. He said, "I haven't been able to get one of these for a long time. Where did you find these?" I said, "That's my secret." We lit up and had the Opus X cigars for dessert. I got halfway through mine and one of the girls informed me that Suzanne had passed out in a chair. I took leave and went inside.

She was in a chair by the sunroom. The girls were laughing and giggling. I got a friend to help me take her to the car. I drove her home and barely got her inside before she started vomiting. I cleaned up behind her after I got her to bed. Her drinking was getting to be more than I could stand. It was becoming worse and worse.

Saturday morning, Suzanne didn't get up till noon. She had a terrific hangover and fixed a Bloody Mary. Then she tried to fight with me. She blamed me for leaving her at the bar with the girls. I refused to fight with her and left. Quickly, I got in my Cadillac and drove off.

Ken Scott answered my cell phone call. He hadn't had lunch. I stopped at the Subway and got us some subs and Cokes. In less than thirty minutes I was with Ken at Good Stuff Antiques. We were both famished and made short work of the sandwiches. Ken said, "Are you ready for a cigar?" I said, "I'm always ready for a cigar." He went inside and came out with two Bering Churchill's. We lit up and started talking. Some people walked up and Ken went inside with them as they browsed his shop.

I continued to enjoy my cigar and thought about Suzanne. I was not at all happy about last night. My thoughts turned to Anne and I wondered what she was doing. It would be Monday night before I talked with her again. The people left and Ken rejoined me. Our cigars lasted about an hour. I asked Ken, "Would you like a Baccarat Pyramid?" He said, "I sure would." My travel humidor supplied us with the cigars. The Baccarat Pyramids measured seven inches by fifty four-ring gauges.

Pyramids are cigars shaped like an ice cream cone. They are not quite as exaggerated. It takes an experienced cigar roller to fashion one. Cigar companies don't make a lot of pyramids.

After I had been on Ken's front porch for about three hours, I went to a movie. When I returned home, I was alone. Suzanne was nowhere around. This time she didn't even bother to leave a note. I started reading and fell asleep. About eleven she returned home and woke me, trying to fight again. She had been drinking at the club. I refused to fight and went to bed.

Finally, Monday night arrived and I phoned Anne from my office. Her voice sounded angelic. I thanked her again for the holiday candle. Anne said, "I wanted to give you a gift. But I didn't want to cause you any problems at home. You gave me red roses. I gave you a red candle. Do you know what red symbolizes?" I said, "It symbolizes true love." She said, "I disguised it behind a Christmas theme." I said, "You're too much."

We talked about each other's problems. Anne related, "Herb Rhodes is still calling and E-mailing with his threats." I told her about Suzanne passing out at John's Christmas party and trying to fight with me. Anne complimented me on having avoided getting into a fight with Suzanne. She said, "I'd really like to see the Crescent. The way you describe it, it must be something special." I said, "It really is something special. I know a lady that grew up in it when she was a child."

Anne told me that she was planning to spend the holiday at her mom's. Her two kids were going to be there. She said, "My mother has a big roast beef dinner planned." I told Anne, "I'm staying home and my two kids are going to join us. I said, "I'm having a hard time waiting to see you again. I'd like to get on an airplane and be with you for Christmas." She said, "I feel the same way." I said, "I love you and miss you." She said, "I love you and miss you too." We talked on for about two hours. As usual, it was hard to disconnect.

Tuesday, I made a few phone calls and delivered some gifts. Tuesday night I went to a movie. Suzanne spent the evening at the club. When I returned home, Suzanne was drunk. She was watching TV. She was very interested in the TV show, so I avoided her efforts to start a fight and I went to bed. I thought of my conversation with Anne as I fell asleep.

Wednesday was Christmas Eve. I went to the office and made some phone calls. I wished some people a Merry Christmas. Don took everyone to a luncheon party at Muldoon's restaurant. The party was in one of the meeting rooms. Everyone had a choice of a "Muldoon Burger" or a grilled chicken sandwich. There was a dessert bar on the side of the room. The waiter served drinks. I got an O'Douls and a burger. The sandwiches were quickly served and people got multiple desserts.

We all exchanged gifts by a lottery. Everyone had "chipped in" and we gave Don a box of H. Upmann Souvenir cigars. Don gave a little speech and wished everyone a Merry Christmas. Then the party broke up and people went their various ways. Don looked at me and said, "'Lucky' Joe, are you ready for one of these H. Upmann's?" I said, "I sure am." We went out on the covered patio and grabbed some wrought iron chairs. Don opened the box and we enjoyed a couple of the Souvenir's. They were great. About an hour later, Don and I headed to our homes.

Suzanne was preparing for Christmas. She had a toddy on the counter as she cooked. I helped with the decorations and some other preparations. I lit the candle Anne had given me. I burned it through the evening above the fireplace. All evening I kept a fire going. It gave me something to do. I spent a lot of time sitting in front of the fire. As the flames flickered, I was thinking of Anne.

Christmas day our family was together. We opened presents around 10:00 AM. I got the family a ping-pong table. Most of the day, people played ping-pong. Some of our kid's friends dropped by. The ping pong table turned out to be a big hit. We played singles and doubles. Some of the doubles matches were hilarious. In school, I had learned to serve with a lot of 'English'. It was fun to watch people miss the ball. When it hit on their side of the net, it was like a knuckleball in baseball.

I kept a fire going in the fireplace and a certain red candle lit. All day I thought of Anne and how much I would like to be with her. The flames from the fire and candle were small, compared to the flame in my heart for Anne.

Suzanne didn't get drunk, but she had plenty to drink. She served wine with the dinner. Rum nog was handy and was her dessert of choice. The day passed quickly and I went to bed thinking of Anne.

Friday through Sunday were days of leisure for me. I read books and spent some time in the parks. The parks only made me wish that Anne were there to share the beauty. One of Valdosta's parks is on the Withalacoochee River. I smoked a cigar on the bank of the river and wished Anne were there to walk the nature trail. Some of the time I spent in the movie theaters. The holiday films were really good. *Titanic* was the best.

Finally, Monday evening came. At 6:30 PM I called Anne. She answered and I said, "I love you and miss you." She responded, "I love you and miss you too. How was your Christmas?" I said, "It was lonely without you." She said, "Mine was the same way. You were missing in everything I did."

I asked about the aquarium. She told me that she had gotten two clownfish and two sea anemones. She had gotten several pieces of live rock and had put the anemones amidst it. Anne explained that the live rock would blossom with sea life. Anne was excited that the clowns were already hiding in the sea anemone's tentacles. She told me the names of some of other fish she had purchased. I didn't recognize them. So she gave me a detailed description. Anne said, "I put the aquarium under the 'Clown Parade' painting you gave me. That way I can spend time looking at the aquarium and thinking of you." I replied, "That's the nicest thing I've heard in years."

I continued, "I wish for you to have your best year ever in 1998." Anne said, "It will be, as long as you are a part of it. It's less than two weeks till we'll be together." I told Anne that I would get a room for us and give her the information, when I called her Monday, January fifth.

I asked Anne what she was doing New Years Eve. She told me that she was spending it with her mother. She asked what I was going to do. I told her that I was going to Wild Adventures to see Trace Adkins perform. Anne said, "I'd really like to be there with you." We talked on and two hours passed as if only a few minutes. We reluctantly disconnected.

Tuesday morning December 23, I went into the office early. I got my motel guides and Florida Motel Discount Book. There were a lot of motels to choose from. I selected the Waterfall Inn and Suites Motel. It's only three blocks north of the convention center. It's one block west of International Drive on a side street. I got one of the ground floor suites with a hot tub.

The motel has a resort pool with a large waterfall that empties into the pool. The noise of the waterfall is wonderful. I've stayed at The Waterfall Inn and Suites several times. Sitting next to the waterfall and smoking a cigar makes for a pleasant evening.

New Years Eve arrived and I went to Wild Adventures Theme Park with Suzanne. They don't allow alcohol. Suzanne didn't like it one bit. However, she did want to see Trace Adkins. We dressed in layers of clothing. The temperature was in the low forties, with a breeze, giving a wind chill factor in the low thirties.

We brought lawn chairs and some blankets. The concert was out in a large field. Thousands of people had brought lawn chairs and were enjoying the music of the warm up-band. I got us some large Cokes from one of the numerous concession stands. Then I discovered that Suzanne had smuggled in some rum in a fruit jar. She had it wrapped up in the blankets. She made herself a strong rum and Coke. I was not surprised, just disappointed and frustrated. I fully realized that Suzanne is an alcoholic.

The warm-up band played for an hour and a half. They finished and it was forty-five minutes before Trace Adkins would be on. We availed ourselves of one of the two dozen portable toilets. They were lined up fifty feet or so behind the concession stands. Suzanne got another Coke. I got a hot chocolate. My toes were cold as ice, even though I wore two socks on each foot. Suzanne was wearing fur-lined boots, so her feet were warm as toast.

Wild Adventures Theme Park had been a convention center just two years ago. The owner had put in a small zoo. People liked the zoo so much that he expanded it and added rides. Now it's a full-blown amusement park. It has rides like the Tilt-A-Whirl, Ferris Wheel, Tornado, Pharaoh's Fury, The Yo-Yo, a small roller coaster, and a dozen kids rides. I thought about Anne. I would like to be on the merry-go-round with her right now.

There is a nature trail on a wooden boardwalk. It meanders around the edge of a small swamp. Dozens of small animals and birds have cages along the walk. It also has a black bear habitat. On the swamp side are large alligators and other water related animals.

They also have big animals in large fields. You can take a safari ride through the natural habitats. They have narrators on the tour that tell you the names of the animals and something about them. There are lots of large African animals.

I left Suzanne at the chairs and walked over to the nearby pond. It has a concrete sidewalk around it. I lit up a Bering Churchill and started walking around the pond. I was thinking of Anne and how much I wanted to be with her. I got that warm, fuzzy feeling. After about thirty minutes, I heard the announcer introducing Trace Adkins. I prematurely disposed of my smoke and returned to our chairs.

Suzanne was 'feeling no pain'. She had gotten another large Coke and had finished the rum. I ignored some unkind remarks about me smelling like smoke and listened to the concert. I was bound and determined not to get into a fight with her. The concert was great. He played his top hits, to the delight of the crowd. To the right of the concert stage they had erected a huge screen.

At the end of the concert, an announcer informed us of a laser light show. There was a thirty-minute delay after the concert and they showed the laser light show. The show was fantastic. The music was sixties and seventies rock and roll for the most part. The music and show were well-produced. It lasted about thirty minutes. When it was over, there was a mass exodus from the park. Suzanne and I took our time and walked around the rides. We watched the kids having fun on the kid's rides. When the traffic had thinned out, we left and arrived home about eleven thirty.

I lit the red Christmas candle Anne had given me. I wanted it burning when the New Year started. My body was here in Valdosta with Suzanne. My heart was in Waco with Anne.

We turned on the TV and watched the New Years Eve Party in Times Square. The ball dropped and it was now 1998. In a few minutes, Suzanne was asleep in her recliner. I watched a little while longer and went to bed. I fell asleep with thoughts of Anne.

New Years Day I thought about how miserable my life with Suzanne had become. I thought about how well the sales force for the Cigar Tees was coming along. Most of the territories now had a sales rep. I thought about the future. Hopefully, Anne would be a big part of it.

Normally, I spent New Years Day planning for the New Year. This New Years Day, I spent thinking of Anne. I wondered if her wants and desires were the same as mine. I fell asleep in front of the fire, with my heavy thoughts.

The days passed slowly. Finally, it was 6:30 PM, Monday, January 5, 1998. Anne answered the phone. I said, "Anne, its been an eternity." Anne said, "It has been an eternity. Happy New Year!" I replied, "I'm wishing you the best year of your life in 1998." She said, "It will be, as long as you are a part of it." I said, "You can count on that." Anne had mentioned before that 1998 would be great, as long as I was a part of it. I hoped her wishes were the same as mine. I was hopelessly in love with Anne.

She told me how she spent New Year's Eve and New Years Day. I told her about the concert and laser light show at Wild Adventures Theme Park. She laughed, when I told her about my frozen toes.

I told Anne that she was on my mind when the ball in Times Square heralded in the New Year. Anne told me that she was watching the ball and thinking of me at the same time. We were even tuned to the same network. I said, "My red Christmas candle was burning in honor of you. It heralded in the New Year." Anne said, "I'm honored."

We talked about Orlando. She was excited about The Waterfall Inn and Suites Motel. Set up day for the show is Saturday, January 10. We agreed to meet at the motel Friday afternoon. We both planned to arrive around 2:00 PM. Anne was leaving Waco Wednesday the 7th. She was going to spend Wednesday night with a girlfriend in Lafayette,

Louisiana. Thursday she planned to make it as far as Pensacola, Florida.

She told me that Herb was not bothering her as often. However, his tone had gotten meaner. I told Anne there is no doubt that Suzanne is an alcoholic.

We were both almost giddy at the prospect of being together in just four days. We talked about the fun we would have. We agreed to go to Downtown Disney on Friday evening. We both wanted to go dancing at Pleasure Island. I told Anne that Pleasure Island is the central part of Downtown Disney and it has a lot of dance clubs.

We talked for over two hours. Both of us agreed that the gift show was going to be an imposition. We wanted to do and see more things than were possible, in the limited time we would have. Finally, we disconnected with anticipation of our reunion.

The next three days, I made phone calls and readied for the trip. Don and I got samples together for the new reps I would recruit. He said, "I wish I were going with you. However, I can do more here." I agreed with him. Don hadn't a clue, of how serious my relationship with Anne had become.

Thursday evening finally arrived. Packing the Cadillac for the trip was exciting. I set the alarm for 6:00 AM and went to bed. Sleep overcame me, as thoughts of Anne and our reunion danced through my head.

CHAPTER 10

ORLANDO

F riday morning the alarm woke me. Showering and shaving took less than thirty minutes. By 6:30 AM, I was on my way. The radio was tuned to an oldies station that broadcasts out of Tallahassee. I had it turned up loud and was into the music. In a matter of minutes, I had the Cadillac cruising I-75. The oldies station got out of range in about thirty minutes and I put a Yanni tape in the player.

My first stop was to be the rest area on the north side of Payne's Prairie. It's almost halfway. I like to smoke cigars on the scenic overlook. When I got there, it was closed for remodeling. With slight irritation, I drove on to the Disney\AAA Information Center on the south side of Ocala, Florida.

Around 9:00 Am I drove into the center. They gave me some maps of the Orlando Area at the AAA desk. I picked up some brochures of the attractions. One of them showed the times and activities for the month at Downtown Disney. It also showed the bands and acts taking place on Pleasure Island. Having put the information in the Cadillac, I got out a Las Cabrillas Robusto. My thoughts were on Anne as I smoked it while sitting on one of the benches.

A little after 10:00 AM, I was back on I-75. I took out the Yanni tape and tuned the radio to the Orlando 'oldies' radio station. In another thirty minutes I was on Florida's Turnpike. It's the last leg of the journey to Orlando. At Turkey Lake rest area, I gassed up the car and had lunch. At 12:30 PM I pulled into The Waterfall Inn and Suites Motel. Check-in went quickly and I drove down the side of the motel to the room. The room is midway down and is the last room before a center walkway. Trees and hedges landscape the side of the motel.

When I entered the room, the first thing I saw was a huge king-size bed on the left. On the right side of the room was a large chest of drawers. The top has an enclosure for a color TV. A double closet opened past the bed. I went through a door on the right side of the rear into a hallway. On the left side I saw a large room with lavatory, toilet, and shower.

The end of the hallway opens into a great room. Its furnishings include a big pullout couch, a Jacuzzi hot tub, microwave oven, refrigerator, sink, stove, and a table with four chairs. I counted three phones in the suite. The end of the great room is a double sliding glass door. Through the glass is a beautiful view of the waterfall.

After inspecting the room and making sure the phones were working, I unpacked the car and moved in. Then I lay on the bed and relaxed. Thinking of Anne, I fell asleep. At 2:30 PM the ringing of the phone awoke me. Anne was at the motel office. I told her the room number and went out to meet her.

She drove down the drive and parked beside my car. I opened her van door. She got out and we hugged and squeezed each other. Her softness and warmth made me feel wonderful. Tears of joy were in our eyes. I said, "I love you so much." She replied, "I love you too."

We saw another car driving up and proceeded to unload Anne's bags. I took the heavy bag and she carried two smaller bags into the room. When I closed the door, we were drawn to each other like two magnets. We embraced and our lips meshed. Our passion for each other burst into uncontrollable flames. Anne's tongue excited me to no end.

We feverishly discarded our clothing and fell to the bed. Our bodies twisted and turned as we caressed one another. I felt Anne's breasts against my chest. She felt my firmness. Our bodies became one. Slowly at first, then faster and faster and faster our bodies moved, until I erupted like a volcano. I groaned and Anne let out a series of oohs and aahs. Then we collapsed into each other's arms. The feel of Anne's body against mine was wonderful. We both fell asleep.

Anne awoke me around 6:00 PM. We showered together and dressed. Being with Anne made me feel good. By 7:00 PM we were in the car on the way to Downtown Disney. We drove over to Interstate I-4 via Sand Lake Road. Then we headed south toward Disney World. We took the exit marked Downtown Disney and saw the new Disney Sports Complex on the right. We followed the signs to the giant parking lot.

I entered the second entrance and parked ten rows out from the large red AMC Theater sign. We got out of the car and Anne could not believe her eyes. She said, "Downtown Disney is much larger than I ever imagined." We walked between the Virgin Megastore and the 24 screen AMC Theater, to the main street. Our hands were clasped and I could feel a tingle. We strolled to the left and saw the House of Blues complex. Past it, we saw the Cirque Du Soleil building that is under construction. It reminded me of the old OMNI in Atlanta.

We went back up the street past Bongo's Cafe. Anne and I went into the Sosa Family Cigar Store. The walk-in humidor supplied me with some cigars and Anne got a pack of Dunhill cigarettes. There were some small El Imperio Cubana cigars in stock and I got a handful of them. They measure 4" by 32-ring gauge and are an excellent short smoke.

Leaving the cigar store, we walked past the rest of West End to the Planet Hollywood restaurant. It is striking in the dark of the night. The bright blue globe shape, with huge red neon lights spelling out the name, is awesome. Huge, rotating floodlights were sending beams of light dancing through the sky. They were all around the restaurant. A line had already formed. The sign showed, "45 minute wait".

We passed the Planet Hollywood restaurant and looked across the water at Pleasure Island. We went to the east end of Downtown Disney. All kinds of sounds were coming from the island. Anne said, "Look at all the people on Pleasure Island. They all appear to be having a great time." We got to a McDonald's restaurant. On the front of the building, we saw a GRAND OPENING banner. Both of us were thirsty. We went in and got some Cokes.

Anne and I continued our exploring. We came upon a giant LEGO store. We saw lots of kids in front of the store. The LEGO people have a bunch of play stations set up. The kids were building with the LEGO blocks. There are a lot of big statues and models made of LEGO blocks. A LEGO dragon is in the lake, adjacent to the front walkway. Floodlights make the dragon a colorful sight in the night.

Past the LEGO store, we found the largest Disney store in the world. Anne and I walked through it and were amazed at the multitude of Disney merchandise. It's broken up into departments and is as large as a mall department store.

Downtown Disney stretches along the south side of a lake. We looked at the rest of the east end and headed to Pleasure Island. We passed Fulton's Crab House and bought tickets to Pleasure Island. At the turnstiles they put colored wristbands on us. The wristbands have little Pleasure Island designs on them. To get in the clubs and order alcohol, you have to have the right color wristband.

Pleasure Island is shaped like an elongated kidney. We walked around to get a feel for the place. Lots of people were walking on the street. Disney calls its employees cast members. We saw a girl cast member selling single roses. I bought Anne the reddest rose in her basket. Anne said, "I feel loved." I responded, "The rose is red. You are loved."

At each end of the Pleasure Island we saw open air stages. Times were posted for the bands and acts. On the western stage a rock band was playing. People were dancing in the street. We walked back to the eastern end of the island. We had seen a Gyro stand. Anne and I both got a Gyro sandwich. She got a Coca-Cola and I got an O'Douls.

Behind the Gyro stand, we found a patio with wrought iron tables and chairs. Sitting down, we enjoyed our Gyros. When we finished, I lit a Dunhill cigarette for Anne. Then I took out one of the El Imperio Cubana cigars. We both smoked and enjoyed some "people watching". People from all over the world passed by us. My little cigar was great. When we finished smoking, we got up and started walking.

We wound up at 8 TRAX. The sign on the front of the club informed that it played music from the seventies. We could hear the disco music from outside. Entering from the street, our eyes had to adjust to the dark. To our left we saw a giant bar. Lots of little tables and tall stools surround the bar. Waitresses were taking drink orders.

There is a half-story flight of stairs down to the dance floor. Disco lights were flashing on and off. We walked down to the black and white tile checkerboard dance floor. We danced for awhile and decided to 'club hop'. The street was getting more crowded as time passed. People were buying beer, shooters, and tooters from street stands.

We walked up the street to the Rock N Roll Beach Club. After climbing two flights of stairs, we entered the club. The entry floor is a wide circular balcony that's over the stage and dance floor. Several bars were around the balcony. Anne and I walked around to and down the stairs. We got on the crowded dance floor and danced to some of the hottest rock hits. The songs were from the past to the present. The leader of the live band announced that it was ten minutes to midnight and that the New Years Eve blast was about to begin. We walked up the inside stairs and down the outside stairs to the street.

Huge video monitors were counting down the minutes and seconds till midnight. I told Anne that Pleasure Island has a New Years Eve party every night of the year. The brochure informed of a fireworks display at midnight. The seconds counted down and at midnight, fireworks lit up the sky. The fireworks show only lasted a few minutes. Then, cannons from the rooftops blasted clouds of confetti into the air. The confetti swarmed over and around us for a long time. People were screaming 'Happy New Year'. I felt like we were in Times Square at the real New Years Eve celebration.

When the confetti left the air, we walked around the corner to Mannequin's Dance Palace. The attendants checked our wristbands and showed us to an elevator. The elevator carried us up to the third floor. There were costumed mannequins hanging everywhere. Lots of them were wearing Mardi Gras outfits. The decor makes you feel like you are in New Orleans during the Mardi Gras celebration. Some bars were around the floor. We went down two flights of stairs to the main floor.

We saw a huge screen up in the air. It's in the center of the room. All kinds of lights and special effects were playing on the screen. Then Anne and I saw it. We were amazed. Hundreds of people were dancing on a giant revolving dance floor. The strobe lights made it a spectacular sight. We went over to the dance floor. Finally, we found an opening in the crowd and got on. It was too crowded to rock and roll. We disco-danced as the floor—and we—went round and round. It almost felt like I was on a carnival ride.

We got the feel of the dance floor and got off. It was too crowded to be enjoyable. But it was some kind of experience. We took the first floor exit to the street. It was now after 12:30 AM. We walked down the street, crossed the western bridge, and exited Pleasure Island, our arms around each other as we walked.

Anne spotted a park-like area overlooking the lake. It's on the east side of Bongo's Cafe. We found a bench with a nice view and collapsed. Anne got out a Dunhill cigarette and I lit it for her. I got out one of the small El Imperio Cubana cigars and lit up. I said, "Anne, you've given me one of the most fantastic nights of my life." Anne said, "'Lucky'

Joe, I don't remember when I've had such a good time." We talked about the fun and decided to come back Monday night, when it would be less crowded. Anne finished her cigarette and I put out my cigar. We walked to the chest high guardrail that runs along the water. When we got to the rail we were in each other's arms. Our lips met softly at first. We teased and then kissed urgently. The world went away, as our passion for each other manifested itself.

We left Downtown Disney and returned to The Waterfall Inn and Suites. Inside the room, we made love and slept curled up together. My dreams were of Anne and our future together.

The phone awoke us at 7:00 AM. We had placed a wake up call before leaving for Pleasure Island. We showered together and teased each other as I shaved and she put on makeup. She fixed her hair and we went to the complimentary buffet breakfast. I volunteered to help Anne set up her display. She said, "I love you, but I'm not quite ready to show you off in front of my sales reps. I'll do the bare minimum and get back here as quickly as I possibly can." I said, "I already miss you."

About nine, Anne drove to the show to set up. I got a Dunhill Churchill cigar and went over to the waterfall. I sat in a lounge chair and lit the cigar. Dunhill's cigars are mild, mellow, and wonderful. This one was no exception. I was enjoying it immensely, as I started to think of Anne. I realized that I wanted to spend the rest of my life with her. However, I didn't know if she felt the same about me. I decided to find out tonight.

The cigar lasted for an hour. It was exquisite. I went back inside the room and fell asleep. The maid awoke me at one. I went back to the waterfall and smoked a Bering Churchill. A little after two, I returned to the room. About two thirty, Anne returned to the room. We kissed. I could tell that she was worn out. I suggested she take a nap while I went to the grocery store. She protested that she wanted to stay with me. However, her exhaustion won out. I tucked her in bed and drove to the store.

I found a supermarket and bought drinks and provisions for the rest of our stay. The store had a floral department. I bought a dozen roses in a vase. A little after four I returned to the room. Anne awoke when I opened the door. We greeted each other and I returned to the car for the roses. I took them to Anne. She squealed with delight. I returned to the car again. As I got the food and drinks, I had an eerie feeling. I felt as though someone was watching me. I looked around, but I didn't see anyone. I shook my shoulders and took the bags to the room.

Anne admired the roses as she helped me fill the refrigerator. We talked about what we could do this evening. She told me that she knew one thing that we could do. I looked up and she planted a kiss. We made love and it was just as exciting as the first time in Myrtle Beach had been.

We dressed about seven. Anne said, "What are we going to do this evening?" I said, "I'm going to surprise you." We got into the car and I drove several blocks down International Boulevard to the East Side Mario's Italian Restaurant. I remembered it from the time I met and hired our Orlando sales rep. I tipped the hostess and got us a quiet corner table.

The waiter took our drink order. When he returned with her Coca-Cola and my O'Douls, he took our food order. Anne ordered Lasagna Al Forno and I ordered the Peppered Chicken Marsala. Shortly, he returned with a bag of warm garlic home loaf bread and their famous 'bottomless' salad bowl. He filled our bowls with salad and asked if there was anything else he could do. We both shook our heads and he left the table. The salad was very good.

We had barely finished the salads, when he brought our entrees. He grated cheese on my side dish of pasta. We thanked him and attacked our food. Anne's lasagna was oven baked from a Sicilian recipe. It had layers of fresh pasta and ricotta, provolone, fontina, mozzarella, and Parmesan cheeses. Each layer had a topping of zesty meat sauce. My Peppered Chicken Marsala included two tender boneless chicken breasts seasoned with cracked black peppercorns. Then they were served with sliced mushrooms and Marsala wine. They were served with a side of spaghetti.

Anne let me try the Lasagna Al Forno and I let her try the Peppered Chicken Marsala. We both agreed that the food was excellent. The waiter refilled her Coca-Cola and brought me another O'Douls without having to be asked. We skipped dessert and had Cappuccino.

I lit a Dunhill cigarette for Anne and we sipped our Cappuccino. I wanted to talk to Anne about our future. She was visibly tired and it didn't feel like the right time. She finished her cigarette. We split the bill and left Mario's. Anne said, "Thank you for taking me to such a good

restaurant." I said, "Wait till you see where I'm taking you tomorrow
night. It's even better." Anne replied, "I can't wait."

Instead of getting in the car we walked south on International Blvd.
We walked a couple of blocks and F.A.O. Schwarz came into view.
Giant building blocks, a giant Teddy Bear, and other giant toys adorned
the outside of the building. A big banner read, 'Now open'. We decided
to go into the giant F.A.O. Schwarz toy store. I had been to their store in
New York City several times. They have outdone themselves with this
new Orlando store.

Anne oohed and aahed in the Barbie Doll department. She remarked,
"'Lucky' Joe, you look a lot like Ken." I picked up a blonde Barbie and
said, "Anne, you look a lot like Barbie." Anne said, "That's okay by me.
Ken and Barbie make a great couple." I wondered if she had a double
meaning to her statement. I hoped with all my heart that she did.

The store is like a wonderland. It took us back to our childhoods.
Only, today's toys are a quantum leap ahead of the toys of the fifties.
I bought Anne a 'Tickle Me Elmo' keychain. When you squeeze it, it
giggles and says, "Ooooh, that tickles." She gave me a big hug and
squeezed the toy. It giggled and giggled. Anne held the toy up to me
and said, "Elmo loves his daddy and so do I." I replied, "I'm not that
thing's daddy."

She acted hurt and said, "'Giggle Box' here is my child and I know
who the daddy is. It's you!" I said, "I give."

We finished exploring the store and walked back up International
Drive to the car. I let Anne in and drove back to The Waterfall Inn
and Suites. We made love and slept cuddled up together. Before I fell
asleep, I promised myself that I would ask Anne to spend the rest of
her life with me tomorrow night. I missed the furniture business. My
no-compete clause did not include west of the Mississippi River. I
planned to move to Waco and open a furniture store if Anne accepted
my proposal. I knew there would be a scene when I told Suzanne I
wanted a divorce.

Our wake up call got us up at 7:00 AM. It was now Sunday morning.
The show opens today. Anne and I showered together. We washed each
other and delighted in our differences. A little after eight, we hit the
complimentary buffet. Anne went on to the show. I went to the waterfall
and smoked a cigar.

When I finished my cigar, I got my sample bag ready and took it to the car. I drove down International Drive to the Orange County Convention Center. The adjacent parking lot was full. The traffic people directed me to the Canadian Court parking garage. I drove a mile further down International Drive and turned onto Canadian Court. I drove down the street a block to the multi-story-parking garage. The attendant got five dollars from me and I drove into the garage. I finally got a parking space on the fourth floor. The elevator took me to the ground floor and I followed the arrows to the shuttle-bus stop.

There was a line for the shuttle bus. After about five minutes, it pulled up to the bus stop. I was the second to last person to board. The shuttle was crowded and there wasn't any standing room left. People were even standing in the stairwells.

The shuttle bus took me from the Canadian Court parking garage to the show entrance. The gift show only takes up one third of the Orange County Convention Center. The rest of the center was occupied by other shows. It's big enough for a National Political Convention. I got my badge and started looking for sales reps. Around 1:00 PM, I walked by the LIZ, Inc. booth.

Anne saw me, grabbed her cigarettes, and followed me outside the building. I lit her Dunhill cigarette and then lit one of my short El Imperio Cubana cigars. Anne said, "Have you done any good?" I replied, "I've recruited two sales reps. I'm very happy with that."

She said, "My reps are asking me when I'm taking them out to dinner. I don't want to. I want to spend the entire show with you." I said, "You can't let your business go because of me. Tell them Monday night. That way we can still go back to Pleasure Island on Tuesday night. It should be slow enough for us to really dance then." Anne said, "OK, but only if you insist." I said, "I insist." She said, "I can't wait for the show to close at five. Then we can be back in our special world."

Anne walked back to the showroom. In a short time, I finished my cigar and went back to work. I saw Candy Royal at the Royal T's booth. She ran up to me and gave me a big hug. She said, "Our friend Anne is the happiest person I've ever seen." I said, "What makes you say that?" Candy said, "She just smiles and smiles. She came by here this morning with a 'Tickle Me Elmo' keychain. I think she's got a boyfriend." I said seriously, "Really." I knew Candy was fishing. At least, I thought she was fishing. I wondered if Anne had told Candy about us. I knew that Candy is her best friend.

Candy and I discussed some possible reps. I asked how the show was going for her. She told me that she had written almost as much business as the first two days of last year's show. I thanked her again for her help and started walking the show.

I happened to pass Angelo's sponge booth. Angelo Onassis was actually in his booth. He spotted me and dragged me to the loading dock. In just minutes, he had everyone laughing, as usual. He smoked cigarettes, while I smoked a cigar. After about thirty minutes, I went back to working the show.

I tried to talk with some more prospects. The reps I wanted to talk with were with customers. I would have to see them tomorrow. I left about 4:30 PM to avoid the rush. The shuttle was crowded, but I didn't have to wait in line for it. By five, I was back in our room. I got on the bed and dozed off. Anne woke me at 6:00 as she came in and said, "You sleepy head. I'm just as jealous as can be."

I made Anne rest on the bed while I showered and shaved. At seven we left the room and went to the car. As I was opening the door for Anne, I got the same eerie feeling I'd had Friday afternoon, when I unloaded the car. I looked around, but didn't see anyone. I piloted the car over to I-4 and headed south.

While we were riding I told Anne what Candy had said. Anne said, "Candy suspects you are my boyfriend. She just doesn't have any proof. I'm not good at hiding my emotions. I'm the happiest with you I've ever been." I said, "I'm glad to hear that, because I'm the happiest with you that I've ever been."

I exited onto U.S. 192 and drove toward Kissimmee. Shortly, I turned into the parking lot beside Charlie's Steakhouse. Since it was Sunday night, we only had to wait about fifteen minutes for a table. We had a fair waiter. Anne got the Filet Mignon and I got the Porterhouse steak. The salads were just good. However, the steaks were super great. I've eaten at half of the supposed top ten steak houses in America. As far as I'm concerned, Charlie's Steakhouse has the best steaks in America.

Anne couldn't believe how good her steak was. She raved over it. I wanted to talk with her about our future. It was too busy and noisy in the restaurant. We got some coffee and Anne smoked a cigarette. I smoked one of the little cigars I had gotten at Sosa's. When we finished the coffee, we split the bill and went to the car.

I drove east on U.S. 192, just past Olde Town. I pulled in the Burger King parking lot and drove through it to another parking lot. I let her out of the car and led her up some stairs to a wooden porch. A small building at the back of the porch served as a ticket booth for the huge attraction in front of us.

A hundred yards in front of us are two huge parallel steel towers. They lean toward each other and are connected at the top by a huge crossbar. They rise up to a height of 300 feet. That's as tall as a thirty-story building. Another hundred yards past the first set of towers is a solitary tower. Large floodlights illuminate the whole area. The solid white towers stand out in the night. They can be seen for miles in any direction.

Two cables are attached to each end of the crossbar at the top of the first two towers. They extend down to about twenty feet above the ground, where they are joined together. There is a hooking mechanism where they connect. Another cable is attached to the center of the crossbar. It goes to a pulley at the top of the single tower. The information sheet they gave us showed that it cost over a million dollars to construct the ride. It also informed that this ride was the tallest of it's kind in the world.

The ride operators strap two or three people into a harness assembly. They have a construction elevator on the ground under the crossbeam. They raise it up to the joined cables and hook up the harness to the cable. Then they lower the single cable down to the platform and attach it to the apparatus.

Once attached, they pull the people up to the top of the single three hundred-foot tower. Just as a skydiver has to pull the ripcord on his parachute, the riders have to pull a release catch. When they pull the release catch, they swing down almost three hundred feet between the two towers and sail back up into the air about two hundred feet.

We watched as three people neared the top of the single tower. A second after they stopped, they dropped. They fell and swung through the double towers. As they rose high over our heads, we could hear one of the girls scream. She screamed, "Oh my god! I'm going to die." They dropped back down and swung back and forth. Each swing cycle the riders traveled considerably less distance. The ride operators raised the elevator. They had a padded pole for the riders to grab onto to stop their swinging.

They undid the group that had just ridden and hooked up another group's harness. Then they repeated the process. It takes them about five minutes to go through a cycle.

Anne couldn't believe anyone could ride the thing. She said, "It takes some kind of nerve to ride that thing." I said, "I need more nerve than that to talk to you about some things I have to say to you." Anne said slowly, "'Lucky' Joe, you can always talk with me about anything."

I walked Anne over to a secluded end of the large porch. I held her hands and blurted out, "I want to divorce Suzanne and marry you." Anne said, "'Lucky' Joe, my darling 'Lucky' Joe, I want to spend the rest of my life with you." We both had tears in our eyes. We embraced and kissed a slow, gentle kiss.

When we broke off the kiss, I said, "Anne, I want to marry you and live in Waco. I'll open a furniture store. You can help me name it. I've been itching to get back in the furniture business." Anne said, "I'd move to the ends of the earth, to live my life with you. I want to marry you with my whole heart and soul." We kissed again.

Some sky riders interrupted us with their screams. I wanted to be alone with Anne and make plans for our future. Anne has given me more happiness than I knew could exist. We went to the car and kissed. As we kissed, I counted my lucky stars. I was truly "Lucky" that Anne feels the same way about me.

We drove back to The Waterfall Inn and Suites Motel. I opened the door for Anne and we walked toward the room. As we neared the door, I saw a figure move in the center walkway. We heard, "If I can't have her, no one can!" Anne said, "Herb!" At the same moment I saw a burst of light as he fired a gun. Anne grabbed her chest and fell into me. She moaned, "'Lucky' Joe, I love you" as she died in my arms.

My right hand reached for the derringer in my pocket. I saw the flash of his gun twice, as my body shuddered violently. When Anne and I were on the ground, I saw Herb put the gun in his mouth and pull the trigger. My body was now paralyzed. I could feel my life forces leaving my body. As a bright light approached, I tried to say, "Anne, I love you."